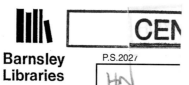

CW00743311

**Barnsley
Libraries**

P.S.202/

HN

Return Date

3805970001585 4

A Future
versus
A Past

MATILDA THORNTON

authorHOUSE®

AuthorHouse™ UK
1663 Liberty Drive
Bloomington, IN 47403 USA
www.authorhouse.co.uk
Phone: 0800.197.4150

© 2018 Matilda Thornton. All rights reserved.

No part of this book may be reproduced, stored in a retrieval system, or transmitted by any means without the written permission of the author.

Published by AuthorHouse 08/23/2018

ISBN: 978-1-5462-9703-1 (sc)
ISBN: 978-1-5462-9704-8 (e)

Print information available on the last page.

Any people depicted in stock imagery provided by Getty Images are models, and such images are being used for illustrative purposes only. Certain stock imagery © Getty Images.

This book is printed on acid-free paper.

Because of the dynamic nature of the Internet, any web addresses or links contained in this book may have changed since publication and may no longer be valid. The views expressed in this work are solely those of the author and do not necessarily reflect the views of the publisher, and the publisher hereby disclaims any responsibility for them.

DEDICATION

To my Nan

ABOUT THE AUTHOR

Matilda Thornton

Born in a town in South Yorkshire, I grew up reading everything from the classics like Louisa May Alcott's Little Women, to more modern works such as Dan Brown's The Da Vinci Code. After completing my A-Level's in English Language, English Literature and Fine Art, I studied English Literature at Newcastle University. I wish to spend my days entertaining people with my works, all people of all ages with varying interests, make them cry, make them laugh, and most importantly, give them a story that stays with them.

ACKNOWLEDGMENTS

Without a handful of people, I would never have been able to write this novel. I would like to thank my teachers, both High School and A-Level teachers for providing me with the skills necessary to write, and for giving me the ability to use linguistic and literary techniques to make the writing more engaging for my readers. Thank you also for being supportive throughout my education, you truly have shaped my future.

Secondly, would also like to thank my family, especially my mum and my dad for being supportive with my decision to publish this novel, without the love they have given me and the faith they have shown that they have in me, I wouldn't have thought that this was at all possible. Even with all the other factors, if I remove you from the equation, it wouldn't add up and I wouldn't be here, writing this, despite the other's, so thank you.

I would also like to thank AuthorHouseUK for their attentive and supportive staff who have helped me through this understandably stressful time.

Finally, the largest thank you I would like to give it to someone who, unfortunately, is no longer with us. My Nan, a retired English teacher, was and still is the main inspiration for everything. The first novels I read were from her shelves and the first in-depth conversations I had about literature, were with her. She passed away shortly before I finished writing this work. She was looking forward to reading it, so this is mainly for her.

Thank you, everyone.

CHAPTER 1

H IS STEP HAD A sense of rhythm behind it. Every step was in time with the next, one after the other as he made his way out of the elevator and towards the bullpen. Darren Thompson, a twenty-five-year-old Detective from Tennessee, was making his way towards his new co-workers and hopefully a new life.

He stopped. As he admired the simple transactions between colleges, unwanted memories came flooding back. He pushed them to the back of his mind.

He glanced around discretely and noticed he had been spotted; a man was already making his way over to him. His palms started to sweat.

The man reached him and instinctively produced his hand which Darren took. The shake was over almost as quickly as it had begun, and Darren was left feeling dazed as the man was already walking away, signalling for Darren to follow.

"Right, my name is Crowley, I am the Senior Agent here, everything that comes into the precinct goes through me, and everything that is leaving it also does. Understood?"

He carried on speaking before Darren had time to answer. After a few moments, they had reached a pleasant looking area which consisted of four desks, each had a pile of folders at least a foot high, papers were scattered across in an organised mess, post-it notes of all colours decorated the edges of their computer monitors, but one desk was empty, this was where Mr Crowley was heading towards. "This is the area where you and your team work, this is your desk." With a brief point and a quick nod of the head towards the intended desk, he was moving again. "Everyone is out, let's see if we can find Bridges."

"Bridges, sir?" Darren asked.

"Agent Bridges, your partner. She must be around here somewhere."

He led him towards the kitchen and told him to get something to drink because the rest of the team should be back shortly. He said that he would then have to introduce himself before he would join in on the case they began investigating early that morning. With that, he left, Darren assumed to find Agent Bridges.

He decided he would make himself a cup of coffee. As the kettle was boiling, he admired the precinct once more. He was immensely impressed with the way people so effortlessly interacted with each other. This place was nothing like the precinct in Tennessee. There, everyone always argued, and most days they never completed their work. When they did finish their paperwork, they did so very poorly. He'd always found it hard to concentrate. He was never a fan of the rowdy, "give me back my pen" atmosphere that was ever present in the office.

The kettle popped. Darren made his coffee and sat at the table, positioning himself so he could continue watching the Agents work.

The cup was an inch away from his lips, so close he could almost taste it, but it didn't quite make it for a woman about his age, 5'5", with long flowing brown hair burst through the door. He looked at her. There was nothing especially striking about her features, but Darren found her very beautiful.

Sadly, something about her expression told him she was unhappy. He didn't know this woman, but still, he felt a pang of sympathy for her.

She was speaking now, "Was I supposed to simply pack up and move to Africa with him, just like that?" She looked at Darren, "With no warning, was I supposed to leave my entire life behind? He hasn't even given me any proper time to think about it. He said I had a week to decide- A week- d'you know what I said?"

He didn't want to upset her further, for his morning may have been short and simple, but hers appeared to have been a long and stressful one, and it had only just turned 9:00 am. He raised his eyebrows encouragingly and replied simply, "What?"

"I told him, 'You can go, but I'm staying right where I am'. We've been together for two years now, and not once has he told me he loves me. Not once has he brought up our future, he hasn't even met my parents," she snorted and took three steps towards him, he could see the desperation in her eyes, she just needed someone to listen to her. "You know, each time I bring up the topic – about our future," she added when he appeared mildly confused, "he changes the subject." She inhaled deeply, placed her hands on her hips, looked up at the ceiling, closed her eyes, and exhaled. He watched as her shoulders dropped as she relaxed.

She looked at him, suddenly aware that she had no idea who she was speaking to, "I'm sorry." She sighed, embarrassed. "Who are you?" He swiftly put his cup down and offered his hand, but before she could take it, the door opened to reveal Mr Crowley.

"Ah, I see you two have met, Agent Bridges, this is Agent Thompson from Tennessee. Agent Thompson, this is Agent Bridges, your new partner."

She took his hand with a surprisingly firm grip, "Pleasure to meet you. Bridges,"

"Thompson," Darren replied with a friendly smile.

Darren continued drinking his coffee as Mr Crowley stayed and talked to Bridges for ten minutes more before Crowley remembered he had to introduce Thompson to his team who were supposed to be back by that time. He paused his conversation with Bridges briefly while he dashed to the bullpen to see if everyone was back, they weren't. When he returned to the kitchen, he seemed entirely oblivious to the awkward tension between two strangers who knew no more than each other's surnames and the shared knowledge that Agent Bridges had just broken up with her boyfriend of two years.

"Thompson," he said as he re-entered the room. "Your team aren't yet back so you can stay here with Bridges and-" he paused, "I-" he was interrupted by someone who appeared at the door, after giving Bridges and Thompson an apologetic look as he swiftly made his way over to the man at the door. Thompson was not interested in the seemingly unimportant conversation, but Bridges was interested. Thompson noticed her fingers twitching, she tucked her hair behind her ear and altered her stance ever so slightly, so the weight was shifted from her left leg to her right, enabling her to move a couple of inches closer to the conversation. This is what he had been missing, the little things - the little things that people try not to show, discrete as they were sometimes, they were unsuccessful in his eyes. It was, after all, his job, his speciality, and he had missed it.

Mr Crowley returned after a couple of minutes, "Would you excuse me." With that and a polite nod, he left.

"So, you want another coffee?" She woke him from his thoughts. "I make a mean cup, in case you're wondering about being poisoned." She laughed. She had a fantastic smile.

"A coffee would be great, thank you." His was probably getting cold. He watched her turn, fascinated by how quickly she manoeuvred around the large kitchen. He sat down in the same seat he had recently vacated and opened the magazine positioned a little to his left, the article on 'mind reading' caught his attention. Despite detesting the way in which the 'skill' was usually labelled, he was intrigued about what the writer had to say about 'reading minds', and decided to take a look.

"Thank you." He said as she placed his cup down above the magazine.

She sat adjacent to him and fiddled with her placemat. She put it down after realising she was doing it on purpose to avoid a conversation. "A man who can read people's minds?" She observed. That was the best she could do. She wasn't great at sparking a conversation. "Is it real or is it a hoax."

He smiled, this seemed to be a natural conversation starter. "It isn't made up, but it is at the same time." She looked at him confused. He continued, "It's not 'reading a mind' exactly, simply reading body language." She looked like she was beginning to understand, so he didn't hesitate to expand. He paused for a moment as he thought of a way to begin explaining. "For example, the man who came to the door, he was nervous, incredibly nervous in fact. He had been asked to chime in on a conversation in which his boss was speaking; he stalled around the corner of the door before realising the conversation wasn't drawing to a close and came through the door. When he got here, the lump in his throat prevented him from voicing Mr Crowley's name the first-time. He had to try again. This time, you and Mr Crowley saw him. He shuffled his feet and fiddled with his clipboard constantly, kept stealing glances around the kitchen. He was worried he would be in trouble for disrupting our conversation. He's new, right?"

She nodded, she looked amazed. "How on earth did you get all that, without even speaking to him. I didn't notice any of those things." She couldn't believe what had happened, what Thompson had done, was tell her precisely what was going on inside a person's head, someone he had only seen for a brief moment. He hadn't even spoken to the man.

He laughed, "This probably sounds a little rude, I apologise if so, but you would have picked up on a lot more if you concentrated more on what you could see, rather than what you could hear." He was smiling, quite broadly, she had amused him.

"Was I that obvious?" She seemed slightly taken back but couldn't help grinning.

"Oh no, honestly, to anyone else you wouldn't have given away a thing, but it's what I do, it's my job to be able to read peoples body language."

"Is it effective?" He scowled as if he didn't understand. "Is it much use in a case? I mean- Does it work?" He smiled, now he understood.

"Yes, it does work, unless you're speaking with someone who is expecting you to watch their every move and guess what they are thinking and feeling."

"Every move?" She sounded surprised.

"Sure, it's like a separate language, each movement, each clearing of the throat, each blink that wasn't in time, is like a separate word, it's quite incredible really."

"Interesting, so the way that I'm sitting isn't just for comfort, it somehow depicts some ulterior, deeper motive, something hidden?" She was laughing nervously now as if she was trying to dismiss the thought that someone could notice her flaws, she suddenly felt insecure. "It is fascinating." She found he conversed easily and she rather liked speaking with him. "Is it easy?"

"Once you get the hang of how people respond to certain news, certain words, you can pretty much figure out how they are thinking, but some interpretation is needed. Why don't you give it a go? Try it on me."

"I thought you said that it doesn't work if someone knows you're going to do it?" She tested.

"I did, but if that person feels confident that you won't see them properly, then it's still possible, you just read what they want you to read," Darren explained.

"Okay, how do I begin?"

"Firstly, think about something you wish to know about me. Secondly, think of a couple of questions which could narrow down your search, the finally, look at my facial expressions, changes in my eyes."

"Your eyes?"

"Yea, eyes show emotion more than any other part of the body. You can tell a lot about a person by looking into their eyes." All the talking about eyes drew her attention to his, they were a pale shade of hazel, the sunlight coming through the kitchen window highlighted the hint of green in the middle, they were beautiful.

"Okay, let's begin." She adjusted her chair so that they were facing. "You will be honest with me afterwards?" He nodded. She gazed deeply into his eyes, completely unaware of the stirring sensation that she was somehow causing inside him. She began, "You strike me as someone who is confident." She looked for subtle movements, "someone who is good with people, the way you're with me," she looked into his eyes, "but, you're not. It's all just an act to hide how you feel. Please, correct me if I'm wrong." He didn't so she continued, "You look lonely, even when you smile, you look sad like you've experienced loss and lots of it." His mouth parted ever so slightly; she was getting somewhere. His eyes said it all. He did look lost. "How far away was I?"

He cleared his throat. His answer was not as she had anticipated, "Right on. You got me in a nutshell." He put on a brave face, not going to show that she made him feel vulnerable, he chuckled, hoping to throw her off. It worked. "No-one has ever been able to read me before." She confessed she had taken a brief class in body language analysis the previous year but had dismissed any thought about it being useful, until now.

She was intriguing, what was it about her that made him defenceless around her he wondered? He was surprised. She had seen right through him, and she was right, everything was an act, all of it. No-one had ever been that far inside his head before; no-one had even broken the surface before. He sat there and smiled at her. She was smiling back, clearly proud of herself. There was more to this woman that he initially thought.

They went back to their coffees. They were both lost in their separate thoughts. When it became apparent that Mr Crowley would not be returning soon, they started talking once more.

"I'm trying to figure out where you're from." Bridges confessed.

"I've just transferred from Tennessee," Thompson answered.

"Yea, but there's something else in your accent. There's some English in there, right?"

"I was born in England. But I haven't lived there since I was eight."

"That explains why it's quite faint."

"Faint as it is now, it wasn't through High School. It was strong enough to cause constant torment." He laughed.

"Why? It sounds quite sweet, quite intelligent." She smiled.

"Thank you." He smiled back at her, grateful for the compliment. He knew it was stupid, but the praise she had given him was the kindest thing someone had said to him in months, years perhaps. Soon after their conversation, Mr Crowley re-entered the room and took Darren and Agent Bridges to the bullpen and introduced him to his team.

It was four weeks since Darren had joined the team, and they were on call out to a crime scene. In the four weeks since Darren had gotten to New York, not only had he developed an impressive solved to unsolved case ratio but also, the team had willingly welcomed him into their group, and for this, he was grateful. He fitted in so comfortably that they figured that he was what they had been missing, a funny, gentle guy with a completely different taste in almost everything. Darren was the perfect man to oppose their opinions in good humour. Everyone enjoyed their arguments as they were never nasty, only ever friendly disagreements over which cover of a specific song is the best, or which X-Men movie is the best.

"Wait up!" Darren called from behind.

Christine Bridges stopped in the middle of the pavement, she rolled her eyes and waited. She cocked her hip so that she was leaning to her left, she placed her hand on her hip and held her watch above her head. "Come on Thompson, or we'll be late." She joked. She got a certain satisfaction when she wound him up. She loved the face's he'd pull when he got all defenceless and pouty.

He caught up to her. He knew she did things purposely to wind him up and figured that the mature thing for him to do was to try and ignore it, but they both knew that he was just as bad as her. "Take it you don't want this coffee then." He teased, gently nudging her on the arm with the hand possessing her coffee.

"Give that here!" She said as she snatched it out if his hand, the other elbow digging sharply into his ribcage, he yelped and spilt his coffee down him. When she noticed, she felt slight guilt, but not enough to prevent her from laughing at him and the mess she had caused. "Oh!" She rushed to him when she realised the coffee was beginning to burn him. She assisted him as he wiped the access away, leaving a definite discolouration, she was still laughing and couldn't stop.

He caught her eye, and it amused him, "simple things," he thought. Nick Davis, the senior agent in the team, caught Darren's eye and waved at him. "We're needed." Darren pointed out. She noticed Nick too. They walked together to the crime scene in almost complete silence; there was some giggling done on her part. "Simple things" he kept telling himself as he silently chuckled.

They continued walking towards Davis and the team. Surrounding the blue tape was almost a hundred people, a lot more people than usual. When they got to the crowd, pushing their way through proved to be useless. They got out their badges, and there was a path through soon enough.

They ducked under the tape and made their way to the body.

Christine got there first. Darren noticed her take in a quick breath upon seeing the victim. He looked down at the body. His heart sank, and he began to panic.

Christine looked at Darren, initially to ask his opinion, but she noticed his eyes, he looked tortured. She asked him if he was okay, but when he answered that he was okay, she saw a slight hesitation. She didn't let on; she just gave an understanding and sympathetic nod. He gave her a small smile, but he had forced it. They went over and collected the evidence, all that there was of it.

The cause of death was a knife wound to the heart, two other knife wounds to the torso. The victim was female, in her early 20's, blonde, quite pretty. She had no shoes. There were no defensive wounds, and her lips were painted red, delicately, perfectly and deliberately, in her blood. But the most haunting thing about this victim was in the way the killer had positioned her. She looked like an angel.

Both Christine and Davis realised, the look in Darren's eyes said he knew it too, the details were too precise, this wasn't just a spur of the moment murder, this was intentionally and successfully, a very intimate and carefully thought out crime. Whoever had done this had purposely included each sickening detail, though their reason was unclear to Darren and the team. It made Christine mad, the idea that someone had thought the murder through before committing, it made her skin crawl. She shuddered.

She stole a glance at Darren, his face was hard and was unchanged. He looked as if he was about to break down. She placed her hand comfortingly on his shoulder. He looked at her. His eyes contained so much pain and hurt. She wanted to make it better, all of it, but she couldn't, she didn't even know why he was reacting this way.

It took a while for Darren to relax, but even then, he wasn't quite himself. The rape test came back negative despite the visible signs of sexual assault. There was a horrifying level of bruising around the top of the victim's legs, leading the Medical Examiner to examine the related area further. His examinations revealed that the victim's cervix had been brutally torn, post-mortem, but by what, he wasn't sure.

Christine pulled Darren over to one side once the rest of the team had left for lunch. She asked him what was wrong, but he brushed her aside and claimed it was nothing.

It had been a few hours since the Police had first arrived at the crime scene, and they still had no evidence to analyse and no idea of who might have killed her and for what reason. The only thing they knew, was her name, Lorraine Casse.

Nick gathered everyone in the kitchen and updated them. The victim was training to become a Primary School teacher. When questioned, her family and friends had said that they couldn't think of anything that would make someone want to hurt her. Upon hearing the news, Darren closed his eyes and muttered the words "Not again, please God, not again" quietly under his breath, before exiting the kitchen.

It was two hours later, and Darren hadn't returned. Mr Crowley entered to inform the team that Agent Thompson had left as he did not seem well at all. Christine couldn't stop thinking about the case. Darren's words, "Not again" rang through her head. "Again"? What did he mean? She decided he would ask him after she got off work. She asked the team where they think he went, Jason, Nick's husband, said he'd probably gone home, Alice suggested that Darren might have gone for a walk, and Nick revealed that Darren once mentioned something about a gym a few minutes away from his apartment that he goes to on Wednesday nights, something to do with Kickboxing. Christine found the gym's address online and put the directions into her phone. It was twenty minutes from work by car; she would go there after work.

She could hear his punches before she entered the room, one closely following the other, each sending an echoing thud through the gym. "So", she thought, "this is where he comes to let it all out".

Christine had different ways of managing with a hard day at work. She would go home, open a bottle of wine and a tub of ice-cream, put on Dirty Dancing or something similar, Pretty Woman, Maid in Manhattan perhaps, and sob to her heart's content. It usually worked.

She continued walking until she reached the entrance to the gym. She stopped. Darren was all alone. There was only one light on throughout the hall, and it was illuminating the punching bag. He appeared exhausted, his bare back was covered with beads of sweat, and his hair was a mess.

She was about to leave him to his business when she heard him call her name, she turned around and saw that he was facing her. She was shocked at the sight that met her eyes, his body was unlike she had expected, his shoulders were broad, his chest was hairless and his abdomen toned, his skin was still evenly tanned still from the summer.

He invited her in before making his way towards his bag. He sat and dried himself with a towel. He seemed stiff as if he had been beating the punching bag for hours. He looked to be in pain. It wasn't long until she saw the bruises that were coming through on his waist. He appeared to have bruised the majority of the left side of his rib cage. He caught her looking and explained that he was sparing with someone earlier that evening and neither of them wore body protection.

"It wasn't a serious fight, but we weren't going easy on each other either." He noticed she looked concerned. She extended one hand out towards his ribs, hesitating at first before she began feeling his side to see if there was any internal damage, "What are you looking for?" He asked her. She replied that she was checking none of the ribs were broken, which they weren't, then scolded him for being so careless, stating that he could have seriously injured himself. Noticing how genuinely concerned she looked, he assured her that he did his opponent damage too.

"Once we had finished, his face was pretty messed up."

She smiled, amused at the thought of Darren hurting someone. She had thought Darren to be a gentleman who was kind through and through, someone who wouldn't intentionally cause someone any pain, mental or physical, but clearly, kind and gentle as he may be, he, like everyone else, needed a way to let it all out. Still, she vowed she would think of him the way she always had.

Darren got dressed, and they began to walk out when a man came to the door. He looked to be in his mid-fifties, tuffs of grey were sprouting their way to the surface amongst the black of his hair. He smiled as they approached him.

"Good evening Darren, how are you tonight? You're here awfully late my boy. Who is this lovely young lady?" He asked referring to Christine.

He began to say they were just friends but the man added, "It's nice to see you're getting over Sarah, jolly good. Good night Darren. Goodnight Miss." He tipped his invisible hat and gave her a wink before leaving.

"What was all that about?" Christine asked him once she knew the man was out of earshot.

"That's just Alan. He's the owner of this gym. He's an old family friend. He's charming, honestly. He speaks a little too fast though." They laughed.

The walk to the car consisted mostly of Darren talking about the Kickboxing class he had taken that evening. He was explaining how he had to teach the entire lesson, not just his usual segment, due to the Grand Master having to go into hospital after having an almost fatal heart attack the previous evening. They reached Christine's car first.

Before they said their goodbyes, Christine asked him if he was okay. When he assured her that he would be fine, she got in her car and went home.

Once she had gotten home, she received a text from Darren, "Thank you for worrying, but today just wasn't a good day, I'll tell you about it sometime when it's the right time. As for the bruises, they'll go away, don't worry. Goodnight, D."

She replied that she wasn't worried about his injuries as it was his fault for not wearing any body armour. She loved making fun of him in a mean but joking way. His replies would always make her laugh, for example, this time he had replied that she was mean, and he hoped she couldn't sleep.

Strangely, that evening, neither of them could sleep. Their minds went over the day's events. Darren couldn't help but feel responsible for the death of the woman that morning. "If only," he thought "I had done my job better, then this wouldn't have happened."

Christine fell asleep pondering about the case, but her mind focused more on Darren's reaction than the case itself. There was something about this case that was bothering him more than any of the other cases had. She knew that it would be on the front of his mind at that very moment, but the one thing she didn't know was why. He had promised to tell her one day when the time was right. But how was she to know when that would be?

CHAPTER 2

H E LOOKED AT HIS reflection in the mirror and poked at his ribs. The bruises from the previous week's fight were almost gone, though the flesh around them was still tender. He buttoned up his shirt and tucked it into his trousers.

He picked up his phone and texted Christine. He wrote: "White shirt and my dark blue trousers, what coloured tie?" After putting his phone down, he took out the shoes he would be wearing that evening.

Midway through tying his second shoe, he heard his phone buzz. He looked up briefly in the direction of his phone before finishing his lace.

"Red. Make sure you wear the matching dark blue suit jacket though, you have to make an effort with your appearance once in your life." She joked. Quickly, he replied that he was offended and that she should be ashamed of herself, upsetting him like this. He smiled.

As he put on the suggested tie, he thought about the last few weeks. Since he had moved to New York, he had made some fantastic friends. Nick, Jason, Alice - the Forensic

Scientist linked to their team - were all great, he thought himself somewhat fortunate to have met them. But then there was Christine; she was something else entirely. They may have only known each other for a few weeks, but she had already become important to him. His feelings for her, however, were beginning to grow in a way that he didn't understand. He may have already married once, but that didn't mean he had ever known what it was like to love someone, he began to worry that he might soon find out.

He banished the thought from his head as he removed his suit jacket out of his wardrobe, the one matching his trousers, as instructed. Once he had put it on, he picked up his watch off his drawers and fastened it on his right wrist. He stopped to look at it. It had been his fathers. It was the only thing he had left of his parents apart from the old and tattered stuffed animal he had as a child. It now sat permanently on the foot of his bed, only to be removed when it was time for Darren to go to bed. The face of the watch, once black, had faded to a pale grey. Despite this, the Roman numerals were still visible, and the gold-plated hands still shone. The glass bore a few scratches, but the watch itself had stayed in perfect condition up until the year before when Darren had needed to replace the leather strap. Nevertheless, he had kept the old one as a memory.

Nick and Jason were the first to arrive at the restaurant. They always tried to get to a restaurant early so that they could find a table away from the door and any windows to minimise the chance of a breeze. These were the first tables to go.

They took their seats and began talking. The first subject of their conversation was the barbecue they were planning on having the following Saturday, but their conversation soon turned to their attire.

"You know, you were right to go with the grey tie rather than the black, it matches your suit better." Nick praised as he admired Jason's suit.

"Thank you, and you were right in suggesting I go with the black shoes, rather than the brown." Jason smiled.

"Anything to make you look more handsome, though you don't need much help from me." Nick teased.

"You also look very handsome this evening." He took his hand and kissed it affectionately. Jason whispered, "However, even though you do look incredible in that outfit, I am looking forward to taking you home and helping you out of it." He winked as Jason replied that he couldn't wait.

It wasn't long before Christine, the designated driver, arrived with Alice. Alice always got a lift with Christine as it meant that she was able to have a drink while she was out. Alice was wearing a long, red, strapless dress, slim fitted to emphasise her slender frame. Her orange hair was down to her shoulders, curled and shimmering, her face was done up beautifully.

Christine, unlike Alice, wasn't wearing any makeup, she didn't need it. Her hair flowed past her breasts, light brown with a slight wave to it, natural, and she was wearing a pale pink dress which came to her knees. It was a light material dress which blew as she walked, it was tight around her waist, and the support around her chest along with the sensible neckline emphasised her shape without showing anything off.

Darren entered the restaurant a few minutes after Christine. She unknowingly stole his glance as his eyes focused solely on her. She looked beautiful.

Before sitting, he greeted everyone with either a shake of the hand or a kiss on the cheek. "You look beautiful." He whispered in Christine's ear as he gently kissed her on the cheek. He took his seat next to her.

"I don't look too plain?" She asked quietly.

"No, no. You look beautiful, trust me." She smiled at his comment and reassurance.

She began to feel strangely uncomfortable, not in a bad way, but her stomach had started to turn. It was the way he had looked at her, his eyes, he had made her feel all warm and fuzzy inside

"You don't look bad yourself," she joked, "except your collars up." His attempt to put it down failed.

"Better?" He asked. She grinned. "I'll take that as a "no". Where?" He was still fumbling around the back of his collar, but couldn't find the bit that was up. He looked at her. She was still smiling. Crossing his arms, he sighed and said, "Very funny." His collar wasn't up.

The dinner was over within the hour, and they had ordered dessert. Nick and Alice had both ordered the lemon cheesecake whereas Jason, Christine and Darren had chosen to share the giant cookie which came with three different flavoured ice-cream sides and multiple toppings. It was too large for the three of them, but they assumed that Nick and Alice would be kind enough to help them finish it.

"I doubt we'll be the only ones eating it," Jason whispered to Christine and Darren when Nick and Alice were busy talking.

They were right in their assumption, for less than ten minutes after the desserts were set down in front of them, Nick and Alice had both finished their cheesecake and had begun to help the others eat the cookie.

"We knew you wouldn't be able to resist," Darren commented, closely followed by a chorus of agreement from Christine and Jason.

"We just thought- We'd give you a hand. We're nice like that, you know." Alice replied, gently nudging Christine.

"How generous of you." Jason mocked. They laughed and finished the cookie.

While the rest of them enjoyed the rest of their evening, Alice noticed that Darren wasn't in such high spirits any more. She continued to watch him, unnoticed, until she couldn't go any longer without asking him if he was okay. She caught his eye and smiled sympathetically, "You okay?" She mouthed. He hesitated but nodded, saying he was okay.

"Do you want to? Darren?" Nick asked.

"I'm sorry, do I want to what?" He gave him an apologetic look as he explained he wasn't paying attention.

Nick laughed and told him it was okay before repeating his question. "Would you be able to make it to our barbecue next week?"

"I sure hope so. What day?"

"Saturday, it begins at four o'clock." Nick gave him all of the details before continuing his conversation with Jason about what meat they should buy.

All Darren could think about was Lorraine's body, laying there. "It's all your fault," he told himself. He was deep in thought when Jason asked him what was wrong.

"Oh, nothing." He replied, trying to shake him off. It wasn't the time or the place to be talking about work.

"Come on. It was something. Is it about work?"

Christine looked at Darren; he had that helpless look in his eyes again.

"No. I was thinking-" He couldn't tell them and he knew it, he sat up and smiled, "if I should get a haircut. Yea, I used to get a trim every couple of weeks, recently I've been missing them, I was wondering what I should do, you know-" He hoped that they would go with it. "What do you guys think I should do?"

They went with it, "I think you should just let it grow, you can always get it cut if it gets too long." Jason recommended.

"I think we all deserve to see what becomes of your hair when it grows." Nick joked, referring to the already curly head of hair Darren had.

"I reckon it retains its 'curliness' and goes off in all directions like he has stuck his fingers in a socket," Alice predicted.

"Whether it does or not," Christine smacked Alice's hand, "I bet it will look lovely."

"Thank you, Chris." Darren stuck his tongue out at Alice who responded by pulling a funny face.

"I think it will look like Josh Groban's hair," Nick commented as he turned to Jason, "What do you think?"

"Yea, I suppose it would, just a little curlier." Jason and Christine agreed.

The following conversations varied from subject to subject as they talked about the weather, what it would be like the next week, what to buy their mothers for their birthdays and how everyone was spending Christmas. When they began talking about the case, Darren withdrew from the conversation and excused himself. He went to the bathroom and splashed his face with cold water. He looked at his reflection in the mirror and reflected on what had happened all those months ago. He tried to convince himself that the events weren't linked, but he knew that they were, and if they weren't, it was the most disgusting and heartbreaking coincidence ever to be identified. When he had returned, he found the conversation was still on the victim. He sat down and attempted to involve himself without appearing out of it.

The evening was over soon, and everyone bid their farewells a little after nine. As they walked to their cars, Jason and Nick mentioned that they wouldn't be at work on Monday as Crowley had given them the day off as it was their Tenth Anniversary. They left, closely followed by Alice. But before she left, Alice mentioned that she too wasn't at work on Monday as her younger brother was going into surgery and Crowley had given her the day off also. When asked, she assured both Darren and Christine that her brother would be okay, it was only a small operation on his knee.

"It's just you and me on Monday then Chris." He opened her car door for her. She got in and replied that she was looking forward to it. With a smile, she left, and Darren made his way to his car. Once inside he turned on the engine but didn't move for a few minutes.

He knew he had to tell Christine about the case and everything that had happened before, including his failure to do his job.

He drove home. By ten o'clock, he was in is Art Room working on his Andrea Bocelli portrait.

He had heard Alice mention something at the table, something that wouldn't leave him alone. She had suggested that the victim wasn't the first one. She indicated that this was someone who had done this before.

He packed up his pencils a little before eleven and got himself ready for bed.

He couldn't sleep. Every time he closed his eyes, all he could see was Lorraine's body lying next to the other woman. He gave up trying and continued with his drawing.

"Not the first one, you say? You are right about that." He said to himself as he got out his sketchpad.

Nick was first through the door, leaving Jason to lock it. As soon as he had, Nick took him in his arms and pulled him into a passionate embrace. Jason helped Nick remove his jacket before taking his own off. They made their way to the bedroom, leaving a trail of clothes all the way from the door.

Nick pulled Jason onto the bed. He organised the protection before they made love, sweetly. Jason came first, and Nick was soon to follow. They laid in each other's arms afterwards, talking about their life and how they couldn't believe how long they had been together.

The calm, fresh night air meant that they could sleep with the window open, something they loved to do as it meant they could wake up to the sound of birds in the trees in the park behind their garden. They laid in bed, both facing the window as Nick held Jason in his arms. He waited for Jason to fall asleep before allowing himself to follow.

Around 2 o'clock in the morning, Darren finally decided to go to bed, but at 04:30 am he was awoken by a quiet flickering sound, which soon stopped. After he had gotten comfortable once more, the noise came back. Reluctantly, he sat up and turned his on the bedside lamp. His eyes wouldn't focus, so he gave them a rub before glancing around the room.

In the top corner of his room, right up on the ceiling, was a moth. "This isn't fair." He moaned as he forced himself out

27

of bed, he turned on the big light, the noise stopped as the moth settled near the bulb. He emptied one of his paintbrush pots and grabbed his chair. "I don't like this." He whispered, he didn't particularly like moths. As he climbed onto his chair, the moth began to move before settling at the other side of the room. The same thing happened twice more before Darren decided he would sleep with his window open, however, after returning to bed, he found he still couldn't sleep. "I may as well get up now." He sighed angrily as he climbed out of bed.

Christine slept like a baby. It was the best night's sleep she'd had in weeks. The tenants upstairs had a habit of keeping her awake, either from the screaming and the shouting or the creaking of the bed and the floorboards around it.

She never liked to stay in bed once she was awake. She believed that a lie-in was over-rated as it wasted part of the day, so, at 07:15 am on this particular Sunday morning, she got up. "Call me crazy." She muttered as she made her way to the bathroom.

The sky was blue and bright, and the sun was shining brightly. She could feel the wind blowing through her hair.

From her balcony she could see for miles, an advantage of living on the 16th floor, she thought. She walked away from the open world and back into her apartment and sat in her favourite lounge chair.

Within a few minutes, she found she was already beginning to miss the cool breeze she had left on her balcony and ached to be out and about. She had an idea but wondered if Darren would be awake. After a moment of consideration, she decided he would be, and if he weren't, then he would be soon.

"How do you feel about cycling?" She asked getting straight to the point.

"Good morning," he joked "I love it, why do you ask?"

"I'm going out, and I wondered if you wanted to come. Do you?" She hoped he would, fun as it may be, it is so much more fun when you're not on your own.

"Sure, when and where do you want to meet?" After she gave him a time and a place he ended the call after a simple reply, "Okay, I'll see you there."

Nick had been awake for almost an hour when Jason began to stir. They had barely moved throughout the night and were both faced with the breathtakingly blue sky visible through their window when they woke. He propped himself up on his elbow and rested his head on his hand.

He waited for Jason to finish stretching before he placed his arm firmly around his waist. Jason reached out behind with his hand and put it affectionately on the top of Nick's leg. "Morning."

Nick felt his heart tug. There were few things he loved to hear more than Jason's morning voice, so raw and raspy, so sexy. "Mmm," he kissed Jason's shoulder and gently began stroking his stomach, "I love you." He kissed his shoulder again.

"I love you too." He felt Nick's hand slide down his body, he exhaled and pressed himself against Nick's naked body. "What time it is?"

To see the clock on his bedside table, he would have to move. Reluctantly he did. However, he soon resumed his position once he had glanced at the clock. "07:49 am." He began to touch Jason, who had pressed himself against him once more. Jason could feel Nick getting harder. While Nick continued stroking him, Jason reached into the draw by the bed. They paused while Nick prepared himself. Jason laid Nick back down and kissed him passionately, beginning at his lips and finishing just below his navel.

Nick sat up as Jason turned over onto his stomach and separated his legs, bending his knees, so his hips were elevated slightly.

Grabbing Jason's waist, Nick pulled himself up and placed his legs between Jason's. He crept forward on his knees until his body pressed against Jason's. Nick leant over and kissed Jason's back and stroked his hips. As he did, he felt Jason quiver. "Oh, Nick," Jason whispered. An involuntary groan escaped from both of their mouths. Within minutes, the sounds of their ecstasy filled the room when they came.

Nick collapsed onto Jason and left his head where it fell on Jason's chest. He ran his fingers through the hairs on his chest as they lay exhausted until the phone rang at 08:27 am.

"Come on!" Christine shouted behind her.

Darren soon caught up, but he did not look amused.

"Did you not see me stop?" His chain had come off about half a mile away, and in the process of putting it back on, the top of his finger was cut open, and it would not stop bleeding.

"Oh!" Christine exclaimed once he had told her. "I didn't realise. I'm sorry!" She dropped her bike by a rock and removed the first aid kit from her bag.

They sat on a large rock and cleaned Darren's finger up, first with bottled water, and then with anti-bacterial wipes, which he did not like at all. "You're like a baby." She accused as he winced, knowing he was pretending. "There." She'd fasted his finger up with gauze and some micropore tape. "All done." But before she packed up, she removed two plasters from a small box and put them over the blisters on her heels. Once packed, with her bag on her back, she slapped her thighs and asked if he was ready. "Ready?"

"Ready." He nodded, and they were off.

They rode for a few more hours, covering another 47 miles, making it around 60 miles covered that day, and arrived back at Christine's apartment just before 17:00. They collapsed onto the couch in unison.

"So how often do you get out?" Darren asked Christine as she took the beans off the ring.

She poured them onto the plates, on top of the buttered toast, "Every Sunday. I just thought you might like to come with me today."

"I did enjoy it." He smiled, he had enjoyed it. When Christine had called him that morning, he wasn't overly fond of going, he initially went so that he could spend time with her out of work, but this he didn't tell her. However, as the day went on, he found that it was the most fun he had had in a long time.

"Good. So, what about you? How often do you get out?"

"Almost every day except Saturday."

As they were sitting down for dinner, the sophisticated delicacy that is beans on toast, they discussed their cycle route and work. Christine did notice, however, that they avoided discussing the new case.

"So, the man is crazy?" Christine joked. They were discussing the reasons why criminals did what they did.

"Well that isn't the technical term for it, but, yes, in a matter of speaking, the man is crazy." They laughed and talked until they had both finished eating, and even continued after, but still, there was no mention of the new case.

Darren could tell that, even though she was trying to avoid bringing it up, she wanted to ask him about it. The conversation died down, and they sat in silence for a few moments before Darren sighed and said she should ask him. She didn't even bother to deny the accusation and say she wasn't thinking of anything relating to the case as she knew her efforts would be pointless. Instead, she just looked at him, "And what about this guy?"

He didn't reply straight away. Instead, he closed his eyes and ran his fingers through his hair before placing them back where they were, one on the table and the other on his knee. He looked at his hand, the one on the table, his eyes followed the scar running from his first finger to his wrist. "Do I think this man is crazy? Of course, I do!" But he didn't say it. Instead, he merely replied, "I don't know, I mean, why would someone in the right mind murder someone?"

He was barely audible, and Christine feared she had gone too far. "Darren, I'm sorry if I,"

"No, no, it's fine, honest." But it wasn't, he thought that he would have been able to handle it. It was all coming back to him. "It's late," he said after glancing at his watch, he hadn't noticed what time his watch had said. "I'd better be going." He stood and began making his way to the door. He grabbed the handle but didn't open the door until he had thanked Christine for the day out. He turned to face her, "Thank you for dinner, goodnight Chris, I'll see you in the morning." He smiled before he turned away to leave.

"It was nothing." She replied, referring to the dinner and their day out. "I'm sorry." She repeated. He stopped and turned to face her once more. He smiled faintly. "Night Darren." She said as the door closed behind him. "Stupid, stupid Chris." She cursed as she repeatedly hit her forehead.

She got a call from Crowley. Throughout their conversation, she managed to say no more than "Bridges?" when she answered and "Okay," before he hung up, he talked very fast and very briefly most of the time. He was calling to let her know where she would be in the morning. "Ah, Bridges, you're going to be with Thompson, he'll pick you up around six in the morning. You're trying to gather

33

evidence linking an attorney with the drug cartel downtown. We have an agent in there undercover. Your job is to listen in and provide back up if something goes wrong. I left the file on your desk; you can pick it up in the morning, it has everything you need. Goodbye."

"Damn!" She thought. She was going to spend the next day in a small confined area with Darren, something she wouldn't mind, had she not asked him that last question. "Why did I ask him?" she asked herself. An early night, she figured, was best.

Crowley called Darren straight after, "Oh, and I told her you'd pick her up around six. Let me know how you get on, goodnight Thompson." With that, he hung up.

"Good conversation, Sir," Darren said to himself as he turned out his light. 10:22 he noticed. "Let's see if tonight's the lucky night." He joked, wondering if he could get a full night's sleep, if he did, it would be his first since he moved to New York.

CHAPTER 3

MY MOTHER WAS CALLING me from upstairs; she had been for twenty minutes now, telling me over and over, that if we didn't hurry up, we would miss our flight. My father has been working in the London Police Precinct for a little over a month now, and my mother and I were flying over there to spend a week with him.

During the day, my mother and I would shop, go to see shows in the West End in the evenings, see all the sights and take in the English Culture. Then at night, my father would join us, we would go out for meals and walk for miles, just talking and catching up, hopefully, if he wasn't too busy like he usually was. It was going to be amazing, or so I'd hoped.

"Christie! Are you sure that you've got everything?" I heard her run across the landing from her room to mine, then back again. "Where's your suitcase?" She screamed. I concealed a snigger as I peered around the book in my hands to see my suitcase, standing by the front door, my backpack on top and my coat draped across.

"Oh good!" She whispered as she came down the stairs, evidently seeing it on her way past.

I continued to read, well, I should say I tried to read, but my mother was in such a state, and a loud one I might add, that I couldn't concentrate, so, I gave in and helped her with the nonexistent problems she was fussing over.

London was even more beautiful than I'd ever thought it could be. I found everything exciting, the lights, the noise and the smells. A man tried to stop us in the middle of the street. My mother later explained to me that he was trying to sell something for a price higher than what it was worth. It took a while for her to relax, but once she was finally at ease after the flight, we made our way towards my father's desk in the precinct, but he wasn't there. We didn't ask anyone if they had seen him as they all looked too busy. It seemed as if something significant had happened that morning. The precinct was half empty, and the remaining detectives were rushed off their feet, running from one place to another.

We didn't want to intrude, so we began to leave, but my father spotted us before we managed to make it to the door. He too appeared on edge and overworked.

We could tell from the bags under his eyes that he hadn't slept the night before.

We took his appearance into high consideration as we realised that he wasn't over the moon to see us at that exact moment. We didn't hold him to it. Instead, we went with him, in silence, to the waiting room where he promptly left us with the promise that he would try and get off work as soon as he could. His shift had finished four hours ago, but they were overworked, and a lot of their people were still out at a crime scene.

The waiting room was empty except for a small, single figure curled up in the far corner.

When my father left, my mother took a seat near the door, but I decided to sit closer to the small shivering figure which now appeared to be a young boy around my age.

The boy's face was as white as the shirt he was wearing and his eyes as red as the blood stains covering it. His eyes were void with emotion as if he had cried his last tear and his eyes had no more to give, leaving them hollow, dark and empty.

I perched myself on the edge of a chair a few feet from where he sat. I glanced at my mother; she had taken out her magazine and had begun to read. Under closer observation, I saw his cheeks were damp with tears, and on one cheek he had a faint patch of dried blood. His knees were tucked tightly under his chin, his arms firmly holding them in place. His hands were covered in blood like his shirt. His coat was sizes too big for him, but he was still shivering. He looked at me, and my heart began to ache, the pain in his eyes seemed to consume his entire body as he continued to shake.

"Hello," I whispered.

He hesitated but then replied in a quiet voice, "Hello."

I smiled at him. "I like your coat," I said.

The boy swallowed hard, "It's my dad's." He wiped his eyes with the sleeve and relaxed his legs, so they were crossed; he rested his elbows on his knees, his head on his hands, and looked down at the floor.

"What's your name?"

He looked up at me and was about to answer when the door opened. A man, as tired looking as the rest, walked in. He was wearing a blue shirt, un-tucked at the back, black tie and trousers, his collar was up slightly. His badge hung at an angle on his left breast, and his shirt was unbuttoned at the top, revealing a white V-neck T-shirt.

The boy froze as the man started towards us. Stopping a few feet in front of the boy, the man crouched down and gently placed his hand on the boy's knee. "I'm sorry, son, but-" he sighed deeply, "We're going to have to take the coat now, it's evidence."

As the man helped the boy remove the coat, he turned his back on me. I don't know if it was because I felt sorry for the man, or if it was because he reminded me too much of my father, but, instinctively, I got up and put his collar down. He tapped me on the hand gently and thanked me.

He gently patted the boy's hair and told him it was going to be okay, and with that, he left, the coat in his hand.

As my eyes remained fixed on the door, the boy spoke. "You sound funny." I looked back at him. His legs were still crossed, but now he had his hands firmly placed on his knees, his back was straight and his head up. "When you talk." He added shortly after.

"That's funny," I said with a smile, "I was about to say the same thing about you."

He smiled back at me, so I sat in front of him on the floor. We were silent for a few moments before he spoke again. "Where are you from? Which state?" He enquired.

"New York. You're from London?"

"Stratford, here in London yes."

When my father came through the door a few minutes later, I had been speaking with the boy about the book I had almost finished reading, Pride and Prejudice.

We had discussed our interests and were delighted to find out that we shared quite a few, he was a few months younger than me, but it wasn't long until he turned nine like me.

"Come on kid, time to go." Even though I had only been talking to the boy for a few minutes, the sound of my father's thick New York accent sounded weird in compassion.

The boy eagerly jumped to his feet at the sight of a detective and began fiddling with his fingers, waiting for my father to look his way. When he did, the boy swallowed hard and cleared his throat. "Excuse me, sir?"

My father sighed, and his voice shuddered as he said there was no news, but they weren't going to stop trying. The boy hung his head, "Thank you, Sir."

My mother and father walked away. My father's eyes held deep regret as if he felt guilty about leaving when the boy's questions were still unanswered.

Reluctantly, I began to follow them. Before I made it out the door, I turned back and asked the boy his name.

"Clark, and yours?" To my surprise, he produced his hand. A faint smile spread across his face.

I took his hand, "Christine."

As we drove to the restaurant, my thoughts consisted only of Clark. "Dad?"

"Yea honey?"

"Who was that boy?"

He sighed as he and my mother exchanged glances.

He purposely perked up his voice slightly as he replied. "That was Clark McAvoy. His parents owned the la- I mean own the largest export business in London."

"You said owned?" I said emphasising the 'ed'.

"No, no, I meant they own, well..." He sighed, "They were- they died early this morning." My heart stopped as I remembered what Clark had said when I asked him about the coat, "It's my dads-" he had said- the detective had uttered the word "evidence"-.

"Murdered," I said quietly. The mere sound of the word made the hairs on my arms stand up as if the word itself brought in a cool breeze that went all the way to my bones.

"Yea honey," he said in almost a whisper, "they were killed."

My father filled us in on what had happened while we were waiting for our dinner. The murder had taken place in the early hours of the morning, there were no eyewitnesses apart from the boy himself, and the CSI's had found no evidence which could implicate anyone.

Clark's statement was incomplete, the only details he could give related to his parents, he could provide nothing relating to the killer.

His parents were putting their suitcases in the boot of the car ready for their departure, they were going on holiday and had an early flight. The man approached them from behind. As Clark watched from his bedroom window upstairs, he noticed that the man had something behind his back. When his father refused to give the man what he wanted, the man revealed what it was. It was a knife.

Clark claimed he screamed out to his mother who was being held by the attacker. The knife was under her chin. Some servants recalled hearing him scream for his mother but dismissed it as they never thought it would have such importance.

Clark ran out to his parents, finding his mother already on the floor and saw the attacker lunging at his father. My father said Clark stopped speaking at this point and sat in silence until asked another question. My father chose to ask Clark what he did next.

"I went over to them" he'd said, "and I sat by them. My father was already dead, and my mother was struggling to breathe."

"Go on son." My father had encouraged when Clark couldn't continue.

It took him a moment, but he continued, "I got up and took one of my father's coats out of the boot and lay it over my mother. I held my father's hand for a moment. It was still warm, and then I put it in my mother's."

"And what about the blood on your shirt son?

How did it get to be there?"

"It's my mother's." The boy's eyes went back to his shirt. "I put my head on her and held her until someone came and took me away. I stayed there even after I felt her die." My father said that this was the first time the boy cried, and even then, it was one single tear which slowly trickled down his blood-stained cheek before it dropped off his chin and landed on his shirt.

My father asked him no more. No-one came for Clark. The servants had packed up and left once they had been questioned and cleared, with no thought for Clark. Somehow, he had developed the maturity to deal with them, give them their pay, with a little extra, before they left him alone with the Detectives once again as they returned to the house to collect their belongings. Neither Clark nor his neighbours had seen them since.

"The poor boy." My mother exclaimed once my father had told us. She didn't say another word on the matter until she and my father were alone later that evening. Whether they knew I could hear or not, I listened to every word they exchanged as I sat against the door separating my room and theirs.

It was my mother's opinion that, if my father wished for me to grow up all "lady-like and proper" as she put it, then the stories would have to stop. The way she saw it, if I grew up listening to my father telling me about the cases he had worked on, then I would grow up fearing the world.

However, my father opinion was very different. He thought that it would open my eyes to the horrors of the world, stopping me from growing up naive and blind, ignorant of the world around me.

He was right. Despite my mother's constant protests, I wanted to be an FBI Agent like my father. In the beginning, she was grieved to discover that I didn't want to take over the family's flower business, but after a while, she began to take my aspirations with a pinch of salt while still insisting that I was making a colossal mistake, blaming my father entirely along the way.

As I sat listening to them talk over one another to be heard, my thoughts once again went back to Clark, as they did quite often for many years to follow.

I never found out what happened to Clark, and my father never mentioned it again, not even to tell me whether they'd found who did it. But one thing he did tell me, was always to follow my dreams and never be deceived by something or someone, a piece of advice I've remembered since.

My father moved out the following month. My parents had had problems for months. He found himself a lovely new apartment on 15th Street and my mother moved back to the place she still called home, Idaho, where she continued her flower business.

They had finalised their divorce by the following Christmas. 2001, the year which my life changed. It was

Christmas at my mothers, Easter at my father's. Summer with my father and Thanksgiving with my mother, only to have it swap around the following year. I stayed at school in New York and went to High School there afterwards, my mother may have moved, but I didn't want to. New York was my home; I'd never even been to Idaho.

I've forgotten almost everything about the boy, I've forgotten what he looked like, and I've forgotten everything he told me. The only thing's I remember, are the things my father said to me that day- and his name.

CHAPTER 4

I T WAS NO USE, yet another night had come and gone, and still, he laid in his bed, as wide awake as ever. His mind would not rest, memories both old and new kept him up as he wondered if he could have prevented it all. He saw them both, side by side, they looked so peaceful, as if they were sleeping.

Only, they weren't.

They were gone, and all he had left was the pain, and the memories that he feared would never leave him.

He laid still as the curtains blew with the breeze coming in through his open window. A single tear escaped his eye. It paused in the corner before it continued its journey towards his pillow. It felt cold against his skin. He closed his eyes tight, allowing the trapped droplets of built up anger and sadness to flow free. He rolled slowly onto his side and buried his face in his pillow. Soon, his eyes began to dry, and he felt the skin around tighten.

A few minutes later, a bird landed on his window ledge and tweeted an excellent morning. Darren sat up and swung his legs around, so he perched on the side of the bed. His eyes gradually began to close as the weeks of sleepless nights continued to catch up with him.

He glanced at the clock above his door, 04:27 am, there was still another hour to go before he needed to pick up Christine.

When he was in the shower, he heard music coming in through the open window. Once he had rinsed himself off, he turned off the shower, got out, and walked to his bathroom window to see where the sound was coming from. If he stood on his tip-toes, he could see. There was a brass band set up in the bandstand in the park behind his apartment. They were rehearsing for the morning show. He had forgotten entirely, it was the Band Stands 120th Birthday, and a special concert was to be held that evening.

Darren left the bathroom after opening the window as far as it would go, he hated it when he returned to the bathroom later to find that the mirrors were still steamed up from the shower. He had forgotten to take a towel into the bathroom, so he had to walk to his room wearing nothing, dripping water along the way. He'd chosen a warm morning though, he thought to himself.

As he neared his bedroom, he heard the music once more, this time they were playing a familiar tune, Glenn Miller's 'String of Pearls'. Upon opening his door, the volume of the music increased.

Humming quietly to himself, he went over to his draws and, from the top draw, removed some underwear at random, and from the second, a pair of socks. He put on the underwear and sat on the edge of his bed so he could put on his socks.

The sun was up and shining through the clouds, but the promise of rain lingered over the city as the clouds continued to darken by the minute. He decided on his dark blue jeans, the ones which were a little snug around his behind. He'd be sitting down for most of the day anyway. He picked out his black V-neck t-shirt. He opened the unit which contained his shoes and selected a pair of white canvas shoes, despite having seen better days, he figured the quality of the shoes didn't matter as he would be in the car.

Once he was ready, he returned to the bathroom and brushed his teeth, splashed his face with cold water and combed his hair, smiling in amusement at the way his hair would straighten with the force of the comb, to spring back into a curl as the comb let go. He then went downstairs, but he closed the window first.

The fridge was full, but he wasn't hungry. Since he knew he would be later, he quickly ate the last banana in the fruit bowl on the worktop and packed lunch with enough food for them both.

The time was 05:01 am, and Darren was already ready, this always happened.

His bookcase covered the majority of one of the walls in his living room. It was 8ft high and 12ft in length. It contained everything from Great Expectations to The Great Gatsby, novels by Harper Lee to the more modern Maureen Lee to Dan Brown. It even had a shelve reserved for autobiographies and regular biographies, John Barrowman to Billy Joel.

Before he sat down to read, he needed to ensure that he'd set off on time instead of getting carried away with his reading, so, he set the alarm on his phone for 5:30. He remembered to turn the volume up before he placed his phone on the coffee table and curled up on the sofa in a way any observer would view as childish, legs tucked underneath him and his elbow positioned at a right angle from the chair arm with his chin resting on his hand.

His mind was transcended into another world as he let the novel pull him in. He didn't want to leave, he never did. He was partway through chapter three of a Maureen Lee novel, an English author whose books he regularly got sent by his godfather in London, called 'The Leaving of Liverpool' when his phone sounded. The young country voice of Brett Eldredge began to sing, "Oh in my mind I keep replaying it, over and over but that's how I found the-" Darren switched it off as quickly as he could. He was unsure whether or not his neighbours would hear it through the walls into the next apartment and he remembered that his neighbours probably wouldn't be up at half past five in the morning. He figured that the bandstand's preparations probably woke them anyway.

It wasn't long until he was in the car and on his way to Christine's. It was too quiet, not only were the roads empty, the only thing he could hear inside the vehicle was the hum of the car itself and the wheels on the way under his feet.

He turned on the radio and put in one of Billy Joel's albums, his 1977 'The Stranger' album and put it on random. A few seconds later, the opening notes of 'Scene's from an Italian Restaurant' began to play, he turned it up enough so that the sound of the car and the road were no longer audible, and began to sing along.

Once again she was awoken by the tenants above her, this time by the creaking of the bed and the floorboards surrounding it, accompanied by loud noises coming from both participants. She became so uncomfortable that she got out of bed and started getting ready at 05:00 am, half an hour earlier than she would have liked.

But before she went into the bathroom to get washed, she put on the CD player and ensured that whatever came on, could mask the sound of the pleasure makers upstairs, while also not bothering the people downstairs.

By the time she was washed and dressed, her bedside clock which stood alone on her bedside table showed the time 5:37.

Realizing she had nothing else to do, she entered her living room area and turned on the TV.

Usually, she would have preferred to read rather than watch the TV, but she had just finished a book the night before, a beautiful Margaret Thornton novel called 'One Week in August', Darren had leant it to her, and was waiting until she had nothing else to do and nowhere else to be before she started another.

There just wasn't enough time now, by the time she'd start getting into it, Darren would get there, and it would be time to go.

She chose to watch an episode of Friends. The episode was almost over when Darren knocked on the door. It was 5:56 and time to go. She desperately wanted to finish her programme but knew she'd have to wait. She knew how it ended anyway.

They had been parked only a few minutes when Christine decided that they needed to talk about certain things. She wanted to apologise, even though she knew everything was alright between them. "Darren?"

"Yes?" In response to her address, he stole a glance at her out of the corner of his eye. She was fiddling with her hands.

"About yesterday-" She began, but Darren cut her off, insisting that there was nothing more to be said as she was right.

"Chris, its fine. Look, you were right to ask, it's my job, and you were asking for my opinion. This case is no different from the others." Even as he spoke the words, he didn't believe them, neither did she.

"But I shouldn't have asked you about this one." She said quietly. Darren couldn't help but feel bad for the way he had responded yesterday when she had asked the inevitable question. "And what about this guy?" She'd said. He had been expecting her to ask him earlier in the evening. "At least not until-" Her voice trailed off as her eyes shot down to her hands once more.

He hesitated before asking. "Until?"

Out of the corner of his eye, he saw her chest rise. It lingered there before it settled down as she took a deep breath. "Until I know why this case bothers you the way it does." She looked at him; his face was unchanged.

He considered telling her that it was none of her business but decided against it. He told her because it was her business and she needed to know about it, and partly because he'd never be as rude as to shoot someone down who showed compassion towards him. She wasn't nosy; she did care and just wanted to know what was wrong. He decided to tell her the truth because she asked with his best interests at heart, not through a common interest.

He knew she'd hear it at some point and much preferred the idea that it came from him.

"Okay, what do you want to know?"

She picked her next words carefully, not wanting to upset him. "Back in Tennessee, what sort of work did you do? Did you investigate Mister Meaners or car theft or-" She paused, she hadn't figured out a way to ask him if he had ever worked a murder case.

"I did what I do here. I worked murders, kidnappings and whatever they decided to throw at me."

"Was the crime anything like it is here in New York? With the population being smaller, is the crime level lower? Is that the case?"

He swallowed as he shifted in his seat, taking a moment to position himself in a comfortable position.

"I was only there for a few months, and in that time, we only had one murder." Time to tell her, he thought.

"How old?"

"She was 24. She'd been stabbed three times. We never found the killer."

"How horrible!" Christine gasped as her hands covered her mouth. After a few moments, she asked in a dull hoarse whisper "And her family?"

"Her mother took badly, as expected." Christine notices Darren's eyes flicker up to the sky. He tipped his head slightly as if in admiration towards the blue and grey speckled blanket up above. She began to look away, but he spoke again "She was married."

Had she heard him correctly? "Married?"

He nodded. "Four years before. She was meant to be meeting him outside the cafe, the one she was found behind." His face was unreadable. He was showing no indication as to what he was feeling or what he was thinking. Before she could ask why he was so reluctant to tell her about the victim, he laughed and said: "I bet you think me ridiculous for wanting to keep it quiet. You probably think that I was stupid."

"No, no! I don't." She assured him. "But I do want to know why you didn't want to tell me."

"That's understandable." He said. Still, his mood was undetermined, but his eyes were beginning to show glimpses of past pain he was trying hard to conceal and push to the back of his mind. "I didn't tell you because certain details in the murder from Tennessee mirrored those of the body here. As the case developed, the similarities became clearer until I was sure. I didn't want to say anything until the case file from Tennessee arrived. I sent for it on Saturday. It should be here within a day or two."

Chris had an idea what he was talking about, but, not wanting to jump to the wrong conclusion, she asked, "Until you were sure about what?"

"Until I was sure that it was the same killer."

Her next question could change things all together. She didn't want to ask as she feared what the answer would be. "And, is it?" She looked at him, his eyes now showed his fear as clear as day, the slight trembling of his lower lip answered her question before he could get his words out.

Still, he answered, "Yes, I'm sure."

"Suspect on the run, Bridges and Thompson in close pursuit. "Christine shouted down the radio as they raced down the alley behind the club.

The suspect, who they identified as Steven Frost, was now beginning to scale the building adjacent to the club he had emerged from a few moments before. Darren followed him up, signalling for Christine to go around the side and cut him off.

Darren was surprised to find how easy it was to make his way up the building without Frost creating distance between them. All that kickboxing was paying off, he thought. Frost was 6'5" making Darren feel insignificant at his 6'2" and only half the size of this machine of a man. If he weren't a bad guy, Darren thought, he'd almost envy him.

They reached the roof where Darren stumbled slightly before regaining his balance and continuing his pursuit.

Where was he? Frost had disappeared.

Darren drew his gun and lightened his step, treading lightly, so his movements made almost no sound as the gravel shifted under his feet.

For a second or two, he froze as he heard what he thought to be a whisper, someone unsuccessfully concealing the sound of their breathing. He soon realised the noise was coming from a fan 30ft to his left.

He continued, but where was Frost?

He heard footsteps around the corner and pressed his back against the wall, readying his gun for his arrest. The steps continued his way, closer and closer until Darren turned around the corner to face Frost in the face, his gun aimed at the space in between Frost's eyes. This area was wrinkled with his disappointment as he realised he had lost. He surrendered his hands in defeat as Darren unclipped his handcuffs from his belt.

Frost made a bold move, he threw a punch at Darren, but Darren blocked, a forward block to free Frost's face for Darren to threaten with a punch of his own. He raised his fist but didn't strike. Instead, he grabbed hold of Frost's arm, the opposite one to the one he had used to cover his face in preparation of Darren's fist, and pressed his thumb into the pressure point on his wrist. While he still held Frost's wrist firmly, he sent his arm over his shoulder, taking him down to the floor where he swiftly turned Frost over, so he was faced down on the gravel. Darren cuffed him quickly and took him down the fire escape, putting him in the back of a police car.

"Thompson!" He heard Christine call from afar, looking around he caught sight of her, she was at the car, sitting on the bonnet. He walked over to her.

She had turned the volume up so high that she was beginning to get nervous, she was worried about upsetting her neighbours. The dial was showing 75 when she decided to turn off the TV altogether. But now she had, the once muffled shouts that were coming from upstairs, were more clear, not only could she not determine who was speaking and when, but she could also tell what they were saying. She whisked out her phone and dialled.

"Thompson," Darren answered.

"Hey, Darren."

"Hello, Chris. What's up, are they still at it?"

"Yea."

"Ah."

"I was ringing to ask you if you wanted to go to a movie or something, I'm getting hungry if you're up for it."

"I would be," he sounded excited "only, I'm almost finished cooking, and I was about to put on a film."

"Oh." She tried to hide her disappointment.

"You're welcome to join me, I've cooked way too much, and I haven't put the film on yet."

"Okay, sounds great. What have you made?" She asked as her stomach grumbled almost painfully.

"Chicken cooked in white wine served with rice."

"That sounds lovely, are you sure?" She knew he'd say yes, but didn't want to appear rude.

"Absolutely."

"Okay, I'll be there in about twenty minutes."

"I'll leave dinner simmering."

"One more thing, what film?"

She noticed his hesitation. His response was delayed and unexpected. "Um, Sen-S-Sense and Sensibility."

"I love that film. Please tell me you mean the Hugh Grant, Emma Thompson version?"

"I do." He sounded pleased.

It didn't take long for Chris to get to Darren's.

"Did you not want to tell me which film you were going to watch, or could you genuinely not get the words out?" She asked him as she recalled his stammering when he tried to pronounce the title.

"I was a little hesitant, to begin with, I admit, but yes, I genuinely couldn't get the words out." She was smiling at him, mocking him, laughing at him. Did she find his film choice funny? "What?" He asked.

"I just never imagined when I asked what film, that you would ever reply 'Sense and Sensibility'." He knew it. Her smile remained.

"What can I say other than Jane Austen is one of my favourite authors. I love every one of her novels. I like the drama based films made from her novels, especially this one and the BBC adaptation of Pride and Prejudice, my Godfather sent over the DVD series over from London. Thinking about it, the BBC version of this," he pointed to the film sitting on the coffee table, "is just as good." He smiled as he took the DVD Case from the table and held it up to his face as he spoke, leaving his eyes the only visible part of his face visible.

It was her turn to hesitate now, but she answered shortly with an approving nod, "Well I think that it's sweet." She assured him sincerely.

Her approval and the look in her eyes sent a chill down his spine, and the butterflies in his stomach began to attack the walls ferociously. Why did he crave her opinion and her approval so much?

The sound of the water in the pan boiling over, took his eyes away from hers. "Oh!" He shot over to the hob and took the pot off the middle ring and turned off the gas.

"That was beautiful," Christine exclaimed as she licked her lips, nodding with approval. "Thank you." She said while she placed her knife beside her fork and pushed her plate away a couple of inches allowing herself room to rest her arms on the table.

"You're welcome." He replied, satisfied with the compliment.

She tucked her hair behind her ear and tried to brush a strand from the corner of her mouth and failed. She tried again but failed. She tried one final time and failed once more.

He raised his hand. "Here." She conceded and let Darren get it for her.

He slid his finger under the strand of hair, gently brushing her cheek as he did. Her breath caught in her throat and he could feel her eyes on him. Once he had the hair, he diverted his eyes, so they met hers. Such beautiful eyes. They looked as if they contained the world, bright, blue and beautiful.

Their eyes remained fixed as he pulled the hair free, tucked it behind her ear and slowly returned his hand to his lap. What was she thinking? He felt as if she could see straight through him, why was this? No-one had ever had this effect on him before. He felt uneasy and open.

Every time their eyes met or their arms grazed, a nauseating feeling stirred inside him. He had never known anyone envoke such a sense. Sometimes he found that its intensity made him feel sick. So far, he had managed to push it away, ignore it, but now it was raging with a force he'd never experienced before. He knew it was wrong to feel like this about his partner; it would only cause problems for the both of them.

His phone rang. They looked down, banishing the accumulate force they had created in those brief seconds.

He answered it. It was Crowley saying a case file had arrived for him from Nashville and that he was bringing it around for him on his way home from work.

The conversation was brief, and by the time he had hung up his phone and placed it back in his pocket, Christine had finished her beer, so they both decided to take their plates to the sink.

They tried to avoid all physical contact as they carefully manoeuvred around each other, but inevitably, their arms brushed past each other, stopping them in their tracks momentarily, but they ignored it and went to sit on the sofa.

Despite being only a two-seater couch, it was rather large, enabling the two of them to sit comfortably, one on each end. Darren decided that it would be best to wait before putting on the film as Crowley would be there shortly. It was only 18:27 and they could watch the movie later, if Christine had nothing else to do, which, when asked, she confirmed she hadn't.

They sat and talked about the man they had caught earlier that day, Frost. Both Darren and Christine stole glances at the three inches of space between their legs. Christine caught Darren looking and gave him a knowing smile, he responded with an embarrassed one. Reassuring him, she nudged his leg with hers a little more than gently and continued to talk about what was going to happen to Frost now that they had him.

Before long, there was a knock at the door.

Crowley stood in his crisp brown suit, polished black shoes which perfectly reflected surrounding objects and his dark-brown trench coat that hung past his knees. His hair was held in place with an appropriate amount of gel, and his glasses were, for once, pushed onto the bridge of his nose. Usually, they sat perched daringly close to the tip of his nose as he scowled over them all from his office, keeping watch. His natural manner was pleasant while his stance oozed with authority.

While his stance remained the same, there was something else in his eyes as he looked at Darren across the threshold. Could it be friendliness? It was something he had never seen in him before, but then again, he'd never seen, never mind spoken to him outside of work before. "Darren, hello." His tone was firm yet friendly as he raised his right hand, it contained an A4 manila envelope which Darren took thankfully.

"Thank you, Sir," Darren asked Crowley in.

"Thank you, I will, but only for a few minutes. My wife is funny about me coming home late. She hates to have to warm up my food. And please, Darren, call me Frank."

As he spoke, he made his way through the door, removed his coat and hung it by the door.

With one look at Christine, Frank turned back to Darren who had closed the door and had begun to follow him through to the living room. "Are you two..." he raised his eyebrows as he searched for the right words.

"No, no, Sir-Frank, were not. Her neighbours were annoying her, so she came around."

"Could've fooled me." He mumbled as he turned towards the living room.

Checking to see if Christine was watching, which she wasn't, Darren gently tapped Frank on the shoulder and diverted him to the kitchen. He asked him what he had meant before.

As Frank explained that he had been watching them for the past few weeks, Darren couldn't keep his eyes away from Christine who was still sitting where he had left her a couple of minutes before. He began to feel a little guilty about leaving her on her own.

"I had just assumed that eventually, something was going to happen between the two of you. I hope you don't mind me saying these things, only, I know what you've been through and was beginning to feel hopeful about the two of you." He looked sincere, and there was no trace of disapproval in his voice.

"Well, I can assure you, there is nothing between us." Darren attempted to conceal his disappointment as he spoke, but Frank's discrete response indicated that he'd failed. But did he want something to happen between them? He pondered this question as he offered Frank a drink, which was politely declined due to the time, and led him into the living room. He kept his eyes on the back of Frank's shoes and away from Christine.

"Hello, Frank." Christine beamed as he reached for her hand.

"Christine." He smiled at her fondly as he asked her about her parents.

"They're fine, thank you. How's Helena? It's been too long since I've seen her."

"She's fine, still moaning at me constantly, but there's nothing new there."

Frank didn't keep his wife waiting long as he left within a quarter of an hour, leaving Darren and Christine alone once more.

"Is that the file relating to the murder victim in Tennessee?" Christine asked almost as soon as Darren had sat down after seeing Frank out.

"It is, yes."

She couldn't wait any longer, she needed to know what they were dealing with and she knew he did too. "Are you completely sure that it is the same killer? Because if you aren't then I don't think it would be appropriate for us to open the file."

"Yes. I'm sure. There's no mistaking."

CHAPTER 5

"IT'S HORRIBLE DAD. I know you will have seen some shocking cases in your career, but nothing I have ever experienced comes close to this. This person, 'The Angel', we have to stop them. What they are doing to these poor girls is-" Christine couldn't even begin to understand why someone would be so cruel and dark.

"That's the way it is with this job, honey. There are going to be plenty of occasions where you lay awake at night wondering what would drive a person to do such things, especially to another person. You'll never get it, and you'll never figure out why because each of the fuckers makes a different excuse." He paused before apologising for his brief outburst of profanity and brought the newly made cups of coffee from the worktop near the window and placed them on their mats.

She thought about the previous evening. Once she and Darren had read through the case file from Tennessee, they had put on the film and had watched it in almost complete silence, "Is it loud enough?", "Popcorn?" and the answers to both were the only words spoken throughout.

Once the film had finished, Christine sat in silence for two or three minutes as her eyes dried and the film credits rolled.

There was only one thing that day regarding Darren which shocked her more than his drama adaptation film choice, and that was the impact the film had on him. As she looked over at him, she noticed that he too had cried.

She looked at him in amazement and did not attempt to look away when he turned to her. He barely suppressed a smirk as he innocently asked, "What?" He quickly and purposely dried his eyes and returned to his original state as he once again asked her, "What?"

"What do you mean "what"? Are you crying?" She asked, shocked.

"No." He didn't lie, and he wasn't crying.

"Okay, were you crying?"

"Maybe." He kept his face straight as he replied.

"That's a yes then."

"No, it's not a yes."

"You still haven't said no." She was testing him now.

"I haven't said yes either. I said maybe."

Their deliberate suppression backfired as it meant the volume of their sudden and synchronised outburst of laughter was amplified.

"So, what happened today? You don't seem yourself, you're thinking about something else, and it's keeping you from your old man." Her father joked.

She told him that she was thinking about her evening with Darren the night before. Her father watched eagerly as his daughter told him about Darren's response to the film. He watched her eyes soften, the corners of her mouth curl up, and he watched her fiddle with her fingers as she spoke of him. There was a faint smile that flashed across her face each time she mentioned his name.

"It's weird, seeing him away from work, he's a lot happier. Last night, despite the crying, I know he had a good time just relaxing and taking his mind off work. Work." She repeated with a sarcastic snort.

"Is there something bothering him at work?"

She looked reluctant at first, but he saw the look of defeat cross his daughter's eyes as she conceded and decided to tell him everything. She explained about the murder of the woman in Tennessee, not revealing any personal details as she did before she explained the connection to the body which showed up a little over a week ago.

"I saw it in his eyes again today dad, when the second body showed up."

"Do you want to know what I think?" She nodded, so he continued. "I think he blames himself for what has happened to these poor girls. Maybe he feels like it is all his fault."

That would explain everything, the way he reacted, his reluctance to cooperate and give in to her constant insistence, and his words came back to her, the ones he'd muttered as he left the office the day they found the first victim. "Not again, please God, not again."

"Christie?" Her father watched as his daughter's face fell as if in realisation.

"He blames himself." She whispered.

After observing his daughter as she spoke of Darren, Albert Thompson decided that it was time he took Christine and her friends out for dinner again like he used to do before his operation. But this time, they would have another chair at the table, and in it would be Darren.

He had never seen his daughter's eyes light up as brightly as they did when she spoke of him or thought about him. She was fond of him, really fond, and Albert figured that it was time to meet him.

He decided that a proper invitation would be more suitable, so, after speaking to Christine about which day would be best for her, she told him where Darren would be.

They left together in separate cars and parted a couple of miles down the road as Christine turned right to go home, and Albert left towards the gym.

Just like his daughter had said, the sound of punches on the punch bags echoed around the reception area and got louder as the ceiling lowered in the narrow hallway as he made his way towards the double doors.

He heard a man's instruction followed by a large number of shouts from children in unison. The man's voice boomed once more as he instructed them, "Twenty push-ups, that shout was pathetic. You're meant to be warriors, and you sounded like a bunch of fairies. Louder!"

He tried the right door, but it didn't open, so he tried the left. It opened to reveal twenty to thirty children, between the ages of eight and sixteen, as the sign had said, in straight lines facing one single man.

The man spoke in a gentler tone now as he told them the commands and demonstrated it briefly.

He controlled his power, and his technique appeared flawless as far as Albert could tell, his concentration was centralised on his imaginary target.

He raised his voice once more as he counted in Korean, one, the children copied his moves, two, they did it again off their other leg. This time, their shouts were considerably louder, which, along with their technique, sparked a faint look of satisfaction and pride in their instructor's eyes.

One of the other instructors had spotted Albert. He was just as tall as the other, but instead of having a blue stripe through the middle of his black belt, his was plain, Albert made a mental note to ask one of them what it meant. As the man made his way towards him, Albert wondered briefly if this was Darren.

Christine had said Darren was 6'2" with untidy dark-brown curls which came halfway down his forehead, this wasn't Darren.

The man was still quite a distance away, giving Albert more time to look around. He looked back over at the lines of children who were now coming back down their lines and were facing towards him. He caught the eye of a child or about eight and smiled. The kid smiled shyly back. He was too busy watching the child, who he thought had a terrific skill for someone so young, that he didn't notice the man appear by his side.

"Sir?"

He jumped. "Hello."

"Can I help you?" The man's smile was bright and his eyes kind.

"Yes, thank you, I was looking f-" He was interrupted as the kids screamed and piled on top of their instructor. Albert briefly saw their instructors head before it disappeared beneath a blanket of children. "Does he let them do that?" Albert asked the man who was still laughing.

"Only when they have done well in the lesson."

"He must be a great teacher."

"He is, somehow he manages to get the kids to do what they are supposed to do, properly and seriously, but have fun with them at the same time. Sometimes, he plays about with them at the end even when they haven't done that well." The man was looking at the pile of children. Their instructor was nowhere to be seen.

"He sounds like a great guy."

"He is. I'm sorry, is there something we can do for you? I'm Bruce." He said as he extended his hand towards Albert. He took it and told him who he was and the reason for his visit.

"You want to see Darren?" Albert nodded. "I'm, afraid you'll have to wait a while," he indicated towards the heap of children across the gym, "he's unavailable at the moment."

The man told Albert that he would let Darren know he wanted to see him whenever he could, then promptly left after a kind farewell and headed towards Darren.

Something touched Albert inside, from what he had seen of Darren so far, he couldn't have been happier. He could tell his daughter liked Darren, even if she didn't know yet. As he managed to climb his way out of the children, Darren was smiling. His smile was contagious as Albert found himself laughing. Albert would have recognised him sooner, but his hair was wet and pushed over his head, hiding the curls that Christine told him would make him unmissable.

As Darren found his feet, he re-organised his suit which had been pulled out of place and twisted as bodies consumed him. As he did so, Albert watched as Darren's huge shoulders moved under the fabric of his suit. Darren hung his head slightly to glance at his uniform, causing a few curls to come loose and drop across his forehead. Albert saw Bruce tap Darren on the shoulder and whisper something in his ear. He pointed to Albert and Darren nodded to Bruce and said something in response.

"One minute." Darren mouthed to Albert as he held up his left index finger. Albert nodded at Darren and watched him stroll over to where two men had just finished sparring. He shook hands with both and congratulated the one which had won. As for the other, he repositioned him and showed which moves would work next time, he praised him nevertheless and began making his way over to Albert once he had said goodbye.

Darren stopped when he was about seven feet away and swallowed hard. Strange, Albert thought. "Hello, Sir. What can I do for you?" Darren said.

"You're Darren?"

"Darren Thompson, sir. And you are?"

"I'm Albert Bridges, Christine's father."

Albert noticed his face light up, "It's a pleasure to meet you, Sir. So, what can I do for you?"

"I called in to ask you if you would like to join the rest of us for dinner next Friday night. Nick and Jason can't make it, neither can Alice, but Mr Crowley and his wife will be there along with Christine and me. Would you like to join us?"

"That sounds lovely, but only if you're sure. I wouldn't want to interrupt anything." Albert liked him even more. He wanted to ensure the invitation was genuine before accepting. Albert admired his pleasant attitude.

"Darren, I used to take everyone out for a meal often, but then I had an operation, and the meals had to stop for a while. A new team member serves as an ideal occasion, Christie agrees."

"I'd be happy to join you. What time?"

"Dinner would be at eight. Is that okay?"

"That's great. Where?"

"There is a lovely restaurant down the road from Christine's' apartment, perhaps you've seen it? It's the one with the blue lights on the front."

"I drive past it every day on my way to work; I always thought it looked nice."

"It is. Are you finished here?" Everyone else had left, and Albert began to feel as if he was preventing Darren from going home.

"I am."

"I'll walk out with you if you like." Darren thanked him with a smile and said he needed to get his bags. "Okay." He disappeared through a door to Albert's right. He heard a locker open. Taking out his phone, Albert decided to call his daughter and confirm that Darren would be there on Friday night, but it was engaged, he couldn't get through. "Damn it", he thought, "she never uses her bloody phone, but when she does, it's always when I want to talk to her".

Albert childishly plotted his daughter's happiness with Darren. He just needed to determine if Darren liked Christine as she did him.

Darren emerged while he was in mid-thought, he had his phone to his ear and was smiling like a fool. "If that's Christine on the phone, then her happiness is guaranteed," he determined.

"That was Christine." He explained as he hung up.

Before he locked it and put it back in his pocket, he studied the caller ID photo for a moment and smiled faintly. Albert knew that look. It was the look that came across his daughter's face when she talked about him, perfect. He was getting ahead of himself, and he knew it, so he wouldn't think about it any further until he got to know Darren better.

They had reached Darren's car first. He began to search for his keys in his bag and found them almost instantly.

"Can I detect quite a bit of an English accent in your southern sound?" Albert smiled.

"You can, yes. Before I moved to Tennessee, I lived there. I was born there." Everything else may be a secret, but he made no attempt to keep this quiet too, it was too obvious.

"Where about?"

Naming a specific district was out of the question, so he responded more vaguely. "East London. I'm going to have to apologise, Mr Bridges, as I have to get to the shop before it closes at eight, my neighbour text me asking to pick up some more dog food." He glanced at his watch and explained that he only had twenty-five minutes left. Albert let him go after shaking his hand and saying that he looked forward to getting to know him better over dinner. They bid each other goodbye and Darren got in his car and drove off, through his rear-view mirror he saw Albert wave briefly before making his way to his car.

"Okay, okay, you can slow down now!" Darren spoke, talking to his heart. "I don't think he recognised me." If he did, things could get complicated over dinner.

"So, you said you'd be there? How was he?" Chris asked him.

"What do you mean?" Darren asked confused.

"He can be a little intimidating when meeting my friends. He wants to ensure I'm in the right company."

He sensed she wanted him to challenge her. "And am I, as you say, the right company?"

"Well, he didn't hit you, did he?" She joked, "Because if he did, probably not. No, I just wondered if he was nice to you, he isn't always."

"He was really polite and inviting actually, pleasant, much more pleasant than you are towards me."

"You sounded very English when you spoke then." She laughed. "It's simple; he likes you. I don't, that's why I'm mean to you."

"So that's why? Is there any way I can get you to like me?" He asked it in context, but secretly meant it in another, he just wished she knew what he meant deep down.

"You can start by lending me another book." There was a knock at the door, and when Darren opened it, Christine was standing before him with her phone in one hand and pressed to her ear, a book in the other.

"This one's too short, I got to the end, and now I need another."

He gestured for her to come in, she did and after taking off her shoes and her coat, and began to make her way towards his bookshelf.

He left her to it and went into the kitchen and turned on the kettle. "I was about to order dinner, are you hungry?" He shouted to Christine.

"I could eat something."

"Get the menus and have a look. Tea or coffee?"

"Coffee please."

A teaspoon of coffee in each mug and two of sugar in one, a single sweetener in the other. "Chicken or Pizza?" She asked him when he put the cups down on the coffee table.

"Well, that's a daft question."

"Fair point. I'll call."

By the time dinner had been eaten, the time was 21:22 pm.

"Did you choose a book?" Darren asked as he realised there was no book laying on the coffee table next to her phone.

"No." She shot up, placed her plate down on the table and once again made her way to the bookcase at the other end of the living room.

When Darren had come back from the bathroom, he was still drying his hands on his trousers. He saw the book which was grasped firmly between Christine's fingers and his heart stopped.

"I know this murder!"

"You couldn't possibly know it. It's based on an English case from sixteen years ago, how could you know it?"

"If it's based on Clark McAvoy, then I only know it because my father was the lead detective on that case."

He managed to find his words, "Was he? Well, erm- Clark refused to be a part of the making of the book, but someone found his parent's murder and the lack of closure interesting and saw an opportunity to mix real life with fiction."

"Interesting. May I borrow this one?"

"Of course." He was struggling to hide the panic in his voice.

She flicked through the pages. "This is me." She pointed to a section of text and read aloud: "The girl was about his age, pretty and kind. She said hello and asked him about his coat. He told her where he'd got it, and they began to talk. He told her she sounded funny."

"So, you're the girl he met in the waiting room? He mentions later that he always wondered what happened to them, I think he said she was, well, you were "pleasantly different to everyone else he had ever met.""

He confirmed that it wasn't because she was the only American person he had met excluding your father. He says there was something about you. I think you'll like it. You'd like it even if you weren't one of the characters."

"I'm sure I will. I always wondered what happened to him. Did they at least find something that could lead them to the murderer?"

No. "You should read it and see. I don't want to ruin it for you."

"Okay, thank you." Her excitement was obvious.

They sat back down on the sofa and turned on the TV. There was nothing good on, so they put on the X Box and logged into Netflix. They put on a random movie which, of the recommended, sounded the best, on went 'Before we go' starring Chris Evans.

As they watched the film, Darren felt as if the book was staring at him, threatening him with its truths. He glanced at the table, but the book was now in Christine's hand as she explained that she'd better be leaving as it was almost 11 o'clock and she was getting tired. They had work in the morning, wicked Wednesday as they called it, the day everyone hated. The day would begin with a mandatory meeting which each member of staff had to attend and was followed by one to ones conducted by Crowley if you required it, and because of the severity of the case they were investigating, they were both asked to attend one the following morning.

They said goodbye and agreed to finish the film another time as they were both enjoying it so far. He closed the door behind her and rested his head against the cold white painted wood. He turned around and leaned against it. Sighing deeply, he slid down its smooth surface until he was sitting on the floor. He tipped his head back so that it was once again resting on the door.

Why had he not seen it before? And how did he feel about it now that he knew? Now everything was clear to him, but what was to happen now?

CHAPTER 6

IN HIS DREAMS, SHE laid in his arms. They would be entwined in a dimly lit room amongst a mass of untidy bedsheets. They would make love and lie still holding each other afterwards. But then he would wake, and he would be alone. Alone in the room that he had dreamt they had been in, alone in the middle of the night aching for her to fill the void. He ached with a pain he yearned to be destroyed with love, her love.

At first, the dreams only came once a week, but now he had them more. In some, they would be talking, in others, they would make love, and in others, they would merely be walking in silence on a beach somewhere Darren never recognised, their hands being the only contact they had.

His dream on this night, in particular, was unlike any other.

They were facing each other in the middle of his living room and, in unison, they began to move towards one another, slowly and deliberately, exciting their passion with each second and with every inch less.

At last, they met in the middle and were now only a few inches away from each other. Their faces leaned gently forward as their anticipation heightened.

They each took half a step forward and encased one another in their arms as their lips touched. There was gentle tugging of hair and pressing of bodies in an encouraging, enticing way until they could both go on no more without the satisfaction they now desperately needed.

He kissed her passionately, she responded with an equally enthusiastic passion. He slowly ran his hands over her body.

She pleaded for him to take her. He did.

He woke at 06:00 Friday morning with his alarm and was surprised to find that he felt a lot better when compared to how he had felt the day before. Crowley had ordered him home once he had seen him Thursday morning and told him to have Thursday and Friday off. But now he had a massive headache which thumped each time he blinked. Albert had booked dinner for 20:00 Darren recalled as he prayed his headache would be gone by then, it wasn't an occasion he wanted to miss, not if he could help it. He was eager to see Chris.

Cautious of his headache, he eased himself out of bed slowly and sat on the edge as he slipped on some socks, the bathroom floor was always too cold on a morning.

He chuckled to himself as he thought about the dreams, they were ridiculous and quite weird. As he brushed his teeth, he heard his phone go off in the next room. Careful not to drop toothpaste on the carpet, he retrieved his phone from his bedside table and unlocked it. It was a message from Christine.

"If you're still as ill as you were yesterday, you'd better not breathe directly on any of us tonight. We don't want to die as well."

"Well, aren't you compassionate towards your ailing friends? I may take extra care to breathe directly on you as often as I please, thank you very much. And by the way, meanie!"

"What do you mean, "meanie"? I'm merely speaking from the heart, and surely, you're not going to hold that against me?"

"I should have thought you'd be at least slightly upset that I may die from this cold, it has been known to happen before!"

"It has. But not, I can inform you, to a man in his mid-twenties in the last 30 or so years. If it has, it is quite unfortunate for the poor guy, and you should stop feeling sorry for yourself."

"Says the woman who required a plaster after you'd pricked yourself with a pin."

"Good point. What time are you planning on getting to the restaurant?"

"Well, since dinner is at 20:00, I thought I'd try and get there for around 19:45 if that sounds okay to you? What time will you and your dad be getting there?"

"Well my dad and I were going to get there for around 19:15 so we would have the chance to sit and talk about you all before you arrive. I'm sorry, I've got to go, some of us have work today. I'll see you later Darren." She sent her last message at 06:22 and finished it with a smiley face. He laughed at her emphasis on the words "some of us" as he wandered back into his room to get dressed. He read their conversation over once more as he randomly chose a t-shirt and baggy jogging bottoms out of his draws.

As much as he looked forward to the evening ahead, a small part of him dreaded it as he knew that his mind would wander off each time he looked at her. It would distract him with its tormenting as it would replay his dreams in his head, over and over. Still, he couldn't wait to see her. He'd wear the blue tie, the one she always said looked nice on him. He once said that he thought it matched her eyes, "the deep blue of the sky on a summer's day", the smile she had responded with was the first of many heart-warming smiles she unknowingly gave him.

Now all he had to do was wait for the evening, it was over twelve hours away, and he had no work to do in the meantime. His head hurt too much to go outside, so training and cycling were out of the question. He decided to draw. He thought that it would divert his mind from thoughts about the upcoming evening and seeing Christine and Albert again. He made his way up to his studio as he contemplated what he was to draw.

For Christine, the highlight of her day was the conversation she had had over text with Darren in the morning. Even though she hated the thought of him being unwell, she was relieved that he wasn't at work on this day. She recalled the day's events as she sat at her desk filling in a case report.

She had arrived at work like usual at 07:00, and as the door of the lift opened a couple of minutes before her shift begun, Crowley met her as the doors opened, his face showed signs of great sadness and remorse as he handed her a file dated the night before.

She had waited until she had gotten to her desk, put away her backpack and logged onto her computer before she contemplated opening the file.

After a few brief moments of contemplation, she opened the file and instantly realised what it had been that had affected Crowley in such a way.

The photograph paper clipped to the front sheet in the file showed a woman in her mid-twenties, blonde, with three red blotches on her otherwise perfect white dress. Her hands-on first look would merely appear to be resting on her stomach to the unknowing eye, but Christine could tell what they were doing. The killer had positioned her like an angel, like the others.

As she thought about it later, she realised her first thoughts should have been of the poor girl's family, but they went to Darren. What would he say? He already blamed himself for the others, and now there would be another innocent victim on his conscience.

She'd stared at the body for what seemed like days until it seemed like she and the victim were the only two people left on earth.

Even though Christine knew the girl was dead, she almost expected her to get up off the ground, she appeared so peaceful and calm, as if she was asleep. Who would do such a thing? What would drive a person to even think about doing this to another living creature, and then, what on earth could possess them to go through with it? These are the questions which were on Christine's mind as she drove back to the precinct as she returned from the crime scene.

She gathered the files from each of the victims and ordered them, oldest case to the newest on her desk. In an attempt to find new evidence which may potentially lead them to the psycho who committed these crimes, Christine started with the oldest one, the victim from Tennessee, and began to read through them.

She'd swiftly skimmed over the victim's details and had begun reading the crime scene report when she decided she should look through the personal information more carefully as a link may be made between the victims that way.

She was grateful she had gone back, for now, she saw something which caught her eye. It wasn't related to the case as far as she could tell, but it was something she found very interesting. As she drove home that night, she realised she was eager to show her father her findings, so she called him.

He answered while she was at a set of traffic lights, where she asked him to wait as she transferred him to the hands-free system installed in her car.

"Are you there?" She asked him once she was sure she had set everything up correctly.

"I am. What's up?"

"Nothing, I was just wondering if we could meet at the restaurant at 19:00, there is something important I need to talk to you about, and I'm not sure how long it's going to take."

"I take it that it is not something you want the team to hear about." He sounded unsure at the thought. She always told the team as much as she could, trusting in them as often as possible.

"It's not something I particularly want to discuss with them, no. But, it is no secret so don't assume anything yet, it is merely something you and I would find intriguing as we are the only ones who could know its significance."

"Okay honey, I'll see you there at 19:00. I'm sorry but I've got to go, so I'll see you tonight. I love you, goodbye."

A man of few words, Christine thought. "I can guarantee he'll have a lot to say about my little discovery."

He had been sitting at his desk for over ten hours, only getting up to go to the toilet and to refill his water bottle. He was getting tired, but the piece he had produced was well worth the fatigue it caused. He had, on a sheet of A2 stretched paper, painted a figure amongst the golden glow of heaven standing before a pair of large black metal gates which depicted the gates of heaven.

The clock showed that he had just over an hour before it was time to set off for the restaurant. After painting for the day, his back was stiff and as he stood and as he straightened himself out it cracked in three different places.

He tidied up his desk as quickly as he could but found that the aching in his back wasn't easing. He decided to get a hot shower and let the water fall on his back for a while. His hands and arms were in dire need of a wash as they were layers deep in the paint of all colours.

Once in the shower, he turned the temperature up as high as he could stand before he stood directly underneath it. He hung his head and let the warm water flow over his hair, pushing it into his eyes before the water dripped off the end of his nose. He smiled as he brushed his hair across his forehead and opened his eyes. What was it about a hot shower that made you forget about your troubles?

For a few brief moments, he was just a man, he had no occupation and no past, his future wasn't planned, and nothing was occupying his mind.

Soon, he felt the images of the victims coming back, he felt her touch on his arm coming back, and the faces of his parents started to reappear once more, so he decided to put on some music.

He had bought the radio a few months ago and was one of the only pieces of technology he owned. It was waterproof and portable. He found he could plug it in during the night to charge it, and when it came to the morning, it had enough power to stay unplugged for well over an hour as he readied himself for work and tidied up. It had taken him quite a while to learn how to work it, but was now used almost continuously.

He decided which album he wanted, and after drying his hands and his arms up to his elbows, selected it on the menu and put it on shuffle. He loved the fact that Leon, his godfather, sent him CD's, DVD's and books, especially those which weren't always available in the US, he always preferred them.

As MIKA's 'Talk about you' began playing, Darren was grateful that his headache was going for the music had to be loud enough to be heard over the shower. He began to wash his hair as he sang along. By the time the song had finished, he had cleaned himself fully and had rinsed the shampoo out of his hair completely. He thought about MIKA, about the novels he had read and the BBC drama's he'd watched. Most of the things he loved the most were from England. Maybe it was time to go home?

The song changed as he climbed out of the shower and dried himself off. The steam in the room kept him warm as he dropped the towel he had dried himself with and proceeded towards the sink naked. The bathroom mat had moved and was in a bundle in the corner, so he went to retrieve it as the floor was cold under his feet.

He cleared the condensation off the bathroom mirror and lathered his face up with shaving cream; he couldn't go to dinner with Christine's father looking like he did. He hadn't shaved in three days and was beginning to look a little untidy.

Humming along to 'Hurts', he tidied himself up. Stroke by stroke he began to look better. He ducked his head as he cupped his hands under the running tap and splashed his face. He dried his face with the towel before once again looking at himself in the mirror.

He stopped. Who was he? His hair was almost down to his eyes, and his cheeks had become much hollower since he moved. "You're not right." He told himself. He hardly recognised himself anymore. He was hiding himself behind a facade, one that hid his inner coward, and the one that made everything appear like it was okay when it wasn't.

He was back in his room when he decided that what he had done wasn't as bad as he thought. He hadn't lied to Christine, he didn't tell her everything, he had told her a little more than nothing, but he still hadn't lied.

His parents came back to him as he recalled what his father had said to him once, "Son, lying is wrong, even when you do it for a reason. Even if that reason is to protect someone you love, it doesn't make it right; it makes you a nice, thoughtful person, yes, but a nice and thoughtful person who lied."

"Father." He whispered. "Mother." He opened his eyes in fear of their images coming back to him in the dark.

His headache was back, but the music remained turned up. He got dressed quickly, choosing the blue tie, as promised, and he set off to the restaurant. He ensured he picked out a CD to put in the car. Something was niggling at him. He went upstairs and instantly believed he knew what it was. There was a towel left on the floor, so he put it on the back of the bathroom door. But that wasn't it. He wandered into his studio and saw his pallet still out, which was funny because he'd never left it out before. He took off his jacket and rolled his shirt sleeves up and placed the paint pallet in the sink and slowly filled it with water. He was careful not to turn the tap on too fast as the paint would go all over his shirt. He cleaned his hands, dried them and rolled his sleeves back down and put his jacket back on.

He needed to leave but decided to have one more look at his painting before he went. This was his mistake.

Instead of seeing the woman waiting to be seen by God to ask permission to enter heaven, he saw that the woman's lips were blood red and there was a faint outline of angel wings behind her. He took a closer look, and he realised that her eyes were shut.

What had he painted? Why had he painted it? How had he managed to do it without realising? Maybe he just needed to tell someone, get it off his chest, then perhaps he wouldn't feel as guilty. But it wasn't his fault- Yes it was, it was his fault she was there- but that doesn't make him responsible, does it? "I'll tell Chris, and maybe she can help me." But what would she think of him?

"But Christine love, are you sure?"

"Dad, I'm one-hundred per cent sure. I searched for her on the FBI Database and found a direct link to him. It's the same boy from all those years ago. I'm sure of it."

"Well, at least we know what has happened to him. Poor kid, he's lost so much. How long ago was this?"

"She was killed about eight months ago."

"And what's he doing now?"

"That's the weird thing; there is no record of him since she was killed." Her father's face told her precisely what he was thinking.

"No dad, I don't. I don't think he killed her." She was about to tell him about the book she had borrowed from Darren but decided against it. But he had seen her stop and asked her what she was going to tell him. She tried to tell him it didn't matter, but he insisted. "Okay. I borrowed this book from Darren. It is about the McAvoy murder. It was published a few months ago. It details his parent's murder. Dad, someone turned his life into a fiction novel, creating characters based on real people and only changing the names. There is something honest in the writing though when they write about his wife."

"What does it say?"

"Well, they interviewed Clark, he gave them the minimal information possible but enough so that they would leave him alone. Their marriage was a "peculiar one" he says. He married the daughter of his English Teacher who was also his adopted mother. It was his adoptive mother's wish, but Clark had no feelings for her daughter. Still, he was, I think he said he was "grieved when he found out she'd gone", which you can imagine."

"He's had a miserable life. I do hope he didn't do it. He was such a lovely, good-natured boy. He was strong. He only broke down once when reciting the events surrounding his parent's death. I would like to know what he's up to now."

"So would I." She whispered. There was something about him that had never entirely left her. It was his eyes, eyes she believed she'd seen a million times since leaving him in that waiting room. She sat in silence for a while. After sixteen years, she was finally able to remember their conversation. She replayed it in her head and smiled at his comment about her accent and her reply.

Within a couple of minutes of silent reflection, Darren was standing before her looking as charming as ever. "I like your tie." She said.

"That's why I'm wearing it." He teased.

She stood to greet him. He gently kissed her on the cheek. She felt his hand on her waist as he leaned in to hear her whisper in her ear. "I've asked him to be nice. But he makes no promises." "Confidence boost, thank you. But I can be mean too." He replied. "Mr Bridges." His hand left her waist and extended out towards her father, who took it and stated the extent of his happiness and how glad he was they have finally met properly.

Darren took the seat Albert had informed him was his, next to Christine, and for a few minutes until Crowley and his wife arrived, Darren talked solely to Albert as he was unable

89

to avoid the direct questions fired at him. Albert asked him about work, about his apartment, about Kickboxing and his transfer from Tennessee to New York.

Christine took no notice of his answers, but she did take note of him. Instead of hearing his response, she watched his eyes light up on occasion. She watched him fiddle with his jacket when he was slightly uncomfortable, and she watched him eagerly answer her father as honestly as possible.

As she watched him, something stirred inside her. She recalled the warmth of his hand on her hip, suddenly finding herself wishing it was still there.

Crowley and his wife arrived soon, and once everyone had said their hello's and had sat down, dinner was ordered, and everyone was quickly involved in their conversations with people across the table. Christine could see that Helena was looking at her from across the table waiting for her to finish her conversation with her father. She made it a point to end her conversation with her father as quickly as possible without seeming impolite so that she could talk to her.

Albert ended their conversation abruptly as he needed to ask Darren something. Christine turned to Helena who smiled as their eyes met, "Did you have an interesting case today Christine? I'm sure I heard Frank mention you investigated a murder."

Her eyes went to Darren who had stopped his conversation with her father and was now looking at her. The noise level on the table died down, and all eyes were on

Christine. Her eyes remained fixed with Darren's, and she knew that he had guessed what had happened.

She quickly cleared her throat and replied as soon as she could, she was careful not to show any hesitation as she did. "It was another 'Angel' murder. The same as the others, we still have no idea who's doing it and why." She stopped there as she saw Darren withdraw himself away from the table and sit back in his chair as if hiding himself from what everyone and what they were saying. She looked at her father who was watching Darren. Her dad then looked at her as she looked back at Darren and reached beneath the table for his shaking hand.

CHAPTER 7

EVERYONE WAS IN HYSTERICS, dancing and laughing around me as they all tried to get to us and congratulate us. Why was I unhappy? I thought this was what I wanted, to give back to those who have treated me with such kindness.

The wedding was only announced a few months before, and since then, everything had been more hectic than it usually was. When my mother approached me with the idea, I felt bound to accept, and I felt that if I did so, it would make me a better person and show my appreciation for the last few years. But now that it is all over, I realise that it isn't even what I wanted.

It may feel good to have pleased so many other people, but should that count if I was as unhappy as I was? No, my feelings didn't matter at that moment, all that mattered was my wife and her mother, the ones who have treated me like one of their family. No, I didn't matter right then.

Why aren't you smiling?" She demanded from my side.

"I am, dearest." I grinned through my unhappiness unsure whether or not she believed me.

"No, you're not!" She shrieked as she pinched the back of my arm until I winced from the pain.

My feelings did not matter I reminded myself. "I'm sorry, darling."

"You'd better be. Because if you aren't, there will be trouble, Clark.

I remembered the fierce look in her eyes as I ensured my face was lit up with a bright smile as guests continued to congratulate me. I didn't mean to make her mad. I wished my parents were here. They'd make me happy, actually happy instead of pretending.

"Are you listening to me?" She was shouting at me again. It never mattered what I did, she yelled at me anyway, but I never argued, I deserved it, at least I think I did.

"Yes darling, I was."

"What did I say?" She demanded as her eyes grew red with rage.

"You were saying that we are to meet your mother outside in a few minutes." The last time I didn't listen to her, she hit me, hard, across the face with her shoe.

"Good." She looked annoyed. Had she hoped I hadn't heard her? If so, why? Did she enjoy punishing me?

We met her mother outside, and her face was as bright as ever. My insides warmed, I'd made her happy, but I still wasn't. That didn't matter, though.

"Sarah darling you look beautiful." She kissed her daughter on the cheek and held her hands in hers as they talked in hushed voices.

"Clark!" She shouted. I looked at her and asked her what was wrong. "Come here."

"Yes?"

"Sarah tells me you've been a little distracted, is this true?"

"No Ma'am." I lied, hopeful that she didn't realise. She did.

She looked around the garden before striking me across the face. "Liar." She instantly regained her composure as she asked me once more about what was distracting me.

"I wish my parents were here, that's all." Instantly I realised I shouldn't have added the "That's all" at the end, it sounded too cheeky, and Isabelle didn't like cheeky. She liked it even less that Sarah did. "Well they're not Clark, you know that. You've got me, and that's all that matters. Now you have Sarah, and we can be one happy family." In her tone, I sensed a touch of sarcasm.

Why did she talk to me like that? I'm not stupid. I know my parents aren't coming back.

When I was younger, someone murdered my parents. They had survived through the poverty of their childhoods, fighting through it all to build a vast empire together. When they died, they owned the largest export business in the UK and were loved by all because of their generous nature towards the less fortunate. They were forever founding charity after charity and were always donating generous amounts of money to hundreds of existing Charites. After all this, they were killed in a simple mugging. We were due to leave for a holiday, and they were packing everything in the car when a man came up behind them. They never found the man.

I was sent back to Boarding School by social services where I grew close to my English Teacher Mrs James, who, when I turned ten, adopted me. I stayed at school until I was 18 and then I moved in with Mrs James permanently. Before I graduated, I had spent each holiday at her house with her and her daughter. I went to University after school where I studied English Literature and Fine Art. They pulled me out of University just before I turned 20. Soon after my return, her daughter, Sarah, declared her love for me, and her mother insisted we got married, and we were, quickly.

I guess the only question I asked myself is why did I stay? It's simple. They were the only ones who had been there for me after my parent's death. I lived with them, both at school and at their house. There was only one problem regarding the marriage, not counting my objections, and that was the idea that my adopted mother was now my mother in law. But I had never anticipated the real motive behind their kindness and generosity.

It was the night of my wedding, and reluctantly, I had gone with Sarah back to her house. I was under her mother's instructions and did not want to upset her.

Sarah had told me what was going to happen that night. Her mother had said that it is what we needed to do to make it all legal, consummation was necessary. But despite knowing my feelings did not matter, I still couldn't help but wish I wasn't there. She had taken me upstairs and was telling me how things were going to happen.

I felt awkward listening to her telling me exactly how things were going to go down and my mind wandered back to the waiting room at the precinct in London twelve years before. I was eight, almost nine at the time, it was the day following my parent's death, but the one other thing that came to my mind about that day was the girl that talked to me.

As Sarah undressed me and pushed me onto the bed, my thoughts remained on the girl whose name I had forgotten entirely. Her eyes were the most beautiful I had ever seen, but I couldn't even remember what they looked like anymore.

That night was horrible. Afterwards, I felt abused and beyond a disgrace, I felt dirty and as if I had done something wrong.

The following four years went by slowly. Many nights occurred where, unwillingly on my part, Sarah would have her way with me. I learned to live with it, but I didn't know why. We all moved to America shortly after I had turned ten. I was taken out of the boarding school, Mrs James left her job, and we moved into an apartment south of Nashville in Tennessee. I had managed to make only a few friends in Tennessee and was quite accustomed to staying out with them, going to a pub after work where they drank beer, and I drank orange, I was never fond of drink.

I came home one night to an empty house but thought nothing of it until I was called back into work that night.

There had been a murder. An as yet unidentified young woman in her early twenties. They needed me on duty as all of the other detectives were in their usual Friday night state.

When I got there, I processed the scene; the Medical Examiner had already taken the body by the time I'd got there. I bagged all of the evidence, swabbed each surface for anything unusual and sketched the scene for further analysis back at the precinct.

A few hours later, when I first saw the body, I deduced that the killer must have had very personal influences as the level of intimacy of the crime was beyond words. They had violated the victim and stabbed her three times, once in the in the torso, the second purposely in the heart and the third one, it seemed, was perfectly straight into the victims' stomach.

The ME had been watching me keenly with an amazed look on his face. Disbelief had come across him, and he could no longer keep silent on the subject, so he proceeded to walk over to me and point something out.

I was so busy trying to figure out the nature of the crime that I hadn't even noticed that the lifeless body laid in front of me on a stretcher in the middle of the night, was the dead body of my wife. Still, even after the revelation, I felt nothing. Sure, I was upset at her passing but only as much as I would have been with any victim. I just felt grieved to the extent anyone would feel when presented when a dead body.

I felt for the loss of a fellow human and disgust towards a killer, but nothing in particular for the woman I married. She had abused me for years and destroyed me emotionally for even longer. Again, I tried, but still, I failed to feel anything for the woman who was before me.

The autopsy showed that she was pregnant at the time of death, but a DNA test showed that the baby was not mine. The DNA matched that of a man who I'd thought to be my only real friend.

Her mother made it clear that she no longer wanted anything to do with me as it was my fault her child and grandchild, had died. A note on the fridge door when I returned home later that night after I'd finished at the crime scene, reminded me that I was supposed to have met Sarah in front of the diner around the time that she died. The grief was finally there, but it wasn't for Sarah, it was for her mother. It was my fault her child was dead, I may not have killed her, but it was my fault she was there.

In a moment of anger, I confessed to her mother that I did not love her daughter and told her briefly what had been going on for the last four years. She then admitted that she didn't care, she knew I didn't love her, and she knew her daughter had no affection for me either. It had been an arrangement. Their goal has been for her to have a child with me. Once we had married and had settled down with a child, she and Sarah had planned to kill me to receive the fortune my parents left me upon their death, leaving it all to our child. She did not expect it to take as long as it did for Sarah to get pregnant.

Distraught that the woman who had taken me in all those years ago, had turned out to be whom she was, I left that night never to return. But before I managed to get out of the door, her mother stopped me and told me the full extent of their plan.

The truth was, their plan had been more extensive than I could have ever imagined. The man who visited almost every day and who moved in with Isabelle the same day Sarah and I had moved out, the man Isabelle had said was her brother, was, in fact, her husband, and the man who had killed my parents with the sole intention that Isabelle take me in. I was intended to live with her, to marry her daughter, to make them rich upon my death.

I left Tennessee after legally changing my name and never looked back. We never found who killed Sarah and I left Tennessee carrying the blame both from myself and from all those who knew Sarah.

CHAPTER 8

A S HER HAND REACHED him under the table, Darren looked up at Christine as the rest of the table continued to talk about the case.

Christine took her weight off her chair and moved a few inches towards Darren and signalled for him to do the same. Once they had sat down again and they were sure everyone else was still otherwise engaged, they began talking about whatever came to their minds.

After a while, Christine suggested to Darren that he think of something completely unrelated to the case, something as random as possible to take his mind off it.

He thought about it for a moment before asking her, "Do you remember the first time we met, in the kitchen at work and you were asking me all of those questions to answer one big question?"

"Yes, I remember."

"What was the overall question? What was it you wanted to know about me?"

She seemed hesitant, but instead of avoiding the question as he had thought she would, her grip tightened slightly around his, and her thumb grazed over his knuckles "I wanted to know if you were... hurting." She winced in embarrassment.

"If I was hurting?"

"It was your eyes which betrayed you first. I know it wasn't entirely professional, but- I don't know why I wanted to know, but that's the question I wanted answering."

He stilled, and she knew that she'd gone too far. She expected him to shake his hand free from hers and move away from her to talk to someone else. But he didn't, he looked everyone around the table, and once he was happy that they were too engaged in their conversations to notice him, he inched closer to Christine and took her hands in his and asked, "Did you get what you wanted?"

"Yes and no." She wanted her answer to confuse him and was grateful when it did.

Knowing that he needed to prompt her more specifically to get his answer, he rephrased his question.

"Okay," he smiled and swiftly glanced at everyone once more, "did you get an answer?"

"I got my answer, yes."

He smiled once more as he affectionately played with her fingers. "Then what was the 'no' for when I asked you if you got what you wanted?"

"That was all I wanted... then." His heartbeat became irregular, and his voice caught in his throat when he tried to speak. It was the way she had said it and the way her eyes had shone as she did.

101

He prayed she was thinking the same as him.

"And now?"

"And now, there's only one thing I want."

Unknowingly, they had moved a little closer together and could now feel the other's breaths gently blowing on their faces.

No one seemed to notice anything, for when Darren was about to respond, Helena called Christine's name, and everything between them vanished. "Christine?" Her hands shot out of his, and she turned back towards the table. "Yes?"

Before Helena could answer her, Darren excused himself from the table and headed in the direction of the bathroom. Christine knew she couldn't follow, but ached to continue comforting him and distracting him, keeping it all away.

The conversation around the table remained on the topic until the servers had brought dinner. Darren returned after a few minutes, and the discussion shifted to music.

Throughout the rest of the evening, Albert observed his daughter and the effect she had on Darren. His feelings were evident, as were hers. But if he was right to believe what he did, then he knew there would be plenty of things preventing Darren from loving his daughter willingly.

Nick and Jason had gone to every extreme to make their barbeque the best anyone had ever seen. They had decorated their garden beautifully, and they all agreed that the food smelt exquisite. As they all walked through the back gate they were all greeted by Nick, Jason was over the grill and gave them a friendly wave with his free hand.

"Hello," Nick said as he hugged each of them in turn. They greeted him with a chorus of hums of approval regarding the decorations or the smell coming from the grill across the garden.

Jason ran over quickly and embraced them as a group before making his way swiftly back to the grill from where smoke was beginning to rise.

They had ended up all squished together after their hug from Jason.

"It looks amazing," Christine whispered to Darren as she leaned towards him.

"It does. They've gone to great measures to make it like this." He looked her over with a deliberately slow gaze and whispered to her, "You look beautiful by the way." Instantly he wished he hadn't said it but was relieved to see that his remark provoked a blush in Christine's cheeks and prompted her to look at him once again with her mesmerising eyes.

"Thank you. You look nice too." She gave him a sorry look as she hinted she didn't know what to say in response.

She had chosen to wear a pale grey dress which, despite the half of the dress below her hips leaving her body to blow freely in the wind, the top half of the dress emphasised each of her curves. He was surprised to see that she wasn't as small as he would have thought. Many days of running after criminals had caused him to imagine her thinner, but as she padded the slight bulge of a stomach and placed her hands over the faint love handles as if she was embarrassed, she became more desirable in his eyes. He didn't know why, but what some may see as an imperfection only strengthened his feelings for her, it made her all the more beautiful to him and the only thought that occupied his mind at that moment was the thought of holding her, even if he only had his arm around her or his hand in hers.

The food tasted even better than it smelt and as they all dug in eagerly, they each muttered unfathomable sounds of approval. Jason joined them once everyone had had at least one serving and they all sat down and managed to squeeze into a single picnic bench. As she sat next to Darren, Christine was aware of the lack of space at the table.

She had to sit, so her left arm was pressed into his right which meant she had to eat her hot dog with only her right hand.

She left the table to speak to Alice, and when she returned to the table, she found Darren being teased by Nick because of the length of his hair. It now almost reached his eyebrows and Nick pointed out that Alice was correct in predicting that his hair would remain curly. Jason suggested that it had become even curlier. Christine decided to come to his aid and fight them off with her compliments of his hair. "I think it looks remarkably fetching." She exclaimed as she sat. Her remark was met by a duet of 'whooping' from Nick and Jason as they joked and pretended to be serious when attempting to find a comeback.

The best they could do was, "Yea, well... your hair is barely curly, you have two perfect heads of hair, it's like you were meant for each other." She did not take offence as she regularly commented on her hair and everyone knew that she was happy with it as it was as it made it easier to deal with on a morning as she got ready for work.

As they watched Darren and Christine get up from the table and walk towards Frank and his wife Helena on the other table, Nick and Jason gave each other a look they both understood. Nick's remark when commenting on Darren and Christine's compatibility referred to more than their hair. They knew that they hadn't appreciated when the statement was first made and didn't expect them to, but they would hopefully realise one day.

Both Nick and Jason could see that they both felt something for the other but neither dared to point anything out through fear of causing them embarrassment. They would have to cross their fingers and hope.

"Thank you, Helena, that would be wonderful. Which day would best suit you?" Christine beamed.

"Oh, no dear, you two choose which day would best suit you."

Christine turned to Darren and asked him which day would best suit him, and when he replied that a week on Tuesday would be the best day, she agreed that that day would be good for her too, they then confirmed it with Helena and her husband.

"That Darren is the sweetest young man I've ever met. Are you sure you're right about him? Are you sure he is who you think he is? Could it all be a mistake, there will be more than one person with the same name you know." Even as she asked her husband these questions, Helena knew that Frank wouldn't have gotten it wrong.

"You know the answer to each of those questions dear, and I don't think it, I know it, he told me soon after he transferred." He kissed his wife gently on the cheek before getting up to get them both another plate of food.

"I just wish there was another answer I could give you."

Before he could leave, Helena grabbed his hand and motioned towards Darren and Christine who were standing alone together by the fence on the other side of the garden. "They make a lovely couple, don't they?"

"They're not together Helena love." He looked back at his wife and gave her a disappointed look.

"Are you sure? But the way he looks at her and the way she looks at him..." her voice trailed off before she turned to Frank, "Are you sure?"

"Very sure." He kissed his wife's hand and went to get their food. He looked at Darren and Christine once more. Christine was pointing towards the sea.

"Do you want me to show you?" Chris hoped he would say yes, she wanted to be alone with Darren if only for a moment, with no one looking. Whenever she was in the area, which was often as she had grown up less than a mile from Nick and Jason's house, she would walk down the beach on her own and sit in her special place under the rocks. She'd always thought that she'd never want to share her special place with anyone else but found that now she wished to share it with Darren.

His smile spread across his face as he replied that there was nothing he would like more.

One the way, they couldn't find anything to talk about, but she discovered that watching Darren's eyes light up at simple little things beat any conversation they could have had.

They finally reached her spot and sat on a rock. Darren could see why she liked this place so much, the rocks surrounding the hole in the wall protected them from the breeze, and the sea looked beautiful with the moon shining down upon it, caching in the creases of the waves.

He looked over at her and saw how at peace she was here. She'd told him that she came here often and every time it gets better, there's either new people walking past or another dog who brings her a stick or even a different smell coming from the harbour, all of which she remembered.

Darren recalled being at a similar place when he was younger, but it was in England, and it probably wasn't the same any more. It was a few miles south from Scarborough on the coast. He used to go there each year with his parents to the caravan park Primrose Valley. They would go each year without fail, and each night, if he could, he would walk down the steep path in the woods until he reached a set of wooden stairs halfway to the beach.

If you took the stairs on the right once you reached the bottom and then followed the path around to the left, you would be faced with a way leading directly along the cliff top towards Filey.

Generally, people chose to walk along the beach instead as not many people knew about this path, which he thought wasn't surprising considering how difficult it was to get through the overgrown trees and shrubs which caught in his hair each time he went through. The concealment of the path meant that Darren had never encountered anyone while he was up there.

It was always the place he returned to in his dreams and when he closed his eyes, his special place.

"I've never brought anyone here before." She confessed as she began to fiddle with her finger as she usually did when she was nervous.

"How come?" He asked quietly.

"I've just never thought about bringing anyone. I've never felt like sharing it with anyone."

"And now?"

"And now," she repeated, "I feel like I want to share it with you, and only you." She didn't dare look at him for she feared she had said the wrong thing.

"I like it here." His simple response caused the exact reaction he had expected. She looked mildly disappointed that he hadn't said anything further or anything that resembled what she had confessed. He waited for a moment before adding, "But I'd like it anywhere you were. Thank you for bringing me here, Chris. Knowing that I'm the only one you've shown this to means a lot to me." She looked better now, happier and less uncomfortable.

"Well, you're welcome." She smiled nervously and finally managed to look at him. Many times, she'd badly wanted to tell him how she felt, but he had never given any solid indication that he reciprocated her feelings, so she'd always figured she'd save herself the embarrassment of rejection. She calmed down. "I just find it funny that I can talk to you for hours with ease, but cannot manage to tell you something so simple." She wanted to tell him how he made her feel, how she was kept awake most nights as she wished for him to be near her, holding her.

As he watched her transform back into the nervous state which she had just escaped, he stood up straight and held out his hand for her. "Let's take a walk." He had held out his hand without even thinking about it first and now realised that it may have been the wrong move. Fortunately, she took it with only slight hesitation and stood before him, her hand in his, smiling gently.

He tugged at her hand slightly to signal that they should begin walking. They walked hand in hand until Darren's phone buzzed in his pocket, and he had to let go of her hand. It was a message from Alan at the gym to tell him that he would drop the keys off at Darren's at about 11 o'clock that night. It was 20:39, and the barbecue was soon to end at 22:00.

They continued to walk along the seafront; the breeze was picking up.

She shuddered from the cold but tried to hide it as she knew Darren would offer her his jacket.

She glanced at him out of the corner of her eye and silently cursed as she witnessed him remove his coat, he'd seen her shiver. Despite her protests, he placed his jacket over her shoulders and told her not to argue. As he did so, his fingers brushed her shoulders, and he paused. He extended out a finger and stroked her shoulder briefly. Her breath caught in her throat and she shivered once more, but this time from within, something inside her was recording his touch and replaying it in her head, even as he moved away from her, it was there, engraved in her soul, tormenting her already. She wanted his skin against hers.

To take her mind off the build-up of sensation within her, she once again insisted that she did not need his coat, flatly denying any reference to her being cold.

"I know," he said, "I too shudder for no particular reason from time to time, but I guess your shivering in the cold is simply a coincidence?" His sarcastic tone caused an unpreventable giggle to escape her lips. "For goodness sake Chris, if only you weren't so stubborn." He half-laughed.

He commented on her stubbornness twice more in the conversation that followed and said that she didn't always have to hide her feelings. He accidentally let it slip that he suffered as he continuously hid his feelings and suggested that she always express everything she feels.

"What do you mean by that?" Her question had one ideal answer for which she hopelessly listened.

"All I mean is- I'm trying to say- you..." He stopped walking and turned, so he was facing her. Her face was glowing in the moonlight, its whiteness reflecting in her eyes giving them the appearance of jewels from Heaven itself.

His voice refused to cooperate when he tried to speak. "I mean, I don't think you know-" He looked at Chris powerlessly. "You don't know what you mean to ... all of us." He tried to tell her, but he couldn't tell her how he felt, not until she showed some sign of affection towards him. He had never told her how he felt as it would ruin what they had, should she reject him.

She exhaled quickly; she had been holding her breath as he spoke, hoping he would say something regarding them in some way. She was disappointed in what he had said, or by what he hadn't said, but what she did know, was that she had to leave. She began to turn away, but she stopped when she felt his hand on her arm. He pulled her back, gently and slowly, so she was facing him once more. They were closer together now. She could hear his sharpness of breath. Her heart raced with the thought that he might be nervous.

He glanced down at her body and hesitated before moving his hands from her shoulders to her waist. His heart was racing as he plucked up the courage to utter his next words. "You got me." He joked. He'd gotten her to smile, and now his heart rate began its descent to normal.

"You don't know what you mean, to me." She placed her hands affectionately on his arms and looked deeper into his eyes, silently encouraging him to continue.

"You don't know how much you mean to me." He pulled her in closer and caressed her cheek in his hand, running his thumb over her lips.

A single tear ran down her cheek, but he wiped it away, and with it, he wiped away all her fears of unrequited love, of rejection.

He took her face in both hands and gently pulled her in, watching her every move and ensuring there was no sign of uncertainty. But instead of pushing him away, she closed her eyes and tipped her head slightly, welcoming his kiss.

The second their lips touched their hearts leapt. Their kiss soon became deeper as she wrapped her arms around his neck. The warmth of their tongues as they touched made them hungry for more. They savoured every intimate kiss as they lost themselves in the other's arms.

Darren's phone began to ring, breaking them up. They let it ring as they stood looking into each other's eyes, seeing each other in a different light, what was once mere dreams had now become more reachable. It was Nick ringing to see where they had gone. He informed them that it was time for dessert and that they should make their way back or there would be nothing left for them. Reluctantly, they began to walk again. Even though the path itself was narrow, they still walked on opposite sides, hands in pockets to protect them from the night air as it threated them suddenly with its sharp gusts of ice cold-wind.

In their minds, they went over the events of the past couple of minutes as they walked back to the barbeque in silence. For some strange reason, neither dared to look at the other. Neither couldn't believe what had just happened as they both had thought the other to be indifferent. Both secretly wished they hadn't been interrupted and both wished that it would happen again, soon.

Frank eyed Darren and Christine keenly as they manoeuvred around the party separately now. His wife stood by his side and watched with him. As she did, she expressed her surprise at how moist the cake had kept after being out in the open for two hours.

"Do you like the cake?" Nick asked as he appeared by their side startling them slightly. "I told Jason that I didn't think it would last, but it looks like he was right, it has kept... hasn't it?" They nodded and congratulated him on hosting such a successful party.

Helena heard Darren laugh and diverted her eyes back to him. He was playing with a group of young children, running around in a circle playing tag and allowing them to catch him every time. He was a remarkable man, she thought, it was just a shame about his past. She knew that there was something between him and Christine but dared not say until one of them mentioned anything. Before she and Frank left around 21:30 she hugged Darren fondly, wished him well and said how much she was looking forward to the Tuesday next when he was to come to their house with Christine for dinner.

As they left, Darren and Christine said a quick goodbye before getting quickly into their cars exchanging only a brief smile which expressed all that needed to be said.

Darren was about to start the engine when Frank knocked on his window. They had come back to pick up Helena's scarf which she had left on the bench. Darren rolled down his window and said hello.

"You've got to tell her now," That was all Frank said on the matter, and after, he said nothing more than goodbye. How did he know anything had happened between them? Darren thought about objecting to the comment but knew that Frank was right, he needed to tell Christine before she found out by accident. He decided had to tell her everything and he would, but after the dinner on Tuesday, he didn't want to say anything to her before, just in case she didn't like what he had to say. He turned on the engine and drove home.

"Do you have any idea to where Darren and Christine disappeared? They were gone for half an hour." Nick asked as he lay in Jason's arms that night.

"I have no idea. You?" Jason answered.

"No."

"Something is going on between them."

"I thought that. Something happened tonight, when they came back, they were different." Nick said.

"Yea." Nick had to suppress a chuckle as he felt a pang of guilt as he realised Jason had almost fallen asleep when he asked him.

"It was a good party. We did good honey; we did well." Jason whispered as he finally dropped off. But Nick couldn't sleep knowing that they hadn't cleaned up properly downstairs. He climbed out of bed without disturbing Jason and crept downstairs where he began tidying as quietly as he could.

Jason woke a few minutes after Nick had left and was confused to find the bed empty next to him. He guessed where Nick would be, and the light sound of plates clattering together in the sink downstairs confirmed his suspicions. He got out of bed and went to help Nick tidy up. He'd only get reminded of his lack of help the next time they argued.

His painting still sat on his desk in the exact place he left it the previous evening before he went to dinner. He stared at the figure once more before getting out his paints and filling up a cup with water.

He swiftly walked into his room and removed his clothes before placing them neatly in the wash basket. He caught a glimpse of himself in the mirror as he passed and was surprised to see the figure before him. He had put on quite a bit of weight since he last looked a week before. His eyes no longer bore the shadows under them, and the colour had completely returned to his face for the first time in months. He was finally beginning to look like himself, and it scared him to think about how long it had been since he felt as happy as he did now.

He relayed their kiss in his mind as he put on his painting clothes and made his way back into his studio. It was time he redid the figure and painted over the wings, dye the figure's hair and tweak the rest of the piece until he was happy.

Once he had finished, he admired his final piece and placed it gently back on the easel to dry overnight. He readied himself for bed and got in at 23:51. As he laid his head on the pillow, he instantly felt tired. Were things moving too fast? He'd only been here two months - almost - he'd only known her for two months, was it too short a time? "No, forget the time, you're finally happy - sort of", he told himself as he fell asleep with the evening's events on his mind, hoping that she was thinking about it too. She was.

CHAPTER 9

I T WAS 20:32 MONDAY night a week and a bit after
the Barbeque at Nick and Jason's and everyone except
Darren, Christine and Alice had gone home a couple of
hours before. They were all sitting in the conference room
and were still filling out the paperwork for a case they
investigated earlier that day. There had been another murder,
one more to add to Angel's victim toll. Alice, however, soon
packed up her things and had said goodnight, leaving Darren
and Christine alone.

Not long after she'd gone, Darren moved his papers to
the seat opposite Christine's and pulled a goofy face when
she looked his way. She covered her smile with her free hand
as she continued to write. After a few minutes, he stood and
said he was nipping out. "Are you going to be okay?" He
asked before he left. When she assured him that she could
bear being alone for a short while, he left. He watched him
through the glass walls of the conference room. Her eyes
followed him until he disappeared around the corner towards
the stairs.

Once he'd gone, she found it hard to concentrate on her work as she recalled the events of that Saturday night once more. She closed her eyes and remembered his lips against hers by the beach.

Their kiss had left her breathless and unable to comprehend their situation, she was unable to put her feelings into words as she imagined him standing before her. She needed to talk to him, and she needed to understand what they were if they were anything.

She took out her phone and pulled her earphones out of her pocket. She scrolled down her playlists until she came to one titled 'Bulletproof Picasso', Train's newest album, it had come out the year before, but she still hadn't gotten around to buying it. She put both earphones in and turned it up.

She carried on with her work until Darren returned. He'd been gone almost twenty minutes and was now standing before her with a steaming bag of food, the smell had already filled the room, and her mouth had begun to water.

"What've you got there?" She smiled.

"Food. I got hungry." He answered simply.

"By the looks of it, you're starving." She teased, knowing that he'd bought enough for them both.

"I knew you'd be hungry as well." He placed their food on the table next to the files they were completing. "And I thought that we could do with a break," he paused and looked away "and maybe have time to talk. It's been over a week, and we haven't talked about it." He sat. Christine noticed that he was shuffling in his chair as if he was nervous.

She waited until his eye caught hers before she smiled and said, "Are you okay?"

He looked up and shrugged. "Just a little nervous."

"About?" He raised an eyebrow as if to confess the thoughts circling his mind secretly. "We don't have to talk right now if you don't want."

"No, no. It' fine, I've just never had this sort of conversation with anyone before."

She couldn't hide her surprise so instead asked him about the women before her. When he hesitated, she asked him how many relationships he'd had.

Now was the moment he'd been dreading, he knew he had to tell her at some point, and he knew he had to tell her now. He sat forward in his chair and placed his elbows on the table. She pulled her chair in and sat up straight.

"What?"

He began to fiddle with his fingers. "Christine, I've only ever been in one relationship." Before she could comment, he blurted out his confession.

"What? When?" Christine couldn't contain her shock.

"I was twenty."

"For how long?"

"Four years."

"And now, you're not?"

"No, not anymore."

"Where is she now?"

He hesitated, "She's back in Tennessee."

She noticed that his face held little emotion as he continued to call her "she". Daringly, she asked if he still loved her. When he confessed that he did not, she began to ask him how they had met.

"We met when we were seven. We went to the same school. I spent a great deal of time with her mother who was like a second mother to me. When she told me that she wanted to get married, for some reason, I didn't hesitate despite my lack of feelings for her. Christine, for me to tell you everything, you've got to-" he stopped as he searched her eyes for a sign that told him to stop, to continue or to forget the whole thing.

"I've got to what? What is it you can't tell me?" She felt her eyes begin to fill. "There has always been something you haven't told me, even after you told me about the victim in Tennessee, I could tell there was still something you were still keeping from me. I wish you'd let me in." A single tear travelled down her right cheek, wound its way around her mouth and dripped off her chin.

"Please, don't cry." He took her hand in his and was grateful when she did not refuse it. She ran her thumb over his knuckles. Her eyes remained on their hands as she said that nothing could ever happen between them until he either told her what was always on his mind or promised him that it didn't matter enough to trouble them. She took her hand out of his and packed up her files as he sat helplessly across the table. She could still feel his eyes on her.

She let their eyes meet once more. He was pleading for her to stay. To her relief, he did not try and stop her leaving. Instead, he stood. "What can I do to make you stay?" He asked.

"Why don't you try telling me how you feel? If you can't tell me about your ex-wife or anything like that, then the least you can do is tell me how you truly feel about me." She left before he had the chance to answer. She did not want him to respond out of impulse; she wanted him to think about his feelings and then give her his answer.

He'd followed her out of the conference room but remained at the door as she continued towards the stairs. She stopped and turned. He looked helpless and desperate to speak, but she didn't want to hear it. "I want us to be together Darren, but we can't if you won't let me in." Her words seemed to stay in the air between them as they both stood, still and silent. "Goodnight Darren." She turned the corner and began her descent down the stairs when she heard him close the conference door behind him, hard.

Darren continued with his work until half-past nine when he decided to go home. As he made his way to his car, he was met by Frank who had forgotten the flowers he'd bought for his wife.

When asked about his "sour look" as Crowley put it, Darren told him about the conversation he'd had with Christine. Crowley listened silently and only spoke after Darren had finished. "Well, why don't you just tell her?"

"It's like I'm lying to her, Frank. Do you think she'd hate me for it?"

"Why? You did nothing wrong?"

"Yea, but she might not like it all the same."

"Darren," Frank placed his hand on Darren's arm comfortingly, "you'll never know unless you tell her. Besides, I know Chris enough to know that she wouldn't hold it against you. I don't think it would matter much to her, honestly. I'd tell her if I were you, by not telling her, you're only delaying the inevitable, you're not preventing anything."

"Thank you, Frank."

"You know something, Darren, when I first read your file, I couldn't begin to imagine what such pain would do to a man and I couldn't help but picture a weak-minded man who didn't know what to do. But when you arrived, even the mere sight of you as I approached you on your first morning in the bullpen, told me I'd made a mistake. You're stronger than you think. Your file doesn't define you. Maybe Chris likes you because of you, not because of what you were or what you are on paper. Think about it. Goodnight Darren."

He smiled and continued towards the front door as Darren called out behind him, "Goodnight Frank." As Darren drove home, he knew that Christine's words and Frank's words would stay with him the rest of the night. He had a great deal of thinking to do, and it was time he figured out how to word everything, he was going to tell her, he had to tell her, tomorrow if he could find the time.

"So, for dinner tonight, I thought I'd make us that chicken stew that you love," Nick said to Jason across the bullpen.

Jason made an approving hum and said that it's just what they'd need to warm them up with the day being as cold as it was.

Nick checked that there was no-one else around before he made his way over to Jason, leant over his desk as if to look at his monitor and whispered, "It'll take a couple of hours once we get home so we'll have to find something to do to keep us warm in the meantime."

"I can't wait." Jason teased as he winked at Nick. Their eyes remained locked until, out of the corner of his eye, Jason saw Crowley emerge from his office.

He came over. "Hello, boys." The two men returned his hello in unison before he continued to explain that he was about to leave as his wife had demanded that he help with the dinner that night. "It's a shame you can't come, boys, Helena told me to tell you that you are always welcome. Anytime." He told them with a gentle smile.

"It's a shame, I know, but I think we're due a night in. Since we saw that we could leave early today, we took the opportunity to rent a movie and relax. Thank you though, hopefully, next time." Jason promised.

"Besides," Nick said quietly, "It'll give you and Helena a better chance to get to know Darren."

Jason lowered his voice. "You'll be able to focus more on him and Christine and see if you can figure anything out, you know, about them." He teased.

"Yea, we've got nowhere. If anything is going on between them, they sure are good at keeping it to themselves." Nick remarked.

Crowley stepped in closer so they could communicate in quieter voices as the bullpen was beginning to fill with others walking in and out and they didn't want anyone to hear.

"Well, I may have a little something." Crowley teased. He was pleased to see the eager look in both of their eyes as they demanded to know what he meant. "I nipped to Darren's house, it must have been a couple of weeks ago, maybe more, but anyway, Christine was there, and I asked Darren about it. It's not exactly what he said, but it was the way he said it as if he was disappointed that there was nothing between them."

"Well you'll have to keep an eye out tonight, won't you?"

"I will Nick. Well, I'll see you tomorrow. Goodnight, and whatever you do, do not let either of them know we were talking about them." Crowley warned as he backed away, under no circumstances was he going to tell them about his conversation with Darren the night before. "Kids at heart", he thought as he watched their eager faces as they jokingly gestured their promise with the zipping of their lips and the throwing away of the key. Crowley laughed and turned away as Nick and Jason both returned to their desks with a look of amusement in their eyes. They all knew that they were childish about the whole affair, but they had come to care for Darren as they cared for each other, Christine included, and they just wanted the best for them. Besides, it was just a little bit of fun. They enjoyed playing with them, kindly.

They witnessed Crowley leave about ten minutes after their conversation had ended and watched Darren and Christine return from a crime scene and go home separately after filling out their paperwork. Darren left first, and as Christine made her way to the elevator five minutes later, Jason hinted to Nick that he was almost finished.

As they were making their way out of the building that afternoon at 15:58, they were met by an unexpected gust of wind as they opened the door. The cold blew through them and caused them to go slightly off balance. They continued to walk, but before the door could close behind them, they were called back as there was a call at the front desk. The man on the front desk explained that the woman had asked for Darren, but when told that he wasn't there, she'd said that any member of his team would suffice.

"Hello, Nick Davis," Nick answered dubiously.

"Hello, are you on Darren's team?"

"I am, who may I ask, is this?" The voice was unfamiliar to Nick and sounded as if it belonged to a woman around fifty years old, southern and very loud.

"I'm a friend of his from Tennessee."

"Okay, what can I do for you?" Nick gestured to Jason to begin tracking the call to see if the woman was telling the truth.

"I wanted to know if you could tell me where he is." She sounded impatient.

They hadn't been talking long enough for them to finish locating where she was calling from, but Nick decided to end the call anyway, something told him he needed to. "I'm sorry, but I can't help you." He hung up and apologised to Jason for not keeping her on longer.

"There was just something in her tone of voice that told me that I should hang up, I don't know why." Jason touched his arm affectionately and reassured him that he did the right thing.

"If it's important, she'll call back." He stated.

When Tuesday evening came, Darren went home to get ready for dinner at the Crowley's that evening. As he walked through his front door, he suddenly felt the need to sit down. His head had suddenly become heavy, his eyes heavier, and behind his right eye, there was now a sharp, lingering pain.

After a couple of minutes, the weight his head had forced him to carry for those brief moments vanished, leaving him with a faint pain behind his right eye that he feared would remain there for the rest of the evening.

He got up slowly and made his way into the kitchen where he placed his bag on the table and got himself a drink of cold water. He retrieved two aspirins from the cupboard above the sink and broke them both in half and took them half at a time before he splashed his face with cold water. He picked up his bag and made his way up the stairs and towards his room. He sat on his bed and removed his shoes. As he placed them in their place in the draw, he scrolled down his playlists on his iPod. Before he selected anything, he plugged in the speakers.

Reluctantly, he scrolled past the new Christmas album by Brett Eldredge 'Glow'. It was too early for talk about Christmas, yet he so ached to play it. He silently hoped Christmas would come soon. It would be his first Christmas since the death of his parents which he would hopefully spend happily.

He carefully selected what to put on, deciding on a Josh Groban playlist composed of his greatest hits and the songs from his 'All that echoes' album.

As 'I Believe' filled his room, Darren began to get undressed. He moved in time with the music, and for a moment it transported him back to a happier time. He remembered an occasion where he had attended a formal event with his parents, something to do with their work, he couldn't quite remember. He had watched his parents dance in the centre of the floor with others dancing around them, all in pairs. They had looked at him and smiled. Without even considering how it would seem to those around them, they held their hands out towards him in unison and invited him to join them.

Overcome with joy, he had dashed to them and joined in with them. The world around him seemed to slow as he peered up at his parents. Their brightly lit faces were beaming down at him. His father had winked at him before his eyes diverted back to his beautiful wife. They gazed deeply into each other's eyes until their faces met above Darren's head, where they kissed once, innocently and gently.

Darren watched in awe, he saw the love behind a single gesture and wondered how something so small could mean so much to someone when given.

The song finished and he was once again in his room, alone. People told him that it would get easier, but he had not found that to be the case. What hurt the most about losing them, was that someone had done it purposely, and the killer was never convicted. Darren knew who it was, words exchanged between the two of them provided him with the man's confession, but he never did anything with the information, it seemed too farfetched, and he had no proof. It would just look like he was trying to get back at him for other reasons.

He hadn't seen the man for over a year and didn't care to see him for many more to come. He had once thought of the man as an Uncle, someone he admired and almost loved, but he couldn't have been more foolish, the man had deceived him, and Darren still wouldn't know the truth if it hadn't had been spelt out for him.

He stood in his underwear as he stared into his wardrobe and debated what to wear. He decided on a dark blue shirt and his dark grey trousers. He selected his black shoes and proceeded to put them on quickly as he was becoming quite cold. He reminded himself to put on the heating before he left.

Before he buttoned up his shirt, he undid the top of his trousers and opened his shirt to see if he had seen his reflection correctly. No, he was right, he had been putting on weight, not a lot, but enough to see a difference. He'd first started to lose weight after the day he'd said, 'I do'.

After the move to New York, as he continued to Kickbox on a more regular basis, he had burned off what fat he had left, and while the weight loss defined the muscle he had accumulated because of the training, he thought it made him look too tall and too lanky.

He finished getting dressed and turned on the heating.

He picked up his jacket which was by his bedroom door and began to make his way downstairs. He put his coat down beside the coffee table in the living room and sat down in his favourite chair. The lights from the building opposite were flashing through his window, so he decided to close the curtains.

As he stood at the window, he glanced in the direction of Christine's apartment and recalled the conversation they had had the night before at work. He didn't know why he hadn't told her right then and there.

They were alone, and there could have been no better time to tell her. But he still hadn't; he just couldn't.

After what had happened at the barbeque, down on the beach, Darren was careful not to say anything that could change the way she feels about him.

However, by not saying anything, Christine had ended up walking out on him all the same.

"Darren told me what happened between the two of you, last night." Frank had pulled Christine into the living room once his wife had stopped her fussing over her and had returned to the kitchen.

"He did? Why?" She felt no betrayal over the sharing of their conversation as she would have told Frank herself if he'd have asked her.

"He told me because I asked him what was wrong."

"When did you talk to him?"

"Last night, you'd already gone, and I met Darren as he was leaving work last night. I'd forgotten Helena's flowers." He indicated towards the window ledge where a vase full of white and red roses sat.

"Frank, they're lovely. You know, Helena's lucky to have a husband who still brings her flowers after-" she paused as she tried to remember how long he had been married "almost 12 years?" she asked.

"That's right." He laughed.

"I remembered that your tenth anniversary was about 18 months ago."

"Very good." He smiled. He paused for a moment, so he didn't change the conversation too quickly, he didn't want to seem insincere about his gratitude regarding her comment. "Anyway, I want to hear your side of the story."

"My side? Why, don't you trust what Darren has to say?"

"No, no, I do. However, he may retell the events accurately, but only he can account for his feelings, as only you can do for yours. Let's sit. Dinner isn't going to be ready for another half an hour."

They sat, and Frank listened as Christine retold the previous evening's events. Frank noticed that none of the words which were supposedly exchanged differed from Darren's version to hers, and made a mental note of his next question and hoped that she wouldn't shoot him down when it came to asking it.

"And then I left, and as I went down the stairs, I heard the conference door shut behind him." So far, she had managed to maintain an emotionless face, but that soon changed once Frank asked his question.

"Don't you think you overreacted slightly?"

"Overreacted? In what way?" She sounded irritated but tried not to show it.

"Yes, I think you were unreasonable. I think you should have tried to understand."

"Understand what? Understand that he is keeping things from me. Frank, how can I open myself up to someone who won't even let me in?" Her face shifted, she didn't know what to do or how to feel. At that moment, she seemed lost, as if she was at a crossroads and had absolutely no idea which way to turn. "I mean, what could be so bad that he wouldn't want to tell me? If he knows how I feel, why doesn't he trust me enough? What do you think it could be?" She looked at him as she realised that it's his business to know everything about his agents and for that brief moment, she wondered if he knew what Darren was hiding.

"Christine, dear, I know what it is."

She was taken back by his blunt delivery. She felt a pang of jealousy as she thought of the two of them talking about it.

"And? What is it?" Even as she asked the question, she knew Frank would never tell her, one, it wasn't right to talk about people's private affairs, and two, because she knew Frank would never betray Darren's trust. "I'm sorry, I should never have asked. Please forgive me." She hung her head shamefully as she imagined how much of an idiot she must have looked asking a question for which she knew she wouldn't and shouldn't get an answer.

He put his hand on hers and lowered his voice,

"Christine love, I know what Darren isn't telling you, and I know why. You know I'm not going to tell you what it is, but I will tell you this, it is going to be very hard for Darren to tell you if he ever chooses to, and you should bear that in mind. He'll tell you when he's ready, be patient. You need to understand how hard it must be."

"I understand. Thank you, Frank." She wiped her now damp eyes. At that moment, Darren knocked on the front door. She looked back at Frank and mouthed another thank you.

"Darren, hello love." Helena enthused as she opened the door.

"Hello, Helena." He kissed her once on each cheek before handing her a bottle of wine. She held her hand out for him to enter and as he did, he said "I didn't know if you drank red or white, so I brought red. I hope that's okay."

She brushed his shoulder in a motherly way as she told him not to worry, she assured him that either would have been perfect. She thanked him once more but quickly before she sternly informed him that they were a no shoe house. He glanced over at Christine. He was careful not to let his eyes wander as she raised her right foot a couple of inches off the ground and wriggled it around, shoeless. He obliged instantly.

He felt a hand tap on his shoulder, and when he turned, he saw it was Christine, she had an unusual look on her face. He wanted to ask her what was wrong but he feared she was still l upset with him.

"I'm sorry," she said quickly "about last night." She added a little slower.

"It's fine, honestly. You were right." Darren conceded.

"I should never have gone off like that, so I'm sorry. I didn't mean what I said. I didn't mean any of it well, apart from the part where I said I-" she glanced at the kitchen door awkwardly and finished in a quieter voice "where I said I wanted us to be together." She hid her face from his view "because I do want us to be together, Darren." She looked up at him and was surprised to see a huge smile stretched from one side of his face to the other. She asked him what he found amusing.

"You're cute when you're embarrassed." She rolled her eyes but briefly showed signs of flattery before she looked at him with serious eyes.

"Darren..." She pleaded, asking him to be serious.

"I do too." He whispered.

He took two steps towards her and ran his hand down her arm to her hand which he then took in his. He gave her a reassuring smile before pulling her into his arms. She welcomed his embrace and nestled her head under his neck. Her hands were on his waist until she extended her arms and wrapped them around him and held him as firmly as he was holding her.

Neither of them took any notice of the first dinner announcement, nor did they know who had said it, they remained together until a second call followed a few seconds later.

They parted their bodies, but their eyes fixed on each other once more. Their smiles once again said everything that needed saying. They made their way to the table and sat in their appointed seats. In their thoughts, they were embracing once more as they both secretly rejoiced over the fact that the other reciprocated their feelings.

After dinner, they walked to their cars. "So, I'll see you at work tomorrow?" Christine asked. "Yea. Christine?" He turned to her when they reached her car. "What are you doing after work tomorrow?"

"Nothing, why?"

"I wondered if you wanted to do something." He thrust his hands in his pockets and shuffled his feet slightly.

She smiled at him for reassurance and answered,

"That would be lovely. What do you want to do?"

"I was thinking about dinner. Say, 20:00?"

They decided on a place and arranged for Darren to pick her up at 19:30. They said their goodbye's but stood still and remained face to face.

"You didn't leave." Darren laughed.

"Neither did you." She replied shyly.

Darren took one step closer to her and placed his hands on her waist. He leaned in and kissed her gently on the cheek before saying he had to go as his neighbour was expecting him to walk her dog before they settled down for the night. They got in their cars reluctantly and left after once more confirming their plans for the following evening.

CHAPTER 10

F ROM THE MOMENT HE'D left the office, his head had never ceased spinning. Everything that he'd been managing to keep back, everything that had been tormenting him before, had come back the second his eyes had read the letter on the screen.

Somehow, they'd found him. He needed to figure out how, why and more importantly, who they were. ''The brunette's next, Clark.'' The image was engraved in his memory. He memorised each letter, the way the words had been formed. The style was familiar as if he knew the person who had written it. It was as if he'd seen the handwriting before.

This thought was pushed aside as another took its place, where was Christine? If the people who wrote the letter were severe with their threat, he would need to be near her to try and ensure nothing happened.

He made his way back to his car and drove back to the precinct as quickly, yet safely as he could. He parked across from the car park and saw that her car had gone. He went to call her but found his phone was low on battery and turned off in his hand.

He got out of the car and walked across the car park, into the building and up to their floor. He was met by Crowley who was coming out of his office as Darren walked by.

"Darren!" His voice was full of relief, but as his eyes met with his, Darren could see Frank's face flush with regret as he guided him into his office.

"What's the matter?" Darren asked once he closed the door behind them.

Frank kept his back turned, "I told her." He confessed. He turned to face Darren as he explained that the case had become too deep and that Christine needed to know everything that they did.

"And what about Nick and Jason? Alice? Did you tell them?"

No, they'd already left. I'm sorry, Darren, I didn't want to." Darren told him that everything was okay.

"Why aren't you upset with me?" Frank asked, shocked.

"Because all you did was tell her what I was too scared to tell her." He swallowed hard. "Where is Christine?"

"She left about half an hour after you. I'm sorry if I have ruined everything."

"Don't worry about it." He gave Frank a kind smile as he excused himself. He told him he was going to talk to Christine. As he was halfway out the door, Frank silently wished him good luck.

Once he was in his car, he turned on the radio and inserted a CD without paying any attention to which he was putting in. He'd chosen Bruce Springsteen's 'Born in the USA' album, and as it began playing, he closed his eyes and let the music fill his head. He waited until he felt completely at ease and until his mind was clear before he opened his eyes and started towards Christine's apartment.

For the first time that day, he felt relaxed, a huge weight had been lifted from his shoulders, Christine now knew, and all he had to do now was face the consequences.

The day had started out like usual. They had all gotten to work and were in the bullpen by 08:00. At the time at which Crowley called the four of them into his office at around 09:00, they were all in good spirits. From the look of things, Nick and Jason's evening was just as enjoyable as Darren and Christine's. Alice had come up from her lab and joined them as they all witnessed Crowley's pained face as he explained that there was yet another victim from the Angel.

Something inside Darren had told him that this case was different from the rest, but until they got back to the office a little after 14:00 they had no idea what they were to find.

They had found a letter tucked into the folds of the victim's dress. The envelope in which it was sealed, was blank. Tension accumulated in the bullpen as everyone finished their paperwork and waited for Alice to finish processing the letter.

When she'd finished, she brought it upstairs and declared that she had found no evidence on the letter, no DNA from anyone but the victim and the killer had left behind no prints. No fibres, no hairs, nothing.

She explained that she got no results on the handwriting on the paper inside. She then expressed confusion as to the message's meaning before she left to continue with her work.

Everyone closed in around Frank as he took out the letter and opened it carefully. His face turned white. His mouth fell open in shock, and his fingers trembled slightly. He looked at Darren and flashed his eyes toward Christine. Darren hoped he'd misunderstood what Frank had hinted. He took the letter out of his hand and hesitated before casting his eyes upon the message.

His eyes remained glued to the paper as he heard Frank begin to explain that they would need to start asking around the victim's families, their friends, and anyone else who is even remotely connected to any of the victims and start asking them to provide a handwriting sample.

Darren diverted his eyes towards Christine who was talking to Nick. He heard Jason's voice behind him. "What do you think it means?" He asked.

"I don't know." Darren lied. He handed Jason the note and made his way to his desk. By 16:00 Darren could take it no more. The panic had returned, and it refused to leave.

"Darren, you don't look so good, why don't you get some fresh air?" He looked up, Christine was standing before him with a concerned look on her face.

"I'm fine, it's just, this letter, I'm getting nowhere with it. N-no-none of the-the erm- victims have a- erm relative called Clark." He struggled to get his words out as the panic consumed him further.

Christine didn't budge. "You're not okay." She said.

"I'll be fine." He lied.

"Won't you get some fresh air, please? You look terrible."

He smiled at her and gave in. "Fine, I'll just tell Crowley that I'm stepping out." He stood and touched her hand affectionately.

"Thank you." She smiled before she returned to her desk.

Crowley uttered no work of refusal as he let Darren leave and instead told him to take as long as he needed.

He'd driven for a few miles before he came upon a park. He parked on a nearby road and made his way towards the gate. It was dark within the hour, and he decided that he should be getting back. As he made his way back to his car, a car pulled out of a junction. He was concealed from its view by a stationary van parked by the side of the road. The headlights cast a shadow that seemed to consume him as he continued to walk. It was as if he'd been plunged into darkness, but was constantly tormented by the light in front of him that was just out of his reach. As he continued, the car swung around the corner causing the shadow to move. The shadow seemed to follow Darren as the car emerged from the junction, keeping him in the darkness with the light remaining just that little too far ahead.

It was 17:35, and it was at this point that he suddenly thought about Christine and decided he'd go back to the precinct.

Following his conversation with Frank, Darren decided he would talk to Christine and attempt to make up for not telling her what he should have when he should have told her.

The most natural way for him to get to Christine's was for him to go from his apartment, so he headed in the direction of home and decided he would go from there, it would save any possible confusion.

As he approached the turn of his building, he caught sight of Christine's car parked near the entrance. He turned and parked in his usual space, a hundred yards down the road from her vehicle. He got out and approached her vehicle cautiously as if expecting her to emerge from the car and begin shouting at him suddenly. She didn't as she wasn't in the car.

He turned and checked that he'd locked his car and entered the building. Walking up to the eleventh floor seemed a waste of time, but it would allow him to prepare what he was going to say. However, the delay did nothing for his words, for he had none, none which justified his actions adequately. He was left with no option but to face her with nothing but himself.

He turned the corner so that he was facing his door. Sitting before it was Christine, her back against the door.

The silence between them seemed to last a while, but what was only a few seconds was still enough time to get his heart racing at the thought of her hating him after the conversation that was coming.

"Are you going to open the door?" She asked almost coldly, all sense of affection was absent.

"Okay." He hung his head slightly to break the eye contact as he made his way to the door. She moved aside and followed him in. He took off his coat and hung it up on his peg, removed his shoes and slotted them in between two other pairs sitting by the door. Once he placed his keys on the table near the door and arranged them in a particular position, he stood in the centre of the hallway near the living room door.

She took off her shoes and placed them neatly beside the row of his. She slipped her coat off her shoulders and stood to face him once she'd hung it up.

She watched his shoulders rise and fall with each breath. He turned without saying a word and made his way to the kitchen. He stood at the threshold and turned and asked her if she would like a drink. When she replied that she would like some water, he disappeared. She remained standing at the door. She heard him remove two glasses from the cupboard above the toaster and set them down on the island. The fridge opened and closed a few seconds later. He returned with two glasses of water but he did not stop, nor did he look at her. Instead, he walked straight past her and through to the living room where he placed the glasses down on the placemats and sat in his chair.

She followed a few seconds later and sat in the chair adjacent to him. He would not meet her gaze. His eyes remained on his glass.

"I didn't do it." He said suddenly. Still, he kept his eyes on his glass.

"I know." She whispered.

"No, you don't. You can't tell me that you've never thought that it could have been him - me."

"Darren-"

"Don't please, I need to tell you the truth." He finally looked her way.

"Frank told me."

"I know, but I still need to tell you myself." Even if she already knew, he physically had to tell her.

"Darren, you don't have to do this." Her heart began to ache as she thought of the pain he must be going through. She felt guilty for being mad at him.

"Please let me." He whispered.

"Okay." She mouthed.

He took a deep breath and began. "I don't know how much Frank's told you," Her eyes confessed the extent to their conversation, and he sighed, "but I should tell you that Clark McAvoy doesn't exist anymore. All that is left of him is inside me. I'm Clark McAvoy, well I was." He confessed.

She had no clue what to say. Even though Frank had told already her, it was still a shock to hear it from Darren himself. It made it all the more real.

"It was you, all those years ago, in London?" He nodded. Her face suddenly turned, "But how long have you known that it was me?" She looked hurt as if he'd been playing her.

He said her name comfortingly, "Not long.

Until you told me it was you in that book, I had no idea. And then when I saw your father, it confirmed it all. I'm sorry."

"You don't have to be sorry. Why didn't you tell me before though?"

"I liked where things were going, and I didn't want anything to come in the way of us." He dipped his head in embarrassment. "I know it was wrong to keep it from you, but I thought it would make you hate me. I know I would." He admitted.

She sat forward in the chair, so their faces were only a couple of feet apart. "Darren, it wasn't your fault. It isn't your fault."

"But I could have prevented it all." He looked close to tears.

"But you're not the one doing it, so it isn't your fault. If you're to blame, then so am I, and Nick, Jason, Alice and Frank himself." She smiled at him. He smiled back in defeat. "Okay?"

"Okay." He conceded. He appeared to relax as the overall mood seemed to lighten.

"Are you hungry?"

"We have dinner plans, don't we? I'm not that hungry though." He teased.

"Oh, yes you are!" She stood up and pulled him up with her. They stood before each other, smiling. He held his hand out in jest, inviting her through the door first. She laughed and obliged, he followed.

They put on their shoes in silence and stood with their backs to each other as they put on their coats.

He stopped and turned to face her. "Why are you staying?" He asked.

"Because there is no reason I should leave, none of it matters."

"So, nothing's changed? Well, nothing between us?"

"No." She smiled. "Nothing's changed. I'd say things are a little better." She smiled shyly.

"Good." He replied excitedly. "Shall we?" He asked as he opened the door.

"Why, yes. We shall." She brushed his arm as she walked past him. Once he had locked the door behind them, they began to walk to the elevator. He slowed. She turned to him and watched his face light up as she reached for his hand. His eyes fixed on their entwined hands for a few seconds before he affectionately squeezed her hand and looked up at her. They continued walking.

They sat and talked about nothing in particular until the food arrived. The conversation shifted towards work as they ate, talk about DUI's and other cases they had worked recently. It was only when they had finished eating that conversation focused more on Darren.

He needed no persuading this time though, for Darren willingly told her everything, even the parts he previously thought he still wanted to keep private.

Christine couldn't help but feel that she'd been too pushy, despite not saying anything at all, she felt that Darren was doing this mostly for her, but when she expressed her concerns to Darren, he assured her that he genuinely wanted to tell her. Their conversation resumed but was once again stopped once Darren had retold the story regarding his discussion with Isabelle shortly following Sarah's death.

"And she just told you that?" Christine couldn't conceal the shock in her voice as she imagined how Daren must have felt as he was told who'd killed his parents.

"Yes, just like that."

"What did you do?"

"Nothing." He answered simply.

"Why didn't you tell someone?"

He laughed, "What proof did I have, what proof do I have?"

She sighed, "Good point."

He held his hand out towards her; she took it in both of hers. He felt her foot brush against his leg, sending a pleasant sensation up through him.

He parted his mouth and smiled, pressing his tongue into his tooth, "Shall we get out of here?" He asked with a daring look in his eye.

She nodded shyly and waited while he took the money out of his wallet, refusing her contributions each time she offered.

"Do you mind if I nip to the gym to get my training clothes?" Darren asked once they'd both fastened their belts.

"Not at all." She beamed, still excited about the idea of being out with him.

"Okay then."

Once inside the gym, Darren headed straight for the locker room, but Christine remained in the gym itself. She made her way over to the equipment and picked up a kick pad. She put it down after examining it and wandered over to the punching bag hanging from the wall. She began punching the punching bag lightly and very poorly.

He came up from behind her, startling her when he spoke. "Here, let me help."

"You made me jump." She exclaimed as she gently nudged him in the ribs with her elbow.

"Oh dear." He whispered in her ear as he took hold of her arms from behind. "Here, put this arm here, and this one here. Now try, and make sure your arm doesn't fully straighten before your hand hits the bag. Like this." He showed her slowly. She watched the muscles in his arms flex as his arm extended.

"Like this?" She asked as she attempted to copy.

"Perfect." He praised. "I should go and get my gear."

"I'll come with you." She followed him through to the locker room and sat on the bench near where Darren's things

147

were spread out. "It smells funny in here." She wrinkled her nose as the smell strengthened.

"Chris, it's a men's changing rooms." He said with a chuckle as if to say that was the reason why.

"Does it always smell like this?"

"Pretty much, yes."

She grunted, her nose still wrinkled.

After a few seconds, he zipped up his bag and said that he was all done.

"What's that?" Christine asked as she caught sight of the photographs stuck on the inside of his locker door. As she neared, she saw one of the entire team, one of Darren and his parents and the photo that she and Darren had taken three weeks before while out on their bikes. "So, you're a sentimental kind of guy?" She teased as she closed the door gently. She stood to face him, her back against the lockers.

"I'd say so, yes. Is that weird?"

"No, just unusual. I've been with men who keep photographs of course, but I've never been with someone who cries at Sense and Sensibility." She took two steps towards him, leaving no more than four feet between them.

"I knew you'd bring that up at some point. I told you, I had something in my eye."

"Mmmm." She didn't believe a word he said, and he knew it.

They laughed. "Fair enough, I'm sentimental. But that's me, and if you cannot be with me because of it, then I guess

I'll have to take my things and leave." He joked as he picked up his bag and threw it over his shoulder in a childish way.

"Well, maybe that's for the best." She played along. She stuck up her nose and turned her head away. They laughed again as he put his bag back down on the bench.

He diverted his eyes to the floor and watched his own feet as he shuffled them, kicking invisible stones across the floor.

"Darren?" She whispered, her voice full of emotion. He looked up at her to see she was looking at him. She raised her voice a little. "I meant what I said at yours, none of it matters. I want to be with you."

The look in her eyes caused the funny sensation in his stomach to return stronger and wilder than ever. It was raging with a force that he'd never experienced.

He walked towards her, slowly, his eyes never leaving hers. There was a look in her eyes that drew him to her, pulling him in. She stood still as he neared and smiled a dangerous smile that caused his stomach to spin even further out of control. He reached her and slowed, his face barely two inches from hers, but he didn't stop there. His hands were on her hips as he began walking slowly once more towards the lockers.

Her feet moved in time with his, one step back for each one he took forward. She put her arms around his neck. She could feel his whole upper body rise and fall with each breath. She felt her back against the lockers, preventing her from going any further, but Darren took one more step so that their bodies were touching. He began kissing her neck gently. She gave herself to him willingly. She cupped his behind and pulled him in closer. She could feel him through his trousers, pressing into her, exciting her. She took his head in her hands and pulled him up to her lips. His tongue was warm against hers, and it fought with hers ferociously as they removed their jackets. She reached for the front of his shirt and began to unfasten its buttons as he started pulling up her t shirt. The gym door squeaked, but they ignored it, thinking it was just a draft opening the door, but soon they heard slow footsteps from across the gym and stood still, their bodies still entwined and their heads still together.

"Darren?" They heard Alan call.

Darren moved his head away from Christine's as he replied, "We're in the locker room." He smiled at her before he buttoned up his shirt, hinting that she should tidy up too. As Alan entered the locker room, he found Christine sitting on a chair behind where Darren was standing. "I'm just getting my training clothes. I figured they needed washing," Darren explained.

"I didn't know you were going to be here." Alan smiled fondly at Christine and then at Darren. It was clear that there was more than a friendship between Darren and Alan, and as they talked, it was clear to see that each cared for the other dearly.

"Darren, there's something I need to speak to you about." He looked as if he was about to speak, but caught another glimpse of Christine out of the corner of his eye and stopped, saying that it could wait.

"That's okay. I'll wait in the car." She smiled at Alan before leaving. She was careful not to look directly at Darren.

As she walked to the car, her heart began to pound once more as she closed her eyes and imagined him against her. She walked to the car and leant against it, her eyes on the door. She was shaking now, but it wasn't the cold that was affecting her, it was him, for now, he was now making his way towards her, smiling. He took her hands in his and pulled her off the car. He spun around so that he was leant against the car and gently pulled her towards him, so she stood in between his legs. They remained silent until they heard Alan lock the door, drive away and turn the corner.

"So, what do you want to do now?" He asked casually, his eyes betraying his actual question.

"It's late." She teased.

"I'll take you home then if you'd like." There it was again; she heard a daring question hidden within an innocent remark.

"You could, but there's always something else to do." She teased once more. "We never finished that film, 'Before we go'. We could go to yours and finish it if you like."

"That's fine with me." He replied. He ran his hands up and down her back, sending a delicious sensation through her entire body.

"Okay then." She ran her hands down his body and onto his thighs. She slid her hands inside his thigh, stopping before she went too far. She smiled a devilish smile, "Let's go." She left him feeling dazed with a strange feeling in his trousers. They got in the car and drove to Darren's.

Once at Darren's they removed their shoes and hung up their coats and made their way into the living room and onto the couch. They talked for a while before deciding to finish the film as they probably wouldn't find another chance to do so any time soon. Christine looked at her watch and commented on the time, "Besides, it's only 20:30, we have all night." She teased.

"Excellent point." Darren conceded as he watched her get comfy.

He got up and put on the film before taking his seat once more. Chris continued to fidget while he loaded up the film. She looked at him and smiled before she crawled over to him and lay against him as the movie began. "If you're going to lay there, you can stop fidgeting." He joked, prompting her to dig her elbow into his side.

"I'll try, no promises." She joked in return.

They snuggled as the film began playing and remained as they were until Darren received a phone call about five minutes before the end. Christine went to pause the movie as Darren got up, but he said that she could keep it playing as he'd heard how it ended. He smiled as he took his phone out of his pocket and left the room. He heard her pause it all the same.

"Darren, there's another call for you." It was Sal from the front desk at the office. "It's the same woman. What do you want to do?"

"Has she left a name or anything?"

"No, she just says that she needs to speak to you, no one else."

He took his phone from his ear and looked at the time. It was already 22:01. He sighed, "Connect us, please."

"Connecting you. See you tomorrow Darren."

"Goodbye, Sal."

He waited patiently as beeps and buzzes filled his ears. Once the noises had finished, he could hear faint breathing coming from the other end of the line. "Agent Thompson, what can I do for you?" He asked, wondering who it could be.

"Hello, Clark." His heart began pounding, his head became heavy, and he suddenly felt a little sick. All he could do was repeat his name with a slight emphasis on his first name.

"Well, I know you as Clark, so that's what I'm going to call you." The voice was adamant.

"I wish you wouldn't." He was instantly annoyed at the lack of consideration he was getting.

"Well, I've never really cared about what you want, have I, Clark."

"What do you want?" He snapped.

"Careful now, you do remember what happens when you give me that tone, don't you Clark?" Of course, he remembered, how could he not?

"How the hell did you get this number?" He demanded, his voice as sharp as his question.

"We need to talk. I'm coming to New York."

He began to panic. He knew she wouldn't like seeing him with Christine. "I've got nothing to say to you, so there's no point. Just stay where you are."

"Don't think you can tell me what to do Clark!" Each time she called him Clark, he became more annoyed, he wished he hadn't asked to be connected.

"You have no control over me now, please, leave me alone." There was no point in trying to reason with her, but he still tried, but, as expected, his efforts were fruitless.

"I'm coming to New York. I'll see you soon Clark. Goodbye."

"Goodbye, Isabelle." He hung up.

He composed himself before he returned to the living room where a worried looking Christine met him.

"Who was that?"

He considered telling her that it was no one that it was nothing and that it didn't matter, but he was done lying to her. "It was Isabelle."

"Isabelle? Your mother in law?" The surprise in her voice was obvious. "What did she want?"

"She just said that she's coming to New York because we need to talk. I don't know when that will be, but what I do know is that I don't want you to be here when she does come." He said.

"Why?"

"She won't like you being here, and I don't think she would keep her objections silent."

"Well, I'm staying."

"But I don't want you getting hurt." He pleaded.

"Tough," she walked over to him and placed her hands on his chest "I'm staying." She kissed him once gently before she tucked her head under his.

He wrapped his arms around her and held her. "I love you." He whispered.

She looked at him in amazement before she tucked her head under his once more. She smiled to herself. "I love you too." She began stroking his chest gently with her fingers.

She raised her head and rocked herself onto the balls of her feet so she could reach his lips with hers. He kissed her back with a passion that made her weak. He embraced her tightly as she wrapped her arms around his neck. Their kisses became deeper until they became utterly lost in each other's arms. They parted, and as they did, her hand glided over his behind as her eyes confessed her desires. He took her gently by the hand and began walking backwards, slowly. They had only gotten as far as the bottom of the stairs before there was a knock at the door.

"I'll see you upstairs." She teased as she sensually bit her lip.

His breath caught in his throat as he silently prayed that whoever it was at the door didn't want to stay. He watched her as she walked up the stairs before making his way to the door.

As Darren politely offered Nick and Jason a drink, they replied that they couldn't stay and that they only wanted to see if he was okay. They had seen the way he had been at work earlier in the day and just wanted to make sure that everything was alright.

"I'm fine guys, honestly, but thank you for asking. Are you sure you can't stay?" As he asked them, he prayed they would decline his offer once more and to his delight, they did, saying that they'd better get home as they were beyond hungry and that dinner had been ordered and would be arriving soon.

They said their goodbyes, and once he'd watched them to the top of the stairs, Darren locked the door. He stood with his back against it as he looked at the stairs, he could see his bedroom door from where he stood. He saw a shadow move, and his insides began to turn once more.

Slowly, he made his way to the bottom of the stairs, took hold of the railing and made his way up them, carefully avoiding each creaky spot.

He came to his door and saw her sitting on the edge of his bed facing him. She stood. They each took a step forward before stopping once more. They smiled a celebratory smile as they both thought of how long they had waited for this. They closed the space between them as they were both physically and emotionally drawn to each other once more.

She took hold of his shirt and pulled him towards her. She began walking backwards until her legs hit the bed. She sat and shuffled backwards, so she was sat on the bed properly. She inched back until she was half laying on the bed with only the bottom of her legs off the bed. She leaned forward and took hold of his shirt once more and tugged at it gently, encouraging him to follow her. His eyes never left hers as he effortlessly climbed onto the bed and moved forward until he was directly above her.

He lowered his face towards hers until their lips met. She pulled him down, so he was laying on her as she began playing with the hair at the back of his neck, twisting her fingers in the curls affectionately. He kissed her, and she kissed him over and over until they could no longer go on without the satisfaction they needed. Darren removed his shirt before taking Christine's t-shirt off gently, skimming his hands up her body as he did. He felt her quiver at his touch.

Christine unfasted the button at the top of Darren's jeans and tugged them down slowly as she wriggled out of hers. They were standing separately by the bed now in their underwear. Christine reached behind her to the fastenings on her bra. She fumbled momentarily out of anticipation and mild nerves, but she soon felt the fasteners un-do. She paused slightly before letting the garment drop to her feet.

It was somewhat dark in his room, but Darren could still see the perfect silhouette of her body as the light from the window behind her seemed to illuminate her. He thought of how angelic she looked as she made her way over to him slowly. The small amounts of light which were making their way through the hinges of his bedroom door partially lit her face and her chest as she reached him once more. She was beautiful. She placed one hand on his abdomen as she fingered his muscles gently. She felt his hands on her waist as he began walking her back towards the bed again. She sat and shuffled back as she did before but did not have to wait long until he followed. He planted kisses on her shoulders, her chest, her stomach, her hips and then the inside of her thighs.

He then made his way back up towards her lips. As he reached her neck, he skimmed his nose along her jaw and slowly removed her underwear with his left hand. She pulled his face up to her lips and kissed him once before smiling nervously at him. He flashed his eyes towards his wallet laying on the bedside table. She bit her lip before kissing him once more. She moved out from underneath him as she reached for the wallet.

He took her in his arms as she laid flat on the bed below him. "I love you." He reminded her.

"And I love you." She replied as she kissed him sweetly.

They made love slowly and passionately, both savouring every moment. Somehow, each moment was so much more than either of them had ever thought it could be. Afterwards, Christine laid beside Darren with her head on his shoulder, in silence.

She propped herself up onto her elbow as she watched him, his eyes were closed, but he didn't appear to be asleep. She smiled as she watched his face curl into a broad smile. He opened his eyes and turned his head to face her. She placed her hand on his chest and hesitated before asking him what he was thinking.

He looked at her for a moment before answering. "That was nice," He answered shyly before his face dropped, "but I'm scared that when Isabelle comes that this will all be ruined. I don't want you to get hurt." He laughed. "I don't know which one you should be more afraid of, Angel's vow to get you next, or Isabelle's promise to visit."

It was evident that he was petrified of what could happen to her but didn't want to express the true extent of his fear.

She began stroking his chest as an attempt to comfort him. She watched him relax as he closed his eyes once more as she felt his arm move from her shoulder to her waist.

She felt him move as he looked at the clock on the clock behind her. He faced her entirely now as he smiled and commented on the time. It was almost 23:30.

"I wonder why we're tired." Christine joked as Darren climbed off the bed. She heard his laugh from the bathroom. She slipped back into her underwear after she thought about sleeping without them. He emerged after a few minutes wearing a pair of jogging bottoms but no top.

They slipped under the sheets as Darren commented on how cold the night was.

"I hadn't noticed," Christine confessed as she felt his arm around her waist once more. "Work tomorrow." she sighed. She kissed him once more, a long and gentle kiss. "Someone's brushed his teeth." She commented playfully. "Goodnight Darren."

"Goodnight Chris." She turned away from him reluctantly and rested her head on the pillow next to his.

He felt his face break out into a stupid grin that seemed to touch both his ears as he tried to comprehend what had happened that evening. He fell to sleep the happiest he'd been in years. She loved him too. He would not let anything happen to her.

She felt the arm on her waist grow slightly heavier as she realised he'd fallen asleep. She too fell to sleep with a smile across her face, but her thoughts were both happy and unhappy. The ambivalent thoughts running around in her head remained with her throughout the night for as far as she could remember, she had never felt this happy, but what was to happen when Isabelle came? She didn't bother thinking about the Angel and their threats for fear she would become too scared of them. She pushed all thoughts of Isabelle to the back of her mind as she focused on her and Darren. She fell asleep moments later, not to awake until their alarms sounded the following morning.

CHAPTER 11

I T WAS THE MORNING of the grading, and for some reason, Darren was more nervous this time conducting the grading than he had ever been taking it. It was the first grading to have taken place at the new club since he arrived. The Grand Master had chosen to put him and Bruce in charge to help towards their grades.

He was to watch the students as Bruce warmed them up and stretched them off, watching how far they could stretch. He measured their stamina and their ability and determination to continue even when they were too tired.

After they'd warmed up, he was to put them through their patterns. To grade to the next level, they would have to develop their fighting skills, their self-defence skills would need to be better, and they would have to learn a new pattern. He would take them all through their latest patterns, the older, more advanced Kickboxers would do them individually, the younger, less confident ones would do it in groups. He would then put them in groups and test their knowledge of previous patterns, seeing if they could remember things they learnt from other gradings as those lessons were equally as valuable.

He and had been training recently to take his fourth-Dan black belt, Bruce to take his third, but the frequent absence of the Grand Master since his near-fatal heart attack at the back end of October meant that they weren't ready this time around to take their grading. Sadly, they would have to wait until next time, when they are ready and when the Grand Master is well enough to train them.

As he lay awake, he thought back to the previous week when he had told Chris how he felt about her. It had been so much harder than he could have ever imagined, in fact, in those few days, he had grown to empathise with the male protagonists in Romantic-Comedies, now he knew what they were going through instead of just thinking they were scared.

He tried to think back to a time which he'd been happier. But try as he might, the only occasions which he could remember, were in memories he had of his parents.

As painful as they were, he would still close his eyes and think of them, trying to remember smells, sounds, colours.

He climbed out of bed as his alarm began to sound. He turned it off before making his way to the bathroom. There was no point in him getting a shower considering the amount of physical work he would have to do during the day. He would get one before Chris arrived that evening. He was cooking them dinner which was to be followed by a film, one that they had agreed on two days before to save the time they would inevitably waste while choosing one that evening.

His heart began to race at the mere thought of being with her once more. He pushed the thoughts aside as he brushed his teeth.

On his way back into his bedroom, he flicked the play button on the CD player on his drawers. One of his favourite songs began playing. Andrea Bocelli's 'Canto Della Terra'. There had always been something about that one song. It seemed to flow through him. As the chorus began playing, his heart leapt, and his eyes closed automatically, seemingly to enhance the sound bouncing off the bedroom walls. He re-wound the song to the beginning before he started to get dressed.

He stopped by his bedroom window. The sky was white, but he knew that no snow was to come. Darren loved the snow. It made everything beautiful, it gave everything a new look, a fresh start. It was almost as if the blanket of snow itself hid the moral degradation of the citizens of New York, the imperfections of the landscape and the secrets that everyone had, shielding them from the eyes of the innocent. But Darren, like most, wasn't innocent, even if there were snow, he would still be able to see the dump sites, the wasteland, the heaps of burnt rubble on the horizon. He knew that morally, everyone was corrupt and selfish and as for the secrets, he knew that everyone had them, dark ones, and the snow could never manage to hide them.

"What a grim thought to be thinking at the beginning of the day", he thought aloud. He was needed at work until 11:00 am, and it was from there where he would drive directly to the gym for the grading that was due to begin at 12:30 pm, sharp.

The song finished as he finished lacing up his second shoe. He turned off the CD player after re-winding the track once more, and made his way down the stairs and out of the door for work, picking up his badge, his gun, his keys and his phone on the way out, his training gear was already washed, ironed and in his car.

It had been over a week since the latest victim of the Angel had been found. They felt it was time for another, but couldn't bear to think about or talk about the inevitable. Whoever it was that was killing these innocent women, had to be found, soon. Including Sarah in Tennessee, the victim count was now five. They were officially dealing with a serial killer case.

"Darren, how come you're in today? It's Saturday. I thought that was your day off." Alice asked as she passed him in the corridor.

"Frank needs me to complete some paperwork." He replied as he slowed.

"I see. Will I see you later?" Darren thought he heard the faint desperation in her voice as she asked him. When he explained that she wouldn't, she appeared slightly disappointed but shrugged it off quickly. They had never ceased walking and were almost too far apart to continue their conversation. Darren apologised and said he needed to get going. As he turned back around and kept walking, he had a funny feeling that Alice had stopped and was watching him walk away. Strange, he thought.

As he caught a glimpse of the corridor as he turned the corner, he saw Alice begin to walk away; she had been watching him. But why?

He forgot about Alice entirely as he saw Chris ahead of him. She was coming his way but hadn't seen him. She was too busy reading a case file to notice she was about to walk into a plant by the elevator.

Darren increased his speed enough to grab her by the arm gently and pull her out of the way before she hit it. She looked at him, at the file, at the plant and then at him once more. A smile spread across her face as she realised what had almost happened. He rolled his eyes before stepping out of her way, allowing her to continue in the direction she was going. She thanked him before making a point to close the case file and walk on without reading it. Darren watched as she walked away. He turned away however when he knew that he was smiling stupidly, he didn't want anyone to see them like that, they had talked it through and agreed that no-one was to know about them just yet.

Frank had watched Darren closely throughout the morning and was shocked to find he'd finished with the paperwork quicker than either of them had expected. Frank soon found something else for him to do, he sent him on an errand to collect some evidence from the lockup in the basement.

A couple of minutes after he'd left, Nick came to Frank's door. "Nothing." He said with a sigh. Frank had suggested Nick try searching for Clark McAvoy in the English Database. When asked why Frank improvised and explained that it seemed a good idea and that it was the right sort of extension they needed to take to try and find him.

"Nothing?" Frank found it strange that nothing should have come back, he should still be in the English systems.

"Well, it gives us the same results as when we search for him in the American system. It tells us everything about him up until a few months ago. It says that he changed his name, but it won't even let me request to see the new information."

"I see. Okay, thank you, Nick." Darren would have to think about something soon.

Alice watched as Darren bent over and re-did the laces on his shoe. Maybe she wasn't completely crazy to think that he would like her as she does him. She used to think he was into Chris, but recently, they have started talking less at work, and it seemed like they were purposely trying to avoid eye contact. Sure, earlier that day he'd stopped her walking into a plant pot, but that doesn't mean he likes her, he's just a nice guy like that.

She watched as he stood and walked through the door to the stairs. "That's it," she said to herself, "I'll ask him out." The next time she saw Darren, she would ask him for a coffee.

The grading went better than he could have expected. Despite not being able to tell any of them until the presentation evening the following Tuesday, every one of them had passed, and he was proud of them. He'd been home for just under an hour when he was finally happy with his apartment, it was now tidy, and he had almost finished cooking dinner. He had time for a quick shower.

They had decided on an old war film from the 1950's, a Kenneth More film called Reach for the Sky. Once the film had finished, they began to clean up after the dinner. As they tidied the plates up from the table, they discussed the film further. The film had always been a favourite of Darren's, but Chris had never seen it, but as they washed and dried the plates, Darren was happy to find how enthusiastic Chris was about the film.

There were some films that Darren preferred to keep to himself, but there were others that he felt the need to share. He found the story of this film inspiring, it was one of those that he loved to share, and he was happy to see how much Chris loved it.

He dried his hands as he watched her put the final fork away in the draw. She turned to face him and watched as she sat against the worktop and smiled. He placed the tea-towel on the island and took two steps towards her. He watched as her tongue passed over her lips slowly. She took a step towards him as she sank her teeth into her bottom lip. He took another step forward and placed his hands on her waist. She cupped his face in her hands as she pulled him into a passionate kiss. He picked her up and pulled her closer to him. She wrapped her legs around his waist as he began slowly making his way towards the bottom of the stairs.

They lay on the bed making out until Darren's phone began to ring. As he answered it, Chris smiled at him slyly as she pressed him back against the bed and unfastened the button on his jeans. She straddled him as he removed his trousers. She pulled them off over his feet before climbing back on him and un-fasted his shirt. She began kissing his neck and chest. She had to suppress a laugh as he tried to hide a faint moan in response to her hand moving underneath his boxers. She heard him say goodbye to Frank before he half placed, half threw his phone onto the bed-side table.

He sat up and smiled, unable to hide his amusement at what Chris had been doing. He quickly informed her what they were to do at work on Monday, saying he should tell her now or he'd end up forgetting to before he pulled her in for another kiss.

She rolled onto her back and pulled him onto her. He nuzzled her neck as his hand unfastened her bra. "I want you." He whispered in her ear. She inhaled sharply as her stomach began to twist and turn at the sound of his voice.

"Then take me." She replied, breathlessly.

He did. They made love slowly, savouring each moment. She could tell he was close and as a desperate groan escaped from his lips, she closed her eyes and relished the sounds of his pleasure as they seemed to run through her like her very own blood. She threw her head back against the pillow as they came together. "I love you." He whispered.

"And I love you." She tightened her arms around his neck as he rolled off her and lay next to her. They lay close until the night chill began to cool their bare skin.

Chris fell to sleep soon after they climbed back into bed as she lay in Darren's arms. He was soon to follow but found that something was beginning to trouble him.

He wanted to ask Chris to be his date to the Kickboxing Presentation the following Tuesday, which also served as their Christmas Party, but they had agreed that they weren't to let anyone know about them. He soon realised that there was no-one at the Gym who knew Chris, it would be no problem taking her. With his mind settled, he soon dropped off, not to wake until his alarm sounded at 06:00 the following morning.

As the night of the presentation arrived, Darren found he was more excited than he thought he would be. He'd picked out his favourite grey suit and paired it with his pale blue tie, the one that Chris liked. He'd received a text message from Chris a couple of hours before, asking what coloured tie he was going to wear but he thought nothing of it. However, as the presentation was due to start at 18:30 and he, as one of the chief instructor would be required to arrive before 18:30, they had decided to get there for about 18:00. They would have to set off at about 17:45, she would be at his at 17:30 at the latest. When she arrived, he saw she had put on a fitted but casual baby blue dress that emphasised her figure yet

169

flared suitably for the occasion to just above her knee. It matched his tie almost precisely.

Upon greeting her, he embraced her momentarily before taking hold of her hands, stepping back and holding out her arms so he could get a better look at her dress. "Beautiful." He commented.

She pulled him back into her embrace and thanked him. "The dress is nice too." He whispered in her ear.

They set off for the presentation shortly before 17:45 and got to the pub just before 18:00. They seated themselves near the back of the room yet close enough to the front be seen in spite of the dim lighting. Within a few minutes of their arrival, Darren had been approached by numerous parents, and a couple of adults Chris recognised from photographs and stories Darren had shown and told her.

She watched as he shook the men's hands and kissed their wives politely on the cheek. This was the side of him she never got to see. He was different around her, but there was still something on his mind, even when he appeared more relaxed and at ease. His smile remained long after he had greeted everyone and longer still once he had been mentioned in the Grand Master's speech in which he thanked each one of his team for helping him through the last few months.

When it came to Darren's turn to speak, his smile disappeared for a moment as he rose from his seat. He joined the Grand Master in the middle of the small dance floor. The Grand Master introduced Darren before he handed him the microphone and stepped to the side to allow Darren to take centre stage.

To the unknowing eye, Darren appeared to give an inspirational speech without falter, but Chris knew that he was having trouble with the number of people watching him. She saw a layer of sweat gather on his forehead and his top lip. Thankfully, the room itself was quite warm, and the sweat could easily be blamed on the various spotlights positioned around the hall which were all placed on Darren as he spoke. She heard his voice crack as he thanked everyone for coming. He laughed it off with a humorous remark directed at one of the other instructors. He thanked everyone once more for coming before he handed the microphone back to the Grand Master so he could call out the names of those who had graded up. Darren stood between the Grand Master and a man who Darren had introduced to Chris as Bruce. They occasionally whispered to each other, prompting quiet chuckles from the other, much to the amusement of the Grand Master who ensured the parents that their children behaved much better than his most senior instructors. An embarrassed look flashed across both Darren and Bruce's faces as the audience laughed briefly before another name was called out and another child stood to make their way to the front.

Chris found it rather strange. The child would stand, receive their certificate from the Grand Master as they shook his hand, shake Darren's as he handed them their new belt before they made their way down a long line of people, shaking each hand as they went down. Once he had sat beside her once more, Chris asked Darren why the students shook other children's hands. Darren explained that it was because the children standing in line with him were also black belts who sometimes helped teach the students.

Darren watched as a few of the student's parents stumbled to the dance floor and begun to dance. He was not drunk. He hadn't even had a sip, yet, like them, who had had a few too many, he wanted to dance.

He decided that when the floor became a little more crowded, he would ask Chris if she would want to dance. When the time came, however, he found he was unable to ask for some reason. It wasn't until he caught the eye of Alan, he hadn't even noticed that he was there, who winked at him and tipped his head slightly in the direction of the dance floor, that he found the courage to hold out his hand and ask her simply if she wanted to dance.

"I thought you'd never ask." She joked as she dramatically placed her hand in his. He ran his thumb over her knuckles as he smiled at her. Her smile warmed his insides as he turned and led her to the floor. She placed her hands on his shoulders as he put his on her waist.

Their feet began to move in time to the rather horrible tune coming out of the speakers. Soon enough, however, a theme familiar to both of them started playing. It seemed the D-J had run out of modern music tracks and had nothing left to play but Glenn Miller's 'String of Pearls'. However disagreeable the switch in sound was to the young children, the new sound prompted some satisfied nods from the older members of the audience. Many women aged between sixty and seventy, Darren guessed, joined the other dancers on the floor and swayed in time with the tune they knew so well. Darren watched as some of them closed their eyes as they let the music carry them all the way back to their childhoods.

Apart from the power of words, Darren found the power of music to be a close second to be one of the most inspirational and life-changing forms of motivation.

There was something in the music that somehow transformed people into someone new. Old or young, no matter what religion, race or gender, he knew it would be hard to find many people who did not have that one song they valued more than they would ever admit, one song that touched them deep inside where nothing else ever did. For him, that song was Bryan Adam's 'Everything I do (I do it for you)', a view he knew some people, including Chris's dad, as she had previously explained, would disagree with due to the song's popularity and radio play shortly after release. Many people like Albert found it annoying as they had been forced to listen to it for weeks every time they turned on the radio.

Darren laughed to himself as he thought about how grateful he was that he did not share their view of the song. "What's your favourite song?" He asked Chris.

"My favourite song?" She asked. When he nodded, she replied that she had many.

"But if you had to pick one?" He stressed.

"If I had to pick I guess I'd probably go with Train's 'Drops of Jupiter'." She smiled, clearly proud of her choice.

"Excellent choice, it is a lovely song." Darren agreed. They continued to talk about their favourite things as the music changed three more times. Chris found out that, coincidently, one of Darren's favourite films was 'Robin Hood: Prince of Thieves', the film from which his favourite song comes. As well as that, he liked Sense and Sensibility, obviously, Schindler's list and most of Tom Hank's films. Darren found Chris shared his fondness for Tom Hanks, she liked Tom Cruise too, especially, she explained in Top Gun when he is playing Beach Volley Ball.

"What's so special about that scene?" Darren asked innocently, pretending not to know about what she was referring.

"Nothing, it's just special." She smiled shyly.

Darren pretended to sulk as he expressed his disapproval of such comments. When she replied that she prefers watching Darren beat the punching bag in the gym, in a similar state to the pilots, he thanked her with a smile.

"I could do with practising more often actually," Darren mumbled to himself.

Chris took a small step towards him and moved her mouth closer to his ear. "I'll be watching." She brushed her hand across his cheek before taking his face in both hands as she kissed him once, gently, before stating that she needed another drink.

At the bar, as she was ordering their next round, Chris heard three women gushing over a man. Initially, she paid no attention, but upon hearing Darren's name escape from one of their mouths, she decided she should join in. "Excuse me ladies, but I couldn't help but over-hear your conversation. There are a lot of handsome men tonight aren't there?" They welcomed her into the conversation by three friendly nods of agreement. "Which one were you talking about just now?"

"Darren Thompson." The woman in the middle pointed towards Darren who was talking once again to Bruce by their table.

"Oh yes, I know who you mean." Chris hid her smile behind her drink.

"I've seen him with the kids; he's a natural. It's adorable I tell you." The woman in the middle exclaimed.

"I've watched him train, you know, fight. He's amazing." This comment came from the woman on the right.

The third woman ushered the others, Chris included, in close as she lowered her voice to a whisper. "If you watch him carefully, you can see the way his entire body moves under his suit. His suit flaps open at the top from time to time. He doesn't look bad. I tell you." She sniggered.

Chris saw her opportunity. "You know, I walked into the gym once to find him training on his own, he had no shirt on." She was both amused and shocked at the reaction this comment got from the women. They looked as if they were trying to imagine what Chris may have seen.

They straightened their stance and turned a little towards the bar as they saw Darren look over. "Don't look now, but he's coming over." The woman on the right whispered. They hadn't seen Chris wave him over.

Chris took a step closer to the women as Darren reached her. "We were just talking about you," Chris said merely.

"No, we weren't!" Two of the women snapped desperately in unison.

Chris faked an innocent look, "We were saying how much of a natural you are with the kids."

Their faces softened as they realised Chris wasn't telling on them. "Yes, you are. I'm James's mum." The woman in the right extended out her hand, which Darren took. He held it long enough to realise why he had been called over. The woman inhaled sharply at the touch of their hands. He managed to suppress a laugh as he extended the same courtesy to the other two women as they revealed who their children were to him. "Women." He thought, he knew most men are the same the other way around, so he let it go.

"It's a pleasure." He smiled as he rested his hand on the bar behind Chris.

They all went quiet as Darren took a sip of his drink. The woman on the left broke the silence. "How come we haven't seen you before at one of these presentations?"

"I only moved here a couple of months ago." He replied. They all stood talking about how great New York is, but Darren still wasn't sure which he preferred, London,

Tennessee or New York. They talked until Darren and Chris's glasses were empty.

"Are you ready to go?" Darren asked Chris after looking at his watch. It was almost 21:00. The look of disbelief that spread across the faces of the three women once again amused Chris as she said that she was ready. They said goodbye to the three women and walked away. As they reached the door, Chris felt Darren's hand on her back as he closed the distance between them as they walked.

As soon as they were out of sight, he turned to Chris with a smile on his face. "What was all that about?" He asked.

"Nothing. We were talking about you." She hung her head as she smiled broadly.

"Oh, I get it." Darren understood. They laughed.

"One of them said that they would like to," she looked around her, and upon seeing a couple of people to their right, she stood on her toes and put her lips next to his ear and told him.

The look of shock on his face was evident as she stepped back down. He thought about it for a moment and smiled.

He looked at Chris. He watched a smile creep across her face as she playfully pressed her tongue into her teeth. His stomach began to twist and turn at his thoughts. He pulled her in close so that their faces were no more than two inches apart. "I didn't think that was possible. I say we go back to yours and see."

"You know nothing about this world and the people in it, do you?" She was once again amused at the lack of knowledge he had about specific subjects, knowledge a person generally learns before they reach Darren's age. He was so innocent it made her insides tremble as she thought about all the things she could show him, knowing all too well that she would be the first and hopefully the only one with who he would ever do it.

She let her face linger close to his before she placed her hand in his and walked with him to the car, her breath catching in her throat each time she thought about the night ahead.

The sun is shining, but it's not warm. What did I expect? It's December in New York. It was never like this in Tennessee. Still, it's not too cold. I'm able to sit here writing without my gloves on, thankfully. Have you ever tried writing with gloves on? It's hard; the pen slips through the soft material of the glove before you've managed to write an entire word.

"...this could be to suggest that George Orwell was symbolising that in Nineteen Eighty-Four, the lack of privacy due to the telescreens and microphones located both in the houses of those in the Outer Party and in outside areas which the party members are found in, resembles the lack of privacy Orwell knew was eventually going to be the reality, should the development of technology continue." Okay, that was along the right lines of what I want to say, but I didn't think it would come out like that, way too wordy. Whatever, I'll re-word it later.

I had to get out of my apartment. These urges usually remain unfulfilled, much to my disappointment, but I made a choice not to write, and now I pay the price when I physically feel like I need to write but I can't because I am required at work.

I had started my Kickboxing training a few months before my parents died, but I had never felt as fulfilled fighting as I did writing, I still don't.

But the choice was mine, and I made it.

My English grades never faltered, they were perfect, as close as you could get anyway.

"…Another interpretation of the surveillance cameras and 'Big Brother' themselves could be to show that the Thought Police and Big Brother have the omnipresent ability of God. They, like him, can watch and control their public continuously…" Again, that is what I meant to write, just not quite like that. My mind never rests, these thoughts run through my head regularly throughout most days. Each book I read, I mentally analyse its themes and its characters, they are all put under extreme criticism in my mind once I place the book back on the shelf. What can I do? This sort of thing comes to me naturally. I wish I could stop it but I can't.

I'm sitting trying to write while once again going over my life regrets. What if I had become an English Teacher and not a Police Officer? I wouldn't have met Chris, well,

I wouldn't have met her again. I'd probably still be married to Sarah. Wow, that's a horrible thought, Sarah not Chris. I made the right choice.

I gave up my dream to ensure that no-one has to suffer the way my parents did. This is my job, to keep those who are evil, off the streets to protect those who are good. And what a job I'm doing, ha, a serial killer is on the loose because I was unable to remember I was meeting my wife. Some Detective, I would have been a better teacher than I am a Police Officer. Still, I have no regrets, I do the best I can do, and I get by.

Life can never be perfect, I know that, but when I ignore the fact that the world and the people in it are spiteful, vindictive and selfish, I come to realise that my life is as close to perfect as it could ever be. Listen to me. I have such cynical views of the world. But am I wrong? I wish I were, but the truth is much more dismal than the fairy-tales in which we want to believe.

Still, we must go on hoping that one day it will be better again. It has to be. There has to be a world soon, and by "soon" I mean in the next 1,000 years or so, where no-one kills anyone, no-one steals, no-one lies, and everyone is kind and thoughtful.

Such cynical views and such naïve dreams, isn't that what makes up most people? That and a will to carry on. I should be getting back. Everyone will be arriving soon, and I still need to turn on the oven.

Damn, that's cold! Great, now I need to un-tuck my shirt so I can shake the snow out. Bloody hell that is cold, my back's going numb now. Oh, Christmas Day tomorrow at Chris's mother's house in Idaho, even more, snow, fun.

⌐ CHAPTER 12 ⌐

I N THE RUN-UP TO Christmas, Darren was always watching over his shoulder as he waited for Isabelle's arrival, she had called a few days into December and still hadn't arrived. It wasn't until Christmas Eve that Darren received a voice mail.

He stared at his phone for a few moments before putting the phone to his ear. The operator recording informed him that he had - one - voicemail - and recited the instructions. Darren waited and waited for what seemed like hours before the all too familiar voice began talking. "Hello, Clark. You're probably wondering why I'm not currently there with you, well, let me explain. I knew you'd be left a little upset by my sudden announcement" she sniggered, "and I just wanted to let you worry before I came, I'm nice like that, you know. But mark my words, I'll be there soon. Have a nice Christmas Clark," she did not attempt to conceal the sarcasm from her cold voice, "and I'll see you soon. Goodbye for now Clark."

"Darren? Are you coming back in?" Nick shouted from the living room.

He managed to find his voice, "Yea, I'll be through in a minute." He decided he'd think nothing more of it as there was nothing he could do to stop her coming. He was briefly optimistic when he realised that she didn't have his address, but then he remembered that she knew where he worked and she had somehow managed to get his phone number.

"Darren?"

"Coming." He shoved his phone back into his pocket before he joined everyone else. As tradition demanded, the team were having a Christmas Eve dinner, this year at Darren's. The group had volunteered him as he had the largest apartment and his dining table was far bigger than anyone else's. He seated himself between Nick and Alice on the floor. Despite having more than enough room for everyone on the sofa and the accompanying chairs, everyone was sitting on the floor around the coffee table with their backs against the furnisher. Hot chocolates had been brought through a few minutes before and had been placed on mats in the centre of the table in the same formation as the bodies surrounding the table.

Christine was watching him from across the table. He glanced towards her and watched her as she continued to look his way while still talking to Jason.

The morning after they had spent their first night together, Darren and Christine had laid in bed before leaving for work and talked about what was to happen. They had decided that if everyone were to know that Darren was once Clark, then they would become worried for Chris, so therefore they had decided not to tell anyone that they had begun seeing each other. However, they still hadn't told anyone about Darren's past. A few days before Christmas Eve, they decided that it was about time that Darren came clean to the rest of the team as they were still coming up with empty case files when searching for Clark McAvoy. They needed to know so that they could do their job correctly, Darren could help them fill in the missing information.

"Every time we search for his name, it tells us that he changed his name a little over six months ago. We cannot access his file as it is completely locked, we've tried, but we cannot crack the security protecting his file." As Darren heard Jason mention this to Chris, Darren flashed her a look that told her what he was about to do.

"Clark's from Tennessee." He said aloud once the conversation volume lowered. Everyone stopped their conversations and looked towards Darren. Nick confirmed that he was. "I know Clark, sort of."

Everyone seemed to close in on him as they leaned forwards slightly in anticipation. "What do you mean "sort of"?" Jason asked, confused.

"The reason you can find anything on him is because he changed his name, but you don't know what he changed it to. I do."

"How do you know what he changed it to? What's his name?"

"Because-" he sighed, "because he's me. I changed my name from Clark to Darren when I moved." Everyone was speechless. Their faces were blank as their eyes remained fixed on him.

Nick was the first to try to speak, "You mean you-"

Darren simply nodded at Nick before apologising to everyone.

"Darren, you have nothing to apologise for!" Christine voiced once he'd finished.

"Chris, I do. They couldn't do their jobs because I was withholding information, technically."

"I can't see how it makes a difference," Nick said after giving it some thought. He, as did everyone else, dismissed any possible thought that Darren could be the killer. "It's not as if we've finally found a suspect, all that happens now is we can finally fill in the information on Clark McAvoy. There is no evidence connecting him to the crime so there would be no need to do much more about it." He stopped before looking back at Darren. "Why didn't you just tell us?"

"It's a part of my life that I've tried to escape from."

"But why tell us now?"

"I just decided that it's time you knew. Despite it not making any difference to the case, it's a part of my life that, until now, I wanted to keep secret. It's not who I am anymore, but someone is trying to change that."

"What do you mean Darren?" Alice asked.

"Nick, you remember the woman who called asking for me?"

"Yes."

"Well, she's the mother of the first victim, Sarah. She's my mother-in-law, a horrible woman who is trying to take control over my life once more. You guys needed to know all this before she got here, because my bet is, she would have told you herself."

As they continued talking about Isabelle's promise to join them soon, Christine watched Darren out of the corner of her eye. He was subtly trying to catch her attention. She looked at him.

He winked at her before encouragingly raising his eyebrows. He wanted her to tell the rest of the team about them. She nodded in agreement before becoming visibly excited as she waited for the other conversations to die down.

When the conversations showed no signs of stopping, she got up and made her way over to Darren. She asked to be excused as she passed Alice before she sat in between Darren's outstretched legs. She laid against him as he wrapped his arms around her. He buried his face in her hair and whispered in her ear.

"I know they haven't noticed." She smiled.

There was a knock at the door. "That'll be Frank and Helena," Darren stated as he began to get up.

"I'll go." Jason offered as he rose.

"Thank you, Jas. Still nothing." He whispered to Christine.

The door closed and Frank and Helena joined them all in the living room. They sat behind Darren and Christine on the sofa. "Are we hall having fun?" Helena asked.

When there was no other reply once Darren and Christine had answered her, Darren explained that everybody was overly involved in their conversations.

Helena motioned for Christine to join her on the sofa for a talk. She slid out of Darren's arms and joined her. "Still going strong?" She asked as she tipped her head slightly towards Darren on the floor. When Christine replied that everything was going amazingly, Darren saw her and immediately wondered what the two of them were talking about. When Helena saw him looking, she whispered something to Christine which prompted a nod from her shortly after. They giggled and whispered in each other's ears for the next couple of minutes as Darren tried to ignore them, they were probably trying to wind him up as usual.

"Darren?" Jason asked across the table before he asked Darren to meet him in the middle of the table. Darren obliged. He got up and crawled on his knees towards the table edge before he leant over the table until his face about a foot away from Jason's. "What was all that about?" He asked all excitedly.

"What are you talking about?"

"That whole thing with Chris then. Why was she sitting on you like that?" He smiled mischievously. Are you two-"

"Yes, but I think you're the only one who noticed."

"Oh my goodness!" He expressed as he clapped his hands together fast. "Tell me, how long?"

"A few weeks now." Darren couldn't keep the smile from his face, each time he tried, it became harder and harder as he thought about how happy he was. "We can't think of a way to tell everyone though." He conceded in a whisper.

"Just-" He sighed heavily, "I don't know actually. Just don't hide your affections, you don't necessarily have to tell anyone anything. Remain close, and you know - everyone's sure to notice."

"Good point. Thanks, Jas." He thanked him before returning to his original place on the floor.

"Are we having snacks or what?" Alice asked as she nudged Darren in the arm.

"Damn, yes, the snacks," Darren remembered, he stood swiftly and made his way into the kitchen to get the bowls he'd filled earlier. He stood with his hands on the counter as he closed his eyes and for some reason became very nervous about telling everyone about him and Chris. "Come on," He whispered to himself, "Stop being pathetic."

He remained still for a couple more minutes before he felt familiar arms around his waist and her head on his back. As he turned, she took a step back before stepping into his arms once he faced her. He leant against the worktop once more as he ran his hands up and down her back. She pulled away and placed her hands flat on his chest. She leant on him and tipped her head up so their eyes could meet. "What are you thinking?" She asked.

"Nothing. Just that I love you and I don't want anything to change."

She sighed. "Before you joined us all, that was Isabelle on the phone wasn't it."

"It was, she'd left me a voicemail."

"What did she say?"

"Only that she purposely waited before coming. Knowing I'd worry, she decided to let me stew."

"Bitch," Christine muttered.

"Oh! Naughty word." He pretended to be shocked.

She closed the distance between their faces, "Well, you'll have to punish me later then, won't you?" She teased as their lips met in a passionate kiss. Darren lowered his hands, so they were on her behind as she wrapped her arms around his neck.

"What's this?"

They stopped as they heard the voice from the door. They each stole a glance at the figure before they turned back to each other with amused smiles. They failed to contain their laughter as they burst out in unison.

"Are you two a thing? Or is this just a bit of fun?"

Once he'd calmed down, Darren made his way over to Alice at the door. "Are you two a thing?" She repeated.

"Yes." He answered as he glanced at Christine behind him.

"For how long?" She gasped, her cracked voice full of shock.

"Only a few weeks. Are you okay?" She looked as if her eyes were filling up and her fists were clenched in what he assumed to be a rage.

189

"Fine." She answered, but she didn't look it. "Why, erm... why didn't you tell us?" She forced a smile as she spoke in an equally forced voice.

"We just-" he stopped, her face was becoming redder as the seconds passed. "Are you sure you're okay?" He asked her once more.

Instead of answering, she turned away and made her way quickly back into the living room. "What was all that about?" Darren asked Christine as he turned towards her.

She smiled faintly. "She likes you, isn't it obvious?"

"Not to me." He replied, confused. "You don't believe that do you?"

"I do."

"Oh dear." They remained in silence before Darren asked if she'd help bring in the bowls. They each took two bowls. When they'd set the bowls down on the table, they noticed that Alice wasn't there. "Where's Alice?" Darren asked casually.

"She's gone to the bathroom. She didn't look too well," Frank told him as Darren sat in front of him on the floor.

"Oh, okay, thank you." Christine sat next to Darren but kept her distance. When Alice returned, she willingly sat in the spot Christine had previously occupied, holding her eyes on Darren as she did.

Alice didn't stay much longer, she left around 20:00 but thankfully appeared much more at ease as she wished everyone a Merry Christmas. Darren followed her out.

"Alice?" He called gently. She stopped at the top of the stairs before turning to face him.

"What? I've got a train to catch." She snapped.

"Earlier, you were alright, but then after leaving the kitchen, you were fine with everyone else but me."

"And?"

"And, I wanted to know why."

Somehow, she relaxed as she took her bag off her shoulder and let it fall into her hand. "It's just me, being ridiculous. Just forget about it, please." The look in her eyes as she answered him confirmed that what Christine had assumed, was correct.

"Okay." He replied with a comforting smile.

"I'd better get going."

"Have a lovely Christmas."

"You too Darren."

Once back inside, Darren joined Christine on the floor and placed his arm around her shoulder. She nuzzled her head in the crook of his neck as she closed her eyes and inhaled his scent. It didn't take long for Nick to notice them. He promptly asked if they were seeing each other and when told that they were, he expressed his joy at their newfound relationship and gave each of them a friendly hug. By 21:15, everyone had got their coats on and were saying their goodbye's. Frank and Helena were the first of them to leave, hugging them and wishing them the best. Nick and Jason soon followed with equally loving hugs and wishes, leaving Darren and Christine alone.

"They all left later than I'd expected," Christine confessed.

"They did leave rather late." He checked his watch. "They left too late." He said with a childish pout. "You're packed. I've only got 15 minutes to pack for your mother's." He moaned.

"With two of us, it should take no time at all," Chris commented.

"I don't know if I can do this," Darren confessed as they reached the gate.

"You've met her before." Christine joked.

"Really? You're going there?"

"Fine. You were okay meeting my dad."

"I met your dad at dinner before we were together. Besides, he visited me at the gym before that."

She took his hand and ran her thumb over his knuckles. "I've got you." She comforted as she opened the gate with her other hand. She let go of his hand, allowing him to pick up the suitcases by his side.

"How much did you pack? We're only here for two nights Chris." He said almost to himself as he followed her down the drive.

When they reached the door, he placed the cases either side of him as he watched Christine knock on the door and wait patiently for her mother to answer the door.

Her mum came out and embraced her daughter. For a moment, Darren was transported back to that very night all those years ago. Thankfully, it passed soon enough.

"Mum, this is Darren."

Her mother extended out her warm hand and took his fondly before embracing him in her gentle manner as she expressed her delight regarding them finally meeting. "Your hands are freezing, come on inside the pair of you." She ushered them inside where they removed their snow-covered shoes by the door. Darren then followed Christine into the living room and sat beside her as she continued talking to her mother.

"So, Darren, Christie tells me that you moved to New York about four months ago."

"That's right, yes."

"What made you move from Tennessee if you don't mind me asking?"

He hesitated but hoped she didn't notice, "I needed to get away from my life. Everything had changed, and I didn't like what was happening, so I moved, a 'fresh start' if you will."

"Ah, escaping someone were we? Christie, you'd better look out for jealous girlfriends." Her mother made her way into the kitchen to make them each a warm drink.

"See, I told you you'd be fine." Christine bragged as she placed her head on Darren's shoulder. He glanced over at the clock and sighed. They had caught a 22:06 flight directly from New York to Idaho. The plane had landed at 00:58 and the time was now 02:31.

He hung his head back as he tried to keep his eyes open. Christine had the same problem as she shouted into her mother, telling her that they were going to go to bed.

After a quick goodnight, Darren and Christie made their way upstairs.

''This is the room I stay in when I come to visit.''

"Cosy." He complimented as he put their bags at the bottom of the bed. "I'm just going to do my teeth."

"Okay, I'll be in in a minute." She opened her suitcase. "My mother said that she'd wake us a 08:00 so that we would have time to exchange presents, have breakfast and finish catching up before everyone comes around for dinner at 13:30."

Darren popped his head around the door with his toothbrush in his mouth. "08:00?" He questioned.

"Yes."

"Just checking." He mumbled, causing her to laugh at him.

Once they were in bed, Christine listed the people who'd be coming to dinner that afternoon. "That's a lot of people," Darren confessed, looking a little intimidated.

"You'll be fine, I promise." She placed her hand on his chest. "Besides, you'll have me by your side."

"Thank you." He ran his hand across her waist. He took her nightie in between his fingers, "Now why have I never seen you wear anything like this before?" He teased.

"Sorry, it's all that my mother had for me. I know, it's something my grandma would wear." "Well, I like it, on you that is." He slid his hand down her leg until he reached the hem of the garment. He stroked her bare skin with his fingers before he slid his hand under the material and slowly brought his hand back up her leg. Her breath caught in her throat as he cupped her behind. He brought his hand up and tucked his hand under her chin.

She caressed his cheek in her hand as he gently pulled her face towards his. One kiss became two, and two became more as they lost themselves in the other's embrace. They stopped when they realised where they were going, Christine's mum was only in the next room.

"Did you pass the 'point of no return'?" Christine teased with a sly glance down the bed.

"No, thankfully we didn't." He answered knowing what she'd meant.

"Well," she stroked his chest, "there's always next time."

"There is." He paused. "Goodnight Chris." He said with another kiss, this one gentle and innocent.

"Goodnight Darren."

Darren woke moments before Christine's mum called them from downstairs. Chris hadn't heard, so he woke her gently by nuzzling his nose behind her ear. She quietly moaned, stirring Darren's insides "No, not now," he told himself. "Time to get up." He said aloud as he climbed out of bed, purposely shaking it as he did.

They both agreed to get a good wash. A shower could wait until later when they were getting ready for dinner.

Once downstairs, they along with Christine's mother sat around the coffee table in the living room in the same places they had done earlier that morning.

Christine's mum began to speak, "You know, Darren, it dawned on me as I was in bed, I've seen you somewhere before. I can't for the life of me think where." Darren and Christine exchanged a brief look before her mother proposed that they exchange presents. As her mother made her way over to the table at the other end of the room, Christine turned to Darren and asked him if he was going to tell her mother where she knows him from.

"If she mentions it again, I will."

She appeared to have forgotten about what she'd said before, as, when she returned to her seat after retrieving a small, beautifully decorated box, Flo Bridges asked Darren a semi-related and heart-breaking question. "What do your parents have to say about you spending Christmas away from home?" She hadn't meant any harm, Darren could tell from her tone of voice that she was joking. Still, he felt compelled to tell her.

"I remember seeing you. It's a long time ago now. I'm surprised you remembered." Darren hoped she wouldn't feel too bad about her previous question regarding his parents. He tried so hard to sound positive as he told her that they met in London about seventeen years ago. "I was only young. We met in the waiting room of the police station in London as you waited for your husband to get off work."

Her expression changed from an interested smiled to a knowing look of shock. "You're the young boy whose," she swallowed hard, "whose parents had been murdered." The last word stung in Darren's ears as it always had done when spoken about his parents.

"Yes." He confirmed, not that he needed to.

"Oh, my dear boy!" Flo cried. "I'm so sorry, about that and about what I said before." He leant forward in his seat and reached over the table and put his hand on hers, reassuring her that it was okay. "Your name wasn't Darren, was it?" She said once she had settled down. "No, it was something beginning with 'c' I think, what was it?" She asked.

"Clark." He told her.

"Oh Darren, I'm sorry, I had no idea."

"Please, it's okay." He assured.

She patted his hand with her other hand and gave him a sympathetic, but not overly, smile through which she apologised once more.

"They owned McAvoy Exports, right?" She asked as Darren sat back.

"They did." He began to feel a little uncomfortable as he realised where the conversation might be going.

"Do you own the company now?" She didn't appear to be asking about money. She was merely wondering, so he answered her, telling her that he did.

Knowing that she could only really ask one further question, a question regarding the current success of the company, Flo stopped, the success of the company was nothing to do with her, but she was, however, silently grateful that he would always be able to provide for her daughter.

When Flo left the room to make them another drink, Darren turned to Christine, "I have to go to London for a for a few days mid-January." He said, concealing his intentions for the moment.

"Oh, how long will you have to stay there?" She asked, looking a little sad.

"Two or three days."

"Fair enough."

"Frank gave me the entire week off, so I'm thinking of staying there longer. Would you like to spend the week with me in London?" He asked finally.

"Are you serious?" She was jumping up and down on the sofa excitedly then jumped on him when he confirmed that he was genuinely serious. "Of course I'd like to go!" She said as she kissed him.

"Someone's happy," Flo commented as she re-entered the room with a tray of drinks.

"Darren's invited me to London for a week." Chris slid off his knee so that she was back by his side.

"That's nice of you Darren," She gave him a grateful look, "She's often moaned about only going once all that time ago."

"I can't wait." Christine shuffled in her seat.

It was 21:14 and she had been walking for the last two hours trying to find his apartment building. She stopped and asked a man where she was and asked for the directions to where she needed to be. The man pointed her in the right direction and then bid her goodbye. She finally found the right building, and now she just had to figure out which apartment was his. She stood at the front door and looked down the list of tenants. She found what she was looking for and waited until someone left the building so she could enter. She couldn't be bothered taking the stairs up to the 11th floor, so she got in the elevator. As it took her up to the right level, she began shivering with anticipation. She'd waited for this moment for months.

21:31. She stood before his apartment door. "I'll get his money somehow." She thought to herself as she reached for the knocker.

Darren was at his bookshelf choosing a new book when there was a knock at his door. "That was fast," He commented as Christine walked in, "You said you'd be here at 21:30, you're almost ten minutes early."

"If you're complaining, I can come back later." She joked, half turning to leave.

"I wish you'd stay." He whispered as he wrapped his arms around her.

"Then I'll stay." She replied with a kiss. "So, what do you want to watch?" She asked as they made their way over to the shelves containing his DVD's.

He stood behind her and to the side as they tried to pick a film. She purposely walked backwards until she was pressing into him. She felt his hands on her hips. She shuddered as he began moving his hands up and down her legs.

"Are these new?" He said referring to her jeans. She moved away from him to allow him to get a better look.

"My mother got me them for Christmas, remember?"

"I remember she got you some, but they look different on than they do off."

"Like them?" She asked.

"I do." She smiled at him, inviting him to make the comment she knew he'd be thinking. He began making his way towards her slowly. "I do, however, prefer them off."

Her insides began to stir as her anticipation grew with each step he took towards her. It was a little over a week since they returned from her mother's and they hadn't had a moment to themselves since they got back. He stopped in front of her and placed his hands on her hips. His hands skimmed over her thighs as he reached the button. He unfasted it before unzipping them. Her insides were going crazy. He slowly made his way down, so he was kneeling in front of her. Slowly, he tugged down her jeans, brushing her skin with his fingers as he did. She stepped out of them. He held them up and pretended to admire them as she knelt in front of him on the floor. She placed one arm around his neck and the other around his waist as she sat down and pulled him gently on top of her. They kissed passionately, tugging at each other's clothes until they were both laying on his living room floor naked. "Past the point of no return?" She joked, recalling their encounter over Christmas.

"Getting there." He replied. She could feel him pressing against her, exciting them both further. 21:31. There was a knock at the door. They paused briefly before deciding that whoever it was, would leave, but it seemed that they would not, for a few seconds later there was another knock, this one more demanding than the one before.

"That was so close to being too late," Darren said as he buttoned up his trousers. "Have you seen my top?" He asked.

"Here," She replied with a smirk, "Why don't you keep track of your clothes. I thought you were tidy, fancy just throwing your clothes here, there and everywhere."

"You're no better." He joked as he began towards the door. There was a third knock. "I'm coming!" Darren shouted.

He opened the door and froze as he cast his eyes on the figure before him. Everything around him seemed to slow as he thought of Christine in the room and his parents in the middle of the road, dead. The figure before him was saying something to him in a harsh voice and with an even harsher face. "Aren't you going to invite me in, Clark?" The figure demanded.

"Isabelle," Darren said finally, his voice scarcely more than a whisper.

"Well?" She was becoming frustrated.

"What?"

"Move and let me in."

For some reason, he moved aside and let her in.

"Nice place you've got here, I think I'm going to like staying here."

Darren froze, it was enough for her to show up, he figured she surely couldn't be cruel enough to stay without being wanted. "You're staying?"

"Yes Clark, don't slouch, and take these bags upstairs."

Christine had seen Isabelle walk in and unexpectedly demand that Darren take her bags upstairs, but what she found harder to believe was that Darren stared at her and obliged. She followed Darren up the stairs unseen.

"What is the matter with you?" She asked as she closed the door of the spare bedroom behind them.

"What?"

"Is this what it's going to be like now she's here? Why don't you tell her that you don't want her to stay?"

"Because she wouldn't listen to me if I did, it would only make her want to stay more."

"What if I went down there and asked her to leave?"

"She'd only put up more of a fight. Listen, Chris," he took her hands in his and sat down on the end of the bed, she sat next to him, "I think it'd be best if she didn't see you, it would only wind her up more."

"Darren, I told you before, I'm not going anywhere. I'm going downstairs with you right now."

He knew there was no point trying to argue with her. "I love you so much." They embraced.

"I love you too. Now, let's go." She held his hand as they made their way to the top of the stairs, Isabelle was still fingering the walls and wiping the surfaces, checking for dust it seemed.

Darren went down first with Christine a couple of steps behind. The shock on Isabelle's face when her eyes met Christine's was evident. She made no effort to conceal her disapproval.

"Who's this?" She demanded as if she had a right to know.

"Isabelle, this is Christine, my girlfriend." He might be scared of Isabelle and what she could do to him, well, what she had done to him and probably would do again, but he still found her reaction amusing and had to hide the faint smile that he felt spread across his face as he introduced Chris.

"Girlfriend?" She had the nerve to sound offended. "What do you mean? My poor Sarah hasn't been dead for six months yet."

"We're not having this conversation, Isabelle."

"All I know is that my only child is dead because you failed to be a good husband, no wonder you don't want to have this conversation. And I suppose he's told you everything has he?" She turned to Christine. "All about how he left me to fend for myself after practically causing my daughter's death. About how he was meant to be meeting her on the night she was murdered, I suppose he told you all that, about everything, I bet."

"Actually," now it was Chris's turn to be brave, she wasn't going to let Darren down, "he's told me more than that. He's told me things even you wouldn't know and all the things you definitely wouldn't admit to knowing."

"I don't know what you're talking about." She replied with an evil smile which silently confessed everything. She glanced over to Darren who was shuffling his feet, lining them up with the floorboards, fiddling with his fingers in the way she'd always found weird. "Still a freak?" Her words stung as Darren considered how well he'd been managing with his OCD recently. "Once a freak always a freak." She turned to Chris, "You don't want to be with this one when things aren't going as well as he'd like. He becomes even more of a freak, as you can imagine. You know, he has to walk on different surfaces, like carpet to hard-wood with an even amount of steps, even the same amount of left and right steps. It's weird."

Darren whispered something in Christine's ear before she went upstairs. Isabelle was happy to see the back of her, how dare he have another woman.

"She'd better not come down, not until we've finished our conversation at least." At that moment, Christine came back down the stairs with Isabelle's bags in her hands. She placed them down in front of her and returned to Darren's side.

"This conversation is over," Darren said simply. "I don't think you should stay much longer." Isabelle's hands formed two wrinkly, weak looking fists as she began making her way over to them to scare them. Christine stood still, not at all affected by the woman's advances. Darren also appeared totally at peace until Isabelle spoke. "That's an unfortunate scar you have on your neck, Clark. I can't imagine how you got that. It'd be a shame if suddenly there was one mirroring it on the other side, wouldn't it?" This caused Darren to swallow hard as he appeared to shudder. "I'm going to need a place to stay tonight, and I think that I'll be very comfortable here, thank you." She stopped by her bags and picked them up. "I'll take these upstairs. I'll find my room; thank you very much for letting me stay." As she walked towards them, to save an argument, they parted to let her through.

Once she was upstairs, Darren turned to Christine and apologised. "I'm sorry, I couldn't tell her again."

"You've got nothing to be sorry for. Darren," she said his name sternly, "that woman is horrible to you, she makes you feel horrible for no reason, you've done nothing wrong, remember that."

"Chris, she's got to stay. If I make her leave, she'll only come back stronger and more dangerous. You have no idea what she's capable of, and I have a bad feeling I don't know completely."

"What do you think her plan is?" Christine couldn't for the life of her figure out why someone would purposely ruin someone's life just to let them have their freedom so they could destroy their life again.

"I have no idea. But this is probably bigger than either of us could begin to imagine."

"What do you mean?"

"Chris, her husband murdered my parents simply so she could get close to me and adopt me, she told me herself. She told me that they planned to kill me and make it look like an accident so that they could get my parent's money. If Sarah hadn't died, I don't think I'd be here now."

"Why would she want the money?"

"Why does anyone want a ridiculous amount of money? Chris, the company is worth almost £5 billion, a hell of a lot more than it was when my parents were murdered."

"Do you think she knows how much the company is worth now?"

"I hope not, not unless she's been monitoring it, which I bet she has. I should call them in London, move the meeting up to next week instead of the week after. They should know what's going on in London. We don't know what she might do."

"You think she might try and steal the money?"

"Her brother in law and husband were arrested about eight years ago for attempting to hack into the company's bank account. Her brother-in-law is due to be released in a few months, but her husband was released a couple of years ago. What's to stop them trying again?"

"Oh." She sighed.

His face lit up, "I'll go and speak to Frank now, ask if we can change the week we have off, that's if you still want to go to London?"

"Of course, let's not let Isabelle ruin our week away." She took a step towards Darren. "You'd better not tell me to go home tonight, even though I know you'd only do it to help, I was in the mood for a film and," she paused as an embarrassed look spread across her face, "finally getting around to spending some 'time' with you." She smiled once more.

He was about to take her by the hand and lead her upstairs, but as he reached for her hand, Isabelle came back down the stairs. "Clark, it's been hours since I sat down. Not that I care, but I feel like I have to attempt to sound polite, so, if you don't mind, I'm going to sit down here and watch TV." She walked over to the sofa and sat down. She picked up the film Christine had chosen while Darren answered the door off the table and shook it. "Looks like I'm interrupting your plans." She delivered them a smug smile.

Darren responded as he made his way over to the sofa and took it from her hand, "Don't worry, we were just on our way up. There's a TV in my room. We can watch," He paused to look at which film Chris had chosen, "what is it, 'The Proposal', upstairs. Goodnight Isabelle."

A feeling of pure anger stirred inside Isabelle as she watched Darren take this woman by the hand and make his way upstairs to do God only knows what! How dare he look happy!

Once upstairs, Darren locked his bedroom door behind them, and within five minutes, the film was in, and they resumed where they were when Isabelle had first knocked. She knew that deep down, Isabelle being downstairs was getting to Darren, but from the way they were making love, she knew that it was very deep down inside him and was not affecting him currently. She knew it would soon, but she would ensure that he always had somewhere else better to go when he left the house, whether it be to work or her home or Franks, Nick's and Jason's, wherever, he would not be alone, she knew that they would help too. She glanced at the scar on his neck that Isabelle had mentioned before and briefly wondered how he got it. This thought was banished from her mind as she completely lost herself in Darren.

CHAPTER 13

THEY HAD BEEN CALLED out to another murder victim early that morning. They had all arrived on the scene by 08:00 and had almost finished processing the scene by 10:30. But there was something different about this body, and as they were packing up their things, Jason asked if anyone had any idea what was wrong with the body.

"What, apart from the fact that she's dead and shouldn't be?" Darren asked.

"You know what I mean," Jason replied.

"Her lips aren't red." Darren pointed out.

"That's it!" Jason exclaimed.

"Oh no, they're not," Nick repeated as he walked over to them.

"Christine, come here for a minute," Jason shouted over to Chris who was still digging through the near-by bin.

"Wait!" She screamed. Thankfully she was out of sight and far enough away and couldn't witness them not-so-silently laugh at her. "I'm coming, just let me get out." Darren had ceased laughing and had walked over to the bin to help her out.

As they rejoined the others, they picked food wrappers and scraps of food off her clothes and wiped dust from her jacket. "What's up?" Chris asked as she stood next to Jason.

"Can you spot the difference?" Nick asked.

"Yea, her lips aren't red," Chris replied instantly.

"Right, it's lipstick, look." Jason crouched by the body and indicated for Chris to join him.

"So it is."

"What shade would you say that is?" Jason asked.

She looked at him in confusion. "Apart from when it's an exceptional occasion, have you ever seen me wear lipstick?" She laughed as she stood up.

"No."

"Can Alice determine what shade it is?" Darren asked, he still didn't understand the full extent to which technology can now help them.

"Yea, she can take a sample and run it through a database, figure out the shade, the brand and hopefully give us a list of names of those who have purchased the product recently in stores around here," Nick explained.

"Fantastic. I think we're about done here, wouldn't you say guys?" Darren asked.

A chorus of agreeing murmurs sounded in reply as they made their way back to their cars.

"I'm grateful for the lift that Nick and Jason provided me with on the way here, but I'm going back to the office with you now that you're here. One can only listen to Ed Sheeran for so long, and the five-minute journey was too long at that." Chris whispered to Darren as they reached his car.

"That's fine, but I'll have to move those folders I've put there." He opened the door for her, took the folders out and put them on the back seat. "Here we go."

"Such a gentleman." She teased as she climbed in.

By 16:00, they had all finished their work, Darren the only exception, and were about ready to leave for the day when Frank provided them all with another load of paperwork to complete from various petty crimes that had taken place over the last few weeks. Jason completed his work quite quickly and once finished, sat on the end of Darren's desk.

"Is it tomorrow you're going to London?" He asked when Darren looked up from his computer.

"Yes, we're on the 05:46 flight." He stopped working and put down his pen before turning his chair around, so he was facing Jason. "How are you doing Jason? It's been a while since I asked you that."

Jason laughed. "I'm doing fine thank you, Nick and I have just booked a holiday for April, and I already can't wait."

"Where are you going?"

"Mexico for a fortnight."

Darren was about to tell him how nice that sounded when his desk phone began to ring. He apologetically creased his brow before picking up the phone.

"Thompson." He answered, "Yes Sir- Of course, Sir-hold on one moment please Sir- Jason, could you just…" Darren's mobile phone had begun to ring.

Jason picked it up, stood up and walked a few steps away from Darren's desk and answered it. "Darren Thompson's phone-." He was soon cut off.

"Listen here you little twit, since you're going to London tomorrow, I've decided I'm going to have someone over for the week, they're here now actually. I'm not going to ask if that's okay with you, because I don't care. Now, I have something to say about that bitch that you seem intent of having over most nights…" Jason couldn't believe what he was hearing, how could Isabelle say that- and that- and why did she have to sound so mean? She hadn't noticed it wasn't Darren on the other end of the phone. Jason debated hanging up on her, but judging by the way she was speaking to him, he assumed that if he did, he'd only get Darren in trouble.

He let her finish in silence and remained so until she hung up on him.

"Chris? Could I have a word with you?" Jason asked quietly after he placed Darren's phone back on his desk unnoticed.

"Sure, one second, just let me send this to the printer." After a couple of seconds, she stood and smiled at him as she began making her way towards the printer, hinting for him to follow.

They stood by the printer as Jason repeated what Isabelle had unintentionally told him. "Is she always like this towards him?" Jason asked, shocked.

"Yes, she is. What you've repeated isn't as bad as some things I've heard her say to his face."

"But why? Is it because she blames him for the death of her daughter?"

"Did she say that?" Jason nodded. "Despite pretending that she's not getting to him, each time she mentions Sarah or any of the other victims, it seems Darren only blames himself for them more and more. I don't know what to do. I'm going to tell Darren that we're staying at mine tonight instead of his, we can leave for the airport from my house in the morning."

"That's probably for the best." Jason glanced at Darren who was laughing with Nick.

"We've still got to go to his after work to pick up his things though, for London."

"Oh, Frank wants us. I hope she doesn't bother you both when you collect his things."

They began to walk back towards their desks. "I wonder who she's invited round." Christine wondered out loud as she sat at her desk.

Christine told Darren when they were in the car going to his that Jason had spoken to Isabelle. She told him what she'd told him and was surprised to see how calmly he reacted to the news that there was someone else in his home.

"I can't think of anyone I wouldn't like to see more than I don't like seeing Isabelle, how bad could this be?"

But was he convinced? He didn't know.

He stood by his door with his key still in the lock.

His mind was going crazy trying to figure out who it was that was in there with Isabelle. There only one person who he hated more than her, but he doubted that they'd be in there.

Darren and Chris entered his living room to see two figures laughing on the sofa. One of them stood. Darren stiffened as his eyes met those of the figure making its way towards him. The figure stopped in front of him and extended his hand out towards Darren as a sly smile spread across its face.

"Clark, it's been a long time."

"I am not shaking your hand, and I'm not staying. I'm just here to collect some things. I'll let you guys get back to your conversation."

"Someone's developed a tongue." The figure said.

"No," Darren responded firmly, "someone's developed a backbone." With that, he glanced at Chris who, amused at what Darren had just said, followed him as he made his way up the stairs.

"Who was he?" She asked as she closed his bedroom door behind them.

"If you had one guess, who would you say it is?" He asked as he put things in his suitcase.

"Was he Sarah's father?"

"Yes, that was Julian. I'm ready, are you ready to go?" He seemed uneasy and didn't even try to hide it. She walked over to him and placed her hands on his chest. His heart was beating at an irregular rate, she took his hand in hers and picked up one of his bags as he picked up the other.

"Let's get out of here."

Julian and Isabelle stood by the door. "Where are you going, Clark?" Julian tested.

"If you must know, I'm staying at Chris' tonight."

"I hope you're not leaving because of me." Julian smiled.

"Of course not. When I get back from London next week, I want you gone, both of you." He flashed a glance at Isabelle before fixing his eyes once more on Julian's.

"I mean it." He warned.

"Beg." Julian shrugged.

"Sorry?" Darren's gaze became cold and his mouth set in a firm, hard line.

"Beg, Clark."

"Goodbye Julian, Isabelle." He passed them and opened the door. He followed Chris out into the hallway, but Julian followed shortly behind.

"Beg like your parents begged for their life."

Darren stopped. He turned to face Julian. "What did you just say?"

"You heard me. Beg just like they did."

In a flash, Julian was on the floor, face down with his arms pinned behind him, he hadn't even seen Darren

215

coming. "I want you gone," Darren repeated before taking Chris' hand and leaving down the stairs.

"I'm sorry," Darren whispered once they'd climbed in the car and put on their belts.

"What for?" Chris asked.

"For letting you see that. I shouldn't have let him win."

"Darren, please stop apologising. You shouldn't have to apologise to people like that. Please." She took his hand and kissed it before placing it back on the wheel. They set off. "Besides," Chris said as she tried to remain cool, "it was quite hot."

Darren glanced at her, shocked, before smiling to himself as they continued the rest of the journey in silence.

"We'll have to be asleep by 21:00 if we're to get up in the morning," Darren said as Chris took two bottles of water from the fridge.

"That gives us just over two hours. We have time to watch a film if you like." She pushed past him, purposely brushing against him as she went past.

He wrapped his arms around her waist. "We can put one on in the background."

"Sounds good." She replied as she pulled his face towards hers.

They'd been in London for almost four days when the day of the meeting came. That morning they'd walked from Buckingham Palace to the National Gallery and back again after spending far too long and far too much money in Waterstones near Trafalgar Square. They stood in the middle of Trafalgar Square as Chris turned to Darren and asked him what it was like to be back home.

"Until recently, I'd always considered this to be my home, and that living in America was just a long holiday, but no matter how good it is to be back, I'm happy to call New York my home, finally."

"What changed your mind about America?" She asked.

"You did." He smiled as he squeezed her hand.

"We'd better be getting back. I need a shower before I go."

Once back at the hotel room, Darren got in the shower as Chis took out three suits from his wardrobe and laid them on the bed. She crept into the bathroom and ran the cold tap. She filled her hands with water and threw it on Darren from behind. She laughed as he shouted out from the shock. He took the shower head down from the wall and sprayed her with it before continuing with his shower. She put the lid down on the toilet before sitting down. She admired him as he showered. It always stirred her insides to look at him, watching his muscles clench and release as he washed, he was perfect, and he was hers. She quietly cleared her throat before she asked him what she was to do that afternoon.

"You could go to the Odeon in Leister Square. There's bound to be a film on that sounds interesting."

"I'll do that; I'm not in the mood to walk anywhere. How far away is that?"

"It's about a ten-minute walk from here. I'll walk with you if you like, I'll pass it on my way to the office anyway."

"Sounds good. You'd better hurry up because you've got to leave in twenty minutes."

"I'm done now, could you hand me that towel please?" He turned off the shower and climbed out.

"You mean this towel?" Chris teased as she took the towel off the sink and began to walk backwards out of the bathroom door.

"You're doing this now? It's January, and we're in England. I'll freeze to death." He laughed as he walked towards her. "Thank you."

"Which one?" She asked as she stepped out of the way to let him see the three suits she'd laid on the bed for him.

"Which do you prefer?"

"I like this one," She said as she pointed to a dark grey suit with a pale grey shirt tucked inside, "but this one looks more professional." She held up a dark blue suit with a white shirt and his pale blue tie.

As he put the blue suit on he made a mental note to wear the outfit that she preferred that night when they went out for dinner.

"Do I look okay?" He asked once he'd fastened his tie and put on his shoes.

"Fine."

"But is it smart? I haven't seen them in almost eight years, Chris, I want to look more than fine."

"Perfect. I wish you'd stop worrying. They're going to be so happy to see you that they won't even notice what you're wearing."

"You think?" He looked sceptical still.

"There's no need to be nervous. They're going to love you."

Despite these words of encouragement wrapping themselves around his brain, Darren still found himself standing before the twenty-six storey building he owned, not daring to go in. "Come on. You can do this, stop being stupid." He told himself before stepping into the revolving door he'd spent hours playing in as a child.

"How can I help you?" The receptionist asked him without looking up from her computer.

"I'm here to see Leon Williams."

"He's got a meeting in twenty minutes, could you come back another time Sir?" She still hadn't looked up from her desk.

"I know, I'm conducting the meeting." This made her look up, probably in disbelief. She looked him up and down, a faint recognition passed over her face as she asked his name "Darren Thompson, erm - Cla-."

"Clark!" She jumped up from her desk causing papers to fall to the floor. "I had no idea, I'm sorry."

"Its fine, honestly Gloria, you weren't to know."

"I'm sorry, love. I haven't seen you in, what is it, sixteen years or something like that?"

"Yes, sixteen years is a long time. I visited not long after I turned eighteen, but you were on holiday at the time."

"Leon told me about that, I'm sorry I missed you, I would have loved to see you."

"I was quite disappointed that you weren't here." He smiled comfortingly.

"I'll call up and let them know you're on your way. I'll see you afterwards, won't I?" Slight desperation in her voice caused Darren's heart to tug. He confirmed that she would but that he did have to go upstairs. As he made his way up in the lift, despite hating them, he thought it better not to try twenty-one flights of stairs before the meeting. He remembered back to the times Gloria had taken him out for Ice-Cream because his father was running behind on some work. They'd sat in the Ice-Cream shop around the corner for two hours as the two of them devoured three ice-cream sundaes between them. Gloria had worked for his parents since before he was born, there had never been anyone else on the front desk. Each time Darren had visited his mother or his father after school, which was most days a week, she'd been there, and he couldn't wait to catch up with her after the meeting.

He stood at the door of the conference room and took a breath. He pushed open one of the doors with one hand and entered the room calmly. At the other end of the room stood Leon, his godfather. Leon met Darren's eyes, ceased talking and instantly began to approach him.

"Sorry everyone for the interruption," he addressed the table at which around twenty people were sitting, "but I haven't seen this man in way too long." He reached Darren and half shook his hand, and half embraced him as his eyes remained fixed on Darren's. His eyes dampened as his wide smile told Darren of how much Leon had missed him. "Shall we begin?" Leon asked moments later.

"Yes, let's."

The meeting went as well as expected; they arranged for them to undertake regular checks on the accounts. It seemed that the company was doing just as well, maybe a little better, than it was when Darren's parents ran it.

"See, just as I told you seven years ago, you don't need me here to run things, you're doing brilliantly, Leon, thank you," Darren told him after everyone had left.

"It's my pleasure entirely. Still, it doesn't stop us wanting you here Clark."

"I know."

"You must come to my house tonight for dinner."

"That sounds lovely, could I bring someone with me?"

A look of panic flashed over Leon's face, "It's not that Sarah, is it?"

"No, absolutely not."

"You're not together anymore?"

He paused. "No, we're not, I'll explain tonight, I've got to go, I promised I'd catch up with Gloria afterwards, I'm going to take her for coffee to the Ice-Cream parlour around the corner."

"Bring who you want, as long as you are there. You know where I live, I'll see you there at 20:00."

"I'll see you then. Goodbye Leon."

"Bye Clark."

Ice-cream time. He must take Chris there at some point during the week. She'd love it. He knew what she'd order, the double chocolate sundae with chocolate sprinkles. That or the honeycomb waffles covered with chocolate sauce and strawberries on the top.

CHAPTER 14

"CLARK!" THE WOMAN EXCLAIMED as she opened the door.

"Hello." Darren was shocked not to have Leon answer the door. "Where's Leon?" He asked.

"He's inside." She blushed. "Did he not tell you about us?"

"No, Auntie Sam, he didn't." He was still stuck in her embrace, and his back was beginning to ache because of the height difference between them. "Erm - Auntie Sam, I'm going to have to stand up. Hello Leon." He was approaching them from the back room.

"Clark, how are you?" Leon greeted.

"I'll be better when my spine recovers its original shape. Auntie Sam, Leon, this is Christine, Christine, this is Leon, my Godfather, and my Aunt Sam, my mother's sister."

"Lovely to meet you both." She shook their hands and entered with Darren when Sam complained that they were letting the cold in.

"So, Clark, where did you and Christine meet?" Leon asked once the door had closed.

"Oh, no, we're starting with you. You and Sammie? How did this happen?" He asked as they all sat around the coffee table.

He shrugged. "Not long after your parents died, we took comfort in each other. You know how things go, it just went from there, and now we're here. I wish this could have happened sooner. You wouldn't have had to go with those horrible women." After the death of his parents, Leon has tried to adopt Darren, but due to the amount of time his job required, and his lack of family, he was denied custody. "I'm sorry Clark."

"Leon, it's fine, honestly. We're both happy now, and if things hadn't have happened as they did, you two probably wouldn't have found each other, and I sure wouldn't haven't met Chris here."

"True, still-" He left his sentence to linger as he watched Sam stand to check on dinner. "Sam's made Spaghetti Bolognese. It used to be your favourite, is that okay?" Leon asked as Sam left the room.

"Perfect." Darren smiled.

"Chris, do you like Spaghetti Bolognese?" Leon turned to her.

"Love it." Chris beamed.

Sam came to the door and winked at Leon before asking if Chris would join her in the kitchen. As Chris made her way into the kitchen, Leon moved chairs, so he was sitting next to Darren.

"So, what about you and Chris, she seems lovely?"

"She is," Darren smiled, "what do you want to know?"

"Where did you meet?"

"At work, we're partners of sorts."

"What do you mean 'of sorts'?" Leon asked, confused.

"In our team, there's four of us, and we tend to split up into two twos, I'm usually with Chris."

"Is that wise?" Leon couldn't help but worry that Darren and Chris working together could hurt their relationship.

"It's working so far," Darren answered.

"True. How long have you been together?"

"A month and a bit."

"Is that all? I don't know how but it seems like you've been together longer."

"We've been working together since the beginning of October."

"She's crazy about you, that much is obvious." Leon nudged Darren, and he motioned towards the back door.

"Let's get some fresh air."

"Okay." Darren followed willingly, the scented candles arranged around the room were beginning to overpower him. He walked out of the house to a beautifully paved garden with a small section of grass around the edge. In the middle of the garden was a fountain which flowed with water tinted green which caught in the moonlight. It was warmer than it had been that morning and in the early afternoon, but when the wind blew, you felt the immediate need to wrap your jacket around you tight in a pathetic and useless attempt to shield yourself from the January icy breeze.

"So what happened with Sarah, I thought you were married?"

Despite knowing one of them was bound to ask the question, Darren was no more prepared to answer it when it was asked. "I was married," He confirmed, "but now I'm not."

"Divorced?"

"No, widower." He said bluntly without looking at Leon.

"Jesus!" Leon exclaimed. "What happened?"

"She was murdered, Leon, we never got who did it."

They remained in silence as both thoughts about Sarah. Leon was glad she was gone but was still grieved to find out why she wasn't there with them. Darren, however, was still silently still blaming himself for her death, if he'd have only gotten to the diner a few minutes earlier, then Sarah wouldn't be dead. Darren kept his thoughts to himself as Leon expressed his in a loud whisper, he was careful not to let Sam hear through the open kitchen window.

"There's something else, isn't there?" Leon asked daringly.

Deciding to keep the news about the Angel murderer quiet, Darren proceeded to tell Leon of Isabelle's appearance just before New Year and of Julian's visit, of which he was unsure of the duration, as he was with Isabelle's.

"So, she's been there for over a week?" Leon asked shocked.

"Yea, and there's no sign of her leaving just yet." Darren slumped against the wall next to the door and sighed deeply.

"Is she still-"

"Yes! I reckon she's worse than she was."

"But how?" Leon half laughed at the idea.

"I think it's because she feels she's got something to pin on me now. Before she just used to blame me for things that would go wrong around the house and things like that. If a door was broken, it was my fault and my job to fix it, but now Sarah's gone, Isabelle blames me for her death."

"Why?"

As Darren began to explain the events of that night, how he was supposed to be meeting Sarah but had forgotten, Sam and Chris were finishing up in the kitchen and had gotten onto the topic of the future.

"So what do you think will happen with you and Clark?" Sam asked quietly after glancing out of the window to see where her husband and Darren were. She could no longer hear them speaking.

"I have no idea. Things are quite hectic right now with work."

"And I suppose Isabelle isn't making it any easier for you both."

"Exactly. Besides, we've only been together for a month and a bit. I wouldn't want to rush things by overthinking about the future."

"'Over' thinking?" Sam met Chris' eye and smiled. "Meaning you've thought about it a little bit?" She grinned as Chris blushed and shushed her as Leon entered the kitchen closely followed by Darren.

"Dinner's ready, Christine honey, you and Clark go and sit at the table, those two seats by the fire," she pointed out of the kitchen through the large archway towards a beautifully laid the table in front of a glowing fire set up inside a fireplace constructed with stone and dark wood,

"Leon and I will bring the dinner in."

"Are you sure you don't want any help, Sam?" Darren asked.

"Bless you, no Clark, we'll be fine, thank you," Sam reassured as she guided an unwilling Darren out of the kitchen.

"We?" Darren heard Leon ask from the kitchen as he joined Chris on the table.

Darren took hold of Christine's hand and held it in both his on the table as he smiled affectionately at her.

"They are lovely, Darren, they are," Chris commented.

"I know, I'm lucky to have them. It's our last day tomorrow, what do you want to do?"

Chris thought for a moment before placing her other hand on Darren's leg. "How about a nice long, slow walk, wherever our feet take us?"

"That sounds perfect." Darren longed to kiss her but decided that waiting would make their hotel room seem so much more inviting and make it worth getting back.

Sensing what Darren was thinking, Chris half laughed-half smiled. Neither of them noticed Leon and Sam standing partially hidden by the kitchen wall, watching them, gushing over how happy their Clark was, finally. They both loved him more than he could ever know and were overjoyed to see that he now had someone else to love and to love him.

As Leon and Sam entered the room, Darren and Chris parted and shuffled in their seats, so they were straighter on. "Despite your constant insistence that the English weather forecast is completely unreliable, tomorrow's weather is supposed to be okay, and I like to believe our last day here will be as perfect as the others," Chris said to Darren jokingly.

The weather was as predicted. They spent their final day in the English sunshine. However, the January chill remained slightly, like a constant reminder of what had happened and what was to linger for a while longer, but both banished any thought of work and America while they enjoyed their last day. A perfect end to an ideal holiday. But their joy was to be short-lived as a surprise awaited them back home.

The flight home had been short as far as they were both concerned as they had both slept the majority of the way. They got a taxi from the airport straight to Darren's where they planned on leaving the bags. They'd take Chris' round to hers that afternoon. They were in the elevator when Darren's phone rang. There had been another murder and despite the two of them still officially on holiday, Frank had felt the need to call them as the crime was another victim of the Angel.

"No problem Frank, we'll come, that's fine. Where is it?"

He noticed the hesitation in Frank's voice as he told him the address before hanging up.

"What's up?" Chris asked.

"Another body."

"I got that, but where?"

"Three blocks from here."

As they walked to the scene, the world around them seemed slow one minute then too fast the next. There was something beyond frightening about the body being no more than three blocks away from Darren's apartment. Now he thought about it, the bodies had started at the far end of town and had gradually made their way closer to the precinct and past it, with the odd exception, but this was a sudden jump, the previous body had been found over five miles from this one.

Looking down on the body felt no different when compared to the others, but there was something different about this one. Nick lifted her arm from the floor once Darren had confirmed that they had taken enough photographic evidence. The results from the previous cases had destroyed all hope of ever finding DNA evidence of an attacker, but still, protocol demanded that the nails of the victim were to be tested for any possible traces. This body, to their amazement, gave them something to go on.

They were all shocked when Nick exclaimed that there was skin lodged under the victim's nails, but, to their dismay, the DNA test result back in the lab later that day gave them nothing but the gender of the possible attacker, a female. But they still couldn't be entirely sure that the skin under the nail belonged to the attacker, it may have been there for some other, unknown reason which would leave them exactly where they had been before, no closer to finding the psycho who was killing these women.

Nick and Jason sat at their dinner table talking, enjoying a well-deserved break from work. They'd finished eating almost an hour before yet had returned to the table once they'd finished the washing up.

Nick reached across the table and took Jason's hand in his own. "How long has it been since we've been home and fed before 21:00?"

Jason ran his thumb over Nick's knuckles as he replied that it had been too long.

Nick stood and made his way round to Jason's side of the table. He pulled his chair out slightly and sat on his lap, so their faces were almost touching.

"Don't you think we should make the most of it?" He suggested as he nuzzled at Jason's neck.

"I-" Jason tried to answer, he swallowed hard, "I think that sounds like a marvellous idea." He pulled Nick further onto him and wrapped his arms firmly around his waist.

They slipped off the chair, so they were laying on the floor. Jason pinned Nick's hands to the carpet as he travelled down his body. He slipped his t-shirt off over his head before he unbuttoned Nick's shirt. He began kissing his bare skin, starting at his neck and making his way slowly to the top of his trousers. He released Nick's hands once more as he unfasted the button on his trousers. As he slipped his hand inside, his lips once more came in contact with Nick's. Nick started to groan in delight as Jason continued to touch him.

They began to make love, gently. Jason watched Nick close his eyes as he began to move his hips, a rhythm Nick was quick to match as he pulled Jason down onto him further as their lips met in a hot kiss which only excited them also.

"Let's go to my mothers' on Saturday," Nick suggested as Jason lay over him.

"You did say she was pestering for you to visit." He was still trying to catch his breath.

"Tired, are we?" Nick teased.

"Yup, getting older."

"42 is not old."

"You're only saying that because you've passed it." Jason smiled as he placed his head on Nick's chest.

"Cheeky!" Nick had turned 45 a few months ago, an occasion Jason had not let him forget. "Do you want to go?"

"Sounds like a plan.

It was evident that when Darren had announced he was taking an overnight trip to Tennessee that he'd decided to go to escape Isabelle. He'd received a phone call from his old boss, saying that since the murders had continued in New York, Tennessee wanted to remain in the loop so they would know the minute the "bastard", he quoted, was caught. Chris knew that whatever was to be discussed could have been done over the phone, but still found that Darren's decision to go sparked no surprise with anyone.

Their week in London had finished almost two weeks before, and thankfully, there had been no other victims since. While they were away, Chris had seen a considerable change in Darren. She saw the man he was before Isabelle had arrived. Despite his insistence that her being there wasn't affecting at all, Darren was often nervous and seemed irritated continuously around Isabelle and would often seem out of sorts even when it was just him and Chris.

He'd told her on Thursday that he was leaving that Friday and would be back on Saturday night.

She sat in bed that Friday night, unable to sleep. She received a text message from Darren. Her heart leapt as she read it, it was as if he was already himself again. Why did Isabelle have such a significant impact on him?

"Hello beautiful, I'm sorry if I've woken you. It's been too long since we had dinner. I think that we should go to that Restaurant we went to with your father at that time. The train arrives in New York at 20:18 tomorrow. I'll have a quick change, and I'll pick you up at 21:00? Is that okay with you?" It read, followed by three kisses.

She soon replied, "What's the occasion? That sounds lovely. I'm thinking we come back to mine afterwards."

Three kisses in reply.

"The occasion? We're celebrating the fact that I love you, more and more each day. As for your proposition after dinner, I can't wait. I'll see you tomorrow, good night."

"Goodnight." She placed her phone back on her bedside table before she slipped under the covers and buried her head in the pillow she'd taken from the other side of the bed. She fell to sleep inhaling his scent and pondering what the following evening might bring.

He'd hated leaving so suddenly, but Isabelle had been driving him crazy. They had been back from London just under two weeks, and in that time, not including the time he'd seen her at work, Darren had only seen Chris twice. He'd stayed at hers on both occasions, but the most recent was over a week ago. He threw the phone on the bed next to him as he climbed in. It took a while for him to get comfortable, but once he did, he closed his eyes and thought only of Chris.

Had his old captain just accused him of killing Sarah and the others? He was standing before the man who used to be one of his only friends, but he was speechless. They'd been talking about what changes had occurred in the last six months as if they were still as close as they always had been. Darren couldn't remember his exact words in reply to his old friend's absurd suggestion.

"You see Clark, from the way we all see it, you got rid of your wife so you could start afresh in New York. You look shocked, why? You might not have, we don't know. You'd sure know how to do it as cleanly and as successfully. There was always something weird about you, maybe that's what. Keep us in the loop, now get out of my office."

He hadn't expected a warm welcome, but this had still surprised him. He obliged though after uttering his forgotten line, he was happy to leave.

"Excuse me." A familiar voice said as someone attempted to get past him.

"Sorry." Darren apologised even though he was reasonably sure he wasn't even in the way.

The man turned to face him. "Clark?" The man asked after studying Darren's face for a few seconds.

Darren smiled. "Oh, I almost didn't recognise you there." It was Tim, the only man Darren had ever considered to be a true friend before he moved. "You grew your hair." He said. Until he'd moved to New York, Darren's hair had always remained pretty short, so short that no curls showed, Sarah preferred it like that, she didn't like how naturally untidy she thought the curls looked. "Are you staying for long?"

"No, I'm leaving in a few hours."

"If you wait ten minutes, I'll be on my break. Let me take you to lunch. I'm sure I still owe you that steak." He looked excited.

Darren hesitated. "Okay." He didn't feel like eating but decided to accept the invitation out of politeness.

As they sat in the café four blocks from the precinct, Tim slapped Darren playfully on the arm before asking him how he was doing. "How'ya doin' bud? You don't look that good." Bud!

"I'm doing fine thank you."

"But are you coping?" His eyes showed the sappy sympathy Darren hated.

"Yea Tim, I'm coping." Darren hoped he hadn't sounded too cold and uninterested in his reply.

Tim seemed genuinely interested in what Darren had been doing. Each question he asked resulted in an answer which sparked yet another question. Darren did notice, however, that Tim avoided asking him if he was seeing anyone new.

On his journey there, Darren had decided that if anyone asked, he would lie and tell them that there was no one new in his life. They may disapprove if they found out that he did, believing it was too soon, which, under any other circumstances, under normal circumstances, Darren would probably agree with them. But things were how they were, and even though people would side with him if they knew the truth, lying seemed more natural and not as complicated to explain.

Tim had been recently married and had just received the news that his wife was expecting. Darren thought back to when he'd received the autopsy results from Sarah's body. She was pregnant with Tim's child at the time. He should wish Tim's baby to someone else, but he didn't care enough, he was happy for him, obviously, but he didn't care.

He didn't stay much longer as he was due to catch his train in a couple of hours at the other end of town.

Tim returned to work as Darren made his way back to the train station. Once Tim returned to the office, he removed his coat and knocked on his boss' door.

"Come in!" A voice boomed from inside.

"Hello, Sir," Tim said as he closed the door behind him.

"Well?"

"I took him to lunch, as you asked."

"And?" The man was already becoming impatient.

"Definitely," Tim smirked.

"You think he did it?"

"I do sir."

The man chuckled, "Well if that's the case, you'd better be glad he's gone. After what you and his missus got up to, I wouldn't have been surprised if your body had shown up a couple of days after hers did." For obvious reasons, Tim didn't find this as funny as his boss seemed to, yet he still laughed as he exited the office.

Did he think Clark had killed Sarah? Of course not, but senior management love it when people agree with them, and there was an opening for a team leader in the department. He'd betrayed Clark's trust once before, and he saw no reason why it should be a problem a second-time around.

⌒ CHAPTER 15 ⌒

H E COULDN'T REMEMBER EVER being more eager to reach her door than he did that night. His train had come into the station just over half an hour ago, and already he was changed and was making his way up the final set of stairs in her building, he could see her door now.

She answered the door with the smile he loved before she ran back to her room to retrieve her shoes. She emerged a couple of minutes later wearing them. Closing her bedroom door proved difficult with one arm in her coat and the other tangled in the other. However, she managed it and stood by the bedroom door as she finished putting on her jacket. Once on, she began making her way towards Darren. She picked her keys up off the worktop as she passed. Her arms wrapped around his neck as she reached him and buried her face deep into his throat. His arms were quick to respond and were soon wrapped around her just as firmly as he closed his eyes and rested his head on hers.

"Ready for dinner?" She asked after a few seconds as she slowly removed her head from under his.

"Ready."

Over dinner they discussed which version of Goodnight Mr Chips was their favourite. Darren, who usually preferred the originals to the remakes, stated quite confidently that he preferred the Martin Clunes' version for reasons he couldn't explain. Christine, however, disagreed saying that Robert Donat's portrayal of Mr Chips was far better. Darren agreed that she made a good point but once more expressed that there was something about the remake that he loved.

"You're wrong," Darren claimed.

"Am not," Christine argued stubbornly.

"Sir, you requested the bill." A man who looked to be in his early thirties had approached them with a silver tray containing a piece of paper in his hand.

"Yes, thank you."

The man was beginning to leave when Chris called him back and asked him which version of the film he preferred. He was initially taken back by the unusual question but responded that he preferred the remake as it always seemed more emotional and well produced to him.

"Well, you're no help at all." Chris joked causing the waiter to laugh as he guessed that she preferred the original. "I do, yes."

He quickly paid the bill and generously tipped the waiter. The waiter was being signalled by another table thus ending their conversation. Darren and Chris left the restaurant where Darren took Chris' arm and tucked it inside his own.

"I think we should go on a lovely long ride tomorrow." Darren proposed.

"That sounds great, except you promised to show me your drawings, remember?" Chris pouted.

"That I did." He paused and made a rapid clicking noise with his tongue as he thought about what he was to suggest. "Well, how about we put your bike in my car, drive to mine in the morning, you can look at my work, and we can leave from there?"

"Better. I can't wait, but right now, I can't wait to get you to mine, it's been about two weeks since we were able to 'take advantage' of an early night."

"'Take advantage', that's a euphemism I've never heard before. Let's go."

"What the hell have you done?" Darren demanded as he entered his apartment the following morning.

"Just reorganised, how'ya handling it?" Isabelle joked referencing his need to have things in their specific place. It always did drive her crazy, the way he used to fuss over tidying his room and arranging the furnisher in the house as he cleaned.

"You can't just rearrange my furnisher whenever you please, put it back, please." Darren was beginning to panic slightly as he saw the indentations in the living room carpet where the chair should be.

"It's better this way, trust me, you'll love it."

"I want you gone, now! You being here was enough, but I let you stay. Now I want you to go, and I won't let you stay, no matter what."

There was a knock at the door, but Darren didn't hear it. Chris went to answer it.

"I'm not leaving Clark, I'm staying, so if you want this furnisher back where it was, put it there yourself and I'll be upstairs."

"Isabelle, no."

"What did you just tell me?"

"I said, no. This is my home, and I don't want you here. If you don't leave, I'll have you arrested you for trespassing and taken to the police station."

"Now Clark, that's no way to speak to your mother." Julian's voice sounded from the top of the stairs.

"She's not my mother. I thought you'd gone." The level of cheek in the man's voice annoyed Darren.

"I left for business before you returned from London and returned just before you did from Tennessee yesterday but I had to nip out, Isabelle told me of your little visit on the way back from the train station, I'm so sorry I missed you."

"Both of you, leave," Darren demanded.

"Is everything okay?" Bruce asked Chris as she let him in.

"Darren's mother-in-law won't leave."

"Who's the man talking?"

"That's Julian, her husband."

Sensing it was a lousy time, Bruce began walking backwards until he was once again on the other side of the threshold. "I'll come back. It was nice to see you again."

"Bruce, please, just wait in the kitchen, and I'll tell Darren you're here."

When Christine re-entered the room, Julian had Darren by the scruff of the neck with one hand and the other poised over his shoulder, threatening a punch.

"Darren!" She shrieked as Julian's fist came in brutal contact with Darren's face.

Darren fell to the floor with a thud, prompting laughter from both Julian and Isabelle. Darren didn't stay down for long. He was soon up with one hand against Julian's neck and the other holding his dominant hand in place, as he walked him back quickly, so he was pressed against the wall, his other arm was pinned against the wall by his body.

"I take it you've continued with your boxing." Julian sniggered.

"Kickboxing."

"Sir, I wouldn't joke, he's rather good, and I can tell you that he could pull your windpipe with one hand." Bruce had come into the room after hearing Chris scream.

"I'm not scared of him. He's not allowed to use his moves on me, that much I do know." Julian gasped as he felt Darren's hand tighten around his neck.

"In self-defence, I can," Darren moved his face closer to Julian's, "and there are two people here who would defend me, see, you hit me first." A single drop of blood dripped from Darren's nose and into the cut above his lip.

Darren let him go yet remained close to him as he asked him once more to leave his house. He stepped back and turned away. Julian grabbed him from behind and swung at him once more, but Darren blocked him and shocked him with a punch directly in the gut. Julian's grip released as Darren pulled his shirt free from his grasp and stood back as he and the rest of them watched Julian fall to the floor gripping his stomach.

Isabelle rushed over to her husband and began calling Darren every name she could think off.

"I'm going out. I want you both gone when I come back."

"You'll regret this Clark; you'll see," Isabelle called after him as he left followed by Chris and Bruce. He picked up his bike and cycling clothes from the ironing basket as he passed.

Down at the car, Darren was finally able to talk to Bruce. "Sorry about all that Bruce, what can I do for you?"

"Master Lewis sent me over to bring you your belt back. He's had the old club logo replaced with ours," Bruce replied with a smile. "Is everything okay?"

"Fine, why d'you ask?" Darren laughed as he wiped the blood from his face with a tissue Christine had just handed him. "Thank you for this," he held up the belt, "I'll wear it tomorrow now."

"Well I'd better be going, Kate won't be overly impressed if I don't get home in time to take Danny to football. Goodbye Darren, Chris."

They watched him get in his car and waved to him as he passed. "Chris, please, stop fussing," Darren said as she once again fingered the area around his lip.

"Darren, he could have hurt you."

"But he didn't, please, I'm fine." He took her face in his hands as she placed her hands on his chest. She moved her face towards his and kissed him. She held his head in place with her hand as she pulled his body closer to hers.

"As much as I'm enjoying this, we are in the middle of the street in broad daylight. Let's go out on the bikes, we can finish this," He kissed her once more, "later."

"Why were your cycling clothes in the ironing basket? They're made from lycra."

"Who knows?"

The route they took was almost identical to the one that they had taken the last time. As they reached the top of the hill, they stopped and admired the view. There wasn't a cloud in sight, and the forecast promised that there wouldn't be one for the rest of the day. It was a little after three, and they were due to have a rest. They agreed that the top of the hill would be an excellent place to stop as there was a bench just on the other side. They continued riding until they reached it. They were grateful when they reached it, and as they sat, they let their bikes fall gently to the ground.

They heard voices coming from the other side of the hill, but they couldn't quite see who was coming. Darren swung his legs under the bench, so he was facing Christine who had sat on the other side. He placed his elbow on the table and rested his head in his cupped hand.

He smiled as he watched her finger a scratch on her calf which she'd gotten going over the last hill as a loose thorn had caught in her front wheel.

She winced as she prodded an area which was becoming slightly inflamed. She licked her finger and wiped away what dirt she could, but her saliva wasn't cleaning the wound as well as she'd hoped. He got up and made his way to the other side of the bench where he sat sideways on as he pulled her leg onto his and gently prodded around the wound. He reached for his backpack under the table and removed a packet of baby wipes from the inside. He wrapped one around the end of his forefinger on his left hand as he gently began wiping the scratch, causing her to wince.

"Ouch!" She winced once more.

"Stop you're moaning, it's only a scratch, well…"

"Well? Well, what?"

"It's more of a cut. We should probably rinse it through with Dettol once we get back."

"Why? It's not that bad, is it?"

"No, it's not that. It's just because it happened outside. I think you should clean it properly."

"Ouch!"

"Stop screaming." Darren laughed.

"Then stop hurting me." She slapped him playfully and left her hand laid affectionately on his arm as he continued to clean the area around her scratch.

The couple on the bikes were emerging over the edge of the hill. They could see them pushing their bikes, possibly unable to ride them up the hill. "Isn't that Alice?" Chris asked.

Darren turned to look over his shoulder. "I think so, yes."

"Who's that man she's with?"

"I don't know. He looks familiar though." Darren said as he squinted his eyes to get a better look.

"Anyone would at that distance." Chris laughed. "Alice!" She called.

Alice started towards her with her bike by her side, closely followed by her male companion.

"Chris, Darren, hi!" She placed her bike down beside theirs as she sat on the other side of the table. "Guy's, this is Steven," Steven sat beside her on the bench and reached his hand out towards Darren first and then to Christine, "Steven, this is Darren and Christine."

"I've seen you before, where?" Darren asked him as he shook his hand.

"I was your waiter last night."

"That's right."

"So, these are the two you work with?" He asked Alice who nodded in reply. "I've heard so much about you both, all good before you ask."

"We've heard nothing of you." Christine shot an accusing look in Alice's direction before smiling and telling Steven that there was plenty of time to get to know each other.

The four of them sat and talked as the clouds began to accumulate unexpectedly above their heads. Not one of them noticed the change in scenery until the first drop of rain struck Alice on the cheek. After excessive cursing from each party member, they all mounted their bikes and after saying goodbye and confirming their dinner plans for the upcoming Friday, went back the ways they came in an attempt to get home before being soaked through by the rain which was already beginning to fall quite quickly.

"Are you sure you don't want me to stay at yours tonight," Chris asked as they reached Darren's apartment block.

"Of course I do, you make it sound like I don't want you with me." Darren laughed.

"No!" She assured him. "I just meant that, well… you know what I meant."

"I know. I need to sort out the furnisher in my apartment."

"Are you sure you don't want any help, I wouldn't mind, I think it'd be quite fun."

"You're crazy." Darren joked.

"This coming from the guy who spends the majority of his Saturday mornings cleaning his apartment from top to bottom."

"So, I'm tidy." He shrugged.

"Yes, but you enjoy it. Darren, you enjoy cleaning, and you're calling me the crazy one."

"Fair point. Are you sure you want to help?"

"Yes, now come on, despite being sodden already, I'm beginning to get cold, you're nearest." She gestured for him to open the door. They took their bikes up in the lift and stood them up in his kitchen, amazed to find the apartment empty. They changed out of their wet clothes into dry ones.

It was just after 18:00 when they'd returned, and once they'd changed and made their way back down to the living room to begin re-arranging, it was almost 18:30 and Frank came to the door.

He didn't stay long as he only came to invite them to dinner the following Sunday with the rest of the team. He refused all offers of food and drink and left five minutes after arriving, saying that he'd see them the following morning at work.

It took them until eight o'clock to finish sorting out the apartment, riding the smell of Isabelle's perfume, washing pots she'd left next to the sofa. Darren tried on numerous occasions to deal with specific items being a little out of place but failed each time. After moving the coffee table, he assured Chris that it was okay where it was, not wanting her to help him move it for the fourth time, but when she left the living room to make them each something to eat, he pushed it himself until he was happy with its placement. Chris watched, amused, but he didn't realise.

Once Darren was happy with everything, they sat and ate a very late dinner. "Chris, this is amazing." Darren complimented after a few mouthfuls.

"Thank you." She was surprised at the compliment but tried not to show it. No one had ever said anything remotely nice about her cooking. As she thought about it, she realised she'd never really cooked for anyone before but decided that she should start.

It wasn't long until they'd washed up the pots, so they decided to watch some TV before bed. They watched two episodes of Will and Grace before going upstairs.

Darren soon found, not long after Christine had dropped off, that he couldn't sleep. But after spending an additional hour trying to fall asleep, he decided that it wasn't going to happen. As he watched Chris's chest rise and fall with each breath she took, he felt a horrible feeling begin accumulating in his stomach. A chill went through him suddenly as he sat up. He climbed out of bed slowly, so he didn't shake the bed enough to wake her up and walked to the window. He could see for miles across town. He could even see where the building was which was hiding the precinct almost seven miles across town, he couldn't see the building itself in the night light, but he knew where about to look.

00:18, he'd be on his way there in less than eight hours. He curled up in his favourite chair in the corner of his room, using the armrest as a pillow of sorts. He twisted his head so he could see Chris when he opened his eyes. He closed them in the hope that sleep might find him but was quick to find that the chair wasn't the right shape for him to comfortably curl himself up and sleep.

He stood and stretched to reawaken each muscle he'd crammed into the chair. He smiled as he watched Chris unconsciously throw the duvet across the bed as she followed it with a movement which could only be described as unnatural. She settled once more as Darren gently pulled the covers from underneath her and wrapped her bare legs up once more. He resisted the urge to kiss her on the forehead, knowing he could wake her by doing so. He left the room, skilfully avoiding the loose floorboards as he did. He turned on the light of his art room to find that things had been re-arranged in there too. How did she manage to get into this room? There's only one key, and that's on Darren's chain which remains attached to the belt loop of whichever pair of trousers he has on at the time. It's Isabelle, he thought, she didn't need a key. He took a closer look at the screws fastening the door to the wall, just as he thought, partially stripped, she'd removed the screws from the door, and the lock to get in and screwed them back on afterwards.

It didn't take him long to sort the room out and thankfully each chair and desk either had wheels or was light enough to lift without having to be slid across the floor. He sat at his main desk where he'd left out a half-finished painting of him and Chris on a three by two-foot canvas. He unwrapped the cling film from around the pallet he was using and dipped his paintbrush in the pot containing slightly discoloured water to his left. Before he continued with his piece, he changed his clothes quickly before re-taking his seat where he continued with his work.

When he'd started the session, he'd only got his face and hair to finish as well as the small details in the foreground to finished and had guessed that it should take him around four hours to complete it. He'd finished the bottom couple of coats on his face and hair and was about to make his way onto the foreground detail when he finally felt his eyes becoming heavy. He re-wrapped the pallet and changed back into his night clothes before climbing back into bed. Chris, he observed, had appeared to fall back onto her half of the bed. She was tucked into the covers, allowing him the room to climb back in without needing to shift her limbs. 02:41. He hoped he'd be able to fall asleep now. He was going to be tired at work due to his lack of sleep. He faced the window and watched as the orange glow from the streetlights in the bottom right corner of the window slowly turned to black.

CHAPTER 16

HOW LONG DOES IT take for someone to buy something from a shop at 23:50 at night? She's been in there for almost ten minutes now, shall I find someone else? No, she fits perfectly, this one better not fight back, my arm still hurts from where that last one scratched me as I drove the knife through her. Ha, the look she gave when the blade came in contact with her. I don't know how I thought that this could have been just a one-time thing, it's too exhilarating. Something is exciting about watching the light die from someone's eyes until they go still.

Here she is, time to go. I'll stay out of sight for now. There's no way she can hear my footsteps from here. How far is she going? Wherever it is, we've passed three more convenience stores, why didn't she go to any of those? I had no idea how far she'd gone. The killings went public a little over a week ago, and boy does this girl confirm the stereotype, blondes are stupid. Why, when you know that plenty of people exactly like you have been brutally murdered recently, would you go out? It makes no sense. I like that word though, brutally, there's something beautiful about it.

She's slowed. She's glancing over her shoulder now, and she's smiling at me. What do I do? I smile back as I quicken my pace, hopefully not so much so that she notices. She's spending so long messing with her hair and pulling at her skirt which is so short I can almost see the top of her legs, that she hasn't even noticed that I've gained on her, so much so in fact that I'm no more than six feet from her. I can smell the cheap perfume she's doused herself with. God, how much as she put on? I can almost taste it! TRAMP! You wait until I get a hold of you.

At first, I did this for a reason, a real reason, but now I find that it's enough that they look like her, is that bad? Of course not, apart from the second one who was training to be a teacher, let's face it, none of them was going to go far. No, the second one was a bad call. Still, I think it was an excellent start to what has so far been a good run here in New York. I found the transition from Tennessee to New York quite tricky, but thankfully I managed to figure out my way about quickly enough to start work again within a week of moving here. How long am I going to be able to get away with this? It's been over three months since I came to New York, they aren't exactly the best at doing their jobs. I'm just surprised that I haven't gotten bored yet. The routine is pretty repetitive, and I guess it is boring me slightly, you know, having to do it the same every single time.

She's stopped, crap, I can't stop myself. Ouch! We fall to the floor where we remain for a few seconds as we wait for the pain caused by direct bone coming in contact with concrete to subside before getting up. She's laughing, what is so funny? Oh, honey, laughing is only making it worse, you look and sound more like her now than you did before. This is going to be fun. I slip the knife out of my handbag with one hand while the other is extended out waiting for her to accept my help. She's grabbed my hand, and she's still laughing. She's standing now, but she still hasn't let go of my hand. She's swinging her arm back and forth, taking mine with it. "Thank you." She says as she smiles.

"I'm sorry, I didn't see you stop." I fake a smile as I squeeze her hand affectionately.

"I figured." She laughs again.

"Are you okay?" I may as well ask her, after-all.

"I'm fine, thank you, are you okay? You're not hurt, are you?" A worried look has spread across her face. She may be fine now, but she won't be soon. In 10-

"No, no, don't worry about me, I'm fine." 9-

"Good, I'm glad. What are you doing out at this time of night?" 8-

"Funny, I was going to ask you the same question." I laugh. 7-

"No!" She exclaims in surprise. "I'm just on my way to my mum's house." 6-

"At this time of night?" 5-

"Yes. She called, she's not feeling very well and asked me if I'd nip to the shop and buy some cough syrup and tablets for her. I went to my brother's shop to buy the tablets and told him that she wasn't very well." 4-

"That's very thoughtful of you dear, but don't you think you should be more careful? There's a killer on the loose, isn't there?" 3-

"Oh, I'm not worried about that, it's quite ridiculous actually, there's nothing worse than someone who kills people, especially people they don't know." 2-

"Fair point dear, still, I think it's quite a dangerous chance to take for some cough syrup." 1-

"Yea, I suppose, but my mother's worth it." A stupid smile spreads across her face.

I doubt she's worth what I'm about to do to her. The smile on her face flickers as I drive the knife through her once. "Terribly sorry, at least your mother will be okay, your brother will see to her I'm sure."

Her mouth formed an 'o' shape. I assume she's trying to utter some word in reply. Ha, good luck with that honey. Her hands grip my upper arms as her legs give way under her. Her heels slide across the floor as she falls onto her back. I pull the knife out of her and listen carefully for the inevitable sound. Yes, she unwillingly complied, that sharp intake of breath as the blade slips out.

Wait, 3- 2- 1- I thrust the knife into her once more, this time on the right side of her torso before pulling it out slowly, ensuring maximum pain. I smile at her as her eyes meet mine once more in a shocked look of disbelief and betrayal. The knife slides into the left side of her torso quite quickly; I must have missed the ribs, I'm getting good at this. I watch as her head falls back slowly onto the floor. Her hands released my arms as she begins to grow weaker. She takes one last breath in a desperate attempt at surviving, it's pathetic, just like the rest of them.

What kind of a woman goes out into public with a hot pink tank top on, a, ugh, red leather. Her whole outfit screams hooker. No, this won't do, let's get you in this. I take the white dress from my bag and dress her in it. Oh, the irony, someone like you in colour as pure a white. Just let me put these- there. Perfect, you even look the part now. "I'd thank you for not hurting me, but I doubt you'd make much sense of my gratitude," I say aloud. Okay, time to leave, I don't want to be here when someone comes across her. Oh dear, it looks like I'm going to have to burn this t-shirt as well, this isn't fair. Thinking about it, it would probably make more sense to do this in tops I don't care about ruining. I'll dispose of it in the furnace at the dump. They haven't seen me the last few times.

It's been about ten minutes, and I'm about half a mile from her. Boy, that was fast, I can already hear a police car. Well, Detectives, have fun, I hope I don't see you soon.

CHAPTER 17

AS HE LAY AWAKE with Chris stirring next to him, Darren found that he couldn't shift the funny feeling that had accumulated within him the night before. He had a bad feeling about the day ahead but had no idea why. He rubbed his eyes, hard, until he was sure that there was no sleep left behind. He was left feeling dazed as he began to see strange bright shapes as the room around him appeared to bend and swirl until his eyes returned to normal. He felt the bed shake lightly as Chris rolled over to face him. He turned to face her and smiled. She commented on the time and stated that she was getting up and that he should too if they were to get to work on time.

Darren made no attempt to get up straight away. Instead, he watched as Chris climbed out of bed. She walked briskly to the bathroom where she exclaimed suddenly at the cold surface of the bathroom floor on her bare feet.

He suppressed a laugh as he decided he'd better get out of bed. The hour between getting up and reaching the office consisted of nothing significant. They ate breakfast, arranged the upcoming evening and drove to work in Darren's car as usual. Still, something was bothering Darren, but the worst thing was, he had no idea what.

As they left the elevator, they found that the office was unusually busy. They found out from an officer neither of them knew the name of, that The Angel had taken another victim the night before leaving behind yet another message. Darren and Christine managed to find Frank quickly enough and were instantly sent to the other side of town, the investigation couldn't begin until Darren arrived on the scene as he was the leading investigator on the case.

They got back into the car in silence and remained so for almost the entire journey until Darren asked Chris if she was okay. Chris laughed and said that she should be the one asking that. The address they were on their way to was roughly halfway between their apartments. Darren expressed his confusion as to the location of the murder as it did not follow the same Geographical pattern as the others. Instead of following the almost straight line across town, they had found this victim across town, a lot further east than the rest of the victims. Chris made notes on the way regarding the unusual location and made a note of why they thought it odd.

They had never seen as many people around the tape before. They made their way swiftly towards the people and pushed their way through. Strangers cursed them for trying to get a better view than them but were soon silenced by their embarrassment as they watched Darren and Christine flash their badges and duck under the yellow tape.

Darren stood back as he instructed the others to begin documenting and photographing the scene. He looked at the scene, and he took in each detail until he was confident he could see it when he closed his eyes. He had been given the all clear, everyone had done their job, and now it was his turn. He walked over to the victim and crouched by her side where he memorised the lines of her face and the shape of the blood stains on her white gown. He saw a pink discolouration showing through the white fabric of the dress. He removed a knife from his bag and carefully cut through the material, ensuring he kept her naked body as covered as he could as he revealed her stomach to see the message written in her blood. It read, "Bored?". The nerve of this person sparked a fury inside Darren which he'd never experienced.

There was a scream from behind him. A woman came running through the crowd, knocking a few people to the floor as she did. There was a man behind her shouting after her, but she didn't seem to care. She climbed under the tape frantically and began her approach. Two men grabbed her by the arms and attempted to calm her down. The woman's eyes were red and her face pale. She was dressed in a yellow stained dressing gown and had nothing on her feet. "My baby!" She screamed.

Darren made his way over to the woman and somehow managed to turn her and her attention away from the body of her daughter as he asked her what her daughter was doing out at the time of death, which had been predicted to be between 00:00 and 01:00 early that morning. Her mother, Nicole, explained through muffled sniffles and choked sobs that her daughter had nipped out to buy some cough syrup and tablets for her as she had been stuck in bed with a terrible cold. When asked why her daughter hadn't gone to the shop closest to their house, her mother explained that her brother worked at the shop eight blocks away and she thought it would be best that he knew how ill she was. Darren suddenly felt the desire to wring the neck of whoever was doing this, he wanted to kill them in the most painful way possible, and he'd ensure they'd endure the maximum amount of pain and suffering.

What satisfaction could someone possibly gain from killing an innocent young woman who, despite having to be up at 06:00 for work, as her mother had just explained, was willing to wander the streets at such a time with a killer on the loose to help her mother? He called over another detective to continue talking to Nicole. She was reluctant to leave with the detective at first but willingly went with the detective after Darren promised her that he'd go and see her later at the precinct.

No, he'd prefer to watch this bastard rot in jail for life, being hated by their cellmates, being taunted continuously and abused for their grim technique and apparent lack of motive.

There was a murmur of voices from behind him. He turned to see the crowd of people being forced out of the way by a great camera on wheels closely followed by a reporter dressed in a tight matching skirt and jacket. She gasped at the reality of what she was about to report before she turned her back on the scene and raised the microphone to her mouth. Darren saw the cameraman give her the thumbs up before he heard the reporter begin speaking. She raised her voice so that she could be over the raised voices of the crowd who had become slightly more excited since the appearance of a TV camera. They were now fighting for a spot behind the reporter so the camera could see them over her shoulders.

Darren purposely crouched by the body once more, this time closer to her face. He called Nick and Chris over and told them to crouch next to him, obscuring the victim's body from the view of not only the camera but the crowd as well. He motioned to the Medical Examiner that it was time to take the body back to the lab. The ME saw the camera behind the tape and immediately made his way over to Darren to place the body in the bag.

Somehow, Darren, Chris, Nick, the ME and his assistant Benjy as they called him, managed to get the poor girl in the bag and concealed from view quickly. They lifted her body off the floor together as the ME slipped a stretcher underneath her. They lay her on it and lifted it up so that the wheels extended below. They wheeled her over to the van, still trying to keep her hidden. They closed the van doors behind her, and she was driven away.

Her mother was to follow behind the van with Detective Tass who had previously been asked to continue talking with her. She complied willingly now, her eyes swollen and red but dry.

Everyone watched until the van was out of sight. It was 10:57, and there was still a scene to finish processing. They each returned to their jobs one by one until Darren was left standing with Chris. Chris turned to face Darren who was still facing the direction which the van had gone. She asked him if he was okay to which he responded that he was and that he should go and deal with the reporter who was beginning to climb under the tape.

Chris watched as he walked briskly over to the reporter and gently guided her back under the tape. She thought it better that he deal with the reporter as, if she went over there herself, she would probably say the wrong thing about a woman who relished the thought of a tragic incident as it provided her with a 'great scoop', he could control his words better than she could.

The reporter who had revealed herself as Molly Kingsley was reporting for the New York Times, was adamant that she should be allowed to know at least one detail about the body. Darren responded calmly by saying that the only information she was to receive, was that the victim was dead and that that wasn't going to change, even if he wanted to confide in her, the facts were confidential. The woman managed to coax Darren closer to her as she lowered her voice and asked him once more about the case. She asked for the victim's name, assuring him that she could trust her confidence. Darren faked a smile and motioned for her to move closer to him. "Even if it weren't against the law for me to reveal any detail relating to the victim, I still wouldn't tell you, see, people like you make me sick, I wouldn't even consider telling you my name. My obligation is with the victim and their family." He walked away.

"I know your name, Agent Thompson."

"Good for you." He kept walking towards Jason who was bagging what looked like a lipstick cap.

"I know more than you know." She was shouting now, but Darren doubted that she knew anything that could be of interest to him or the public around her. "I understand that the only reason the killer has been able to claim this victim and the many before is because you failed to catch them in Tennessee." He stopped dead in his tracks.

Nick was over by the reporter and was trying to calm her down, but she would not stop now that she'd started.

"Ma'am, please, think of what you're saying." Nick tried once more to convince her.

"No! I will not keep quiet. Surely you think it's weird that a woman who was murdered, should be married to the lead investigator. Maybe the reason you didn't find who did it was because the man who did it removed all evidence of his guilt, he sure would know how."

"I don't know what you think you know, but you should quieten down." Jason had approached and was climbing under, attempting to drive her away. The crowd became rowdy upon learning of Agent Thompson's secret.

The reporter ran through the crowd and stood on a bench as she called for the attention of the public. "I have it on good authority that on his last visit to Tennessee, Agent Darren Thompson, formally known as Clark McAvoy, was unknowingly observed by a Detective who specialises in reading body language and all things related. As he answered questions relating to the first victim, his wife, he, I quote "acted out of sorts" as the Detective put it, confirming his guilt and providing the Tennessee central precinct with a suspect, finally."

Darren and Nick reached the bench and tried their best to silence her, but it was no good, she'd said what she wanted, everything was out, on film. "I'll be leaving now. You can see yourself on the news tonight at 18:00." She made to run, but her arm was caught in the firm grip of what she assumed to be one of the agents. She turned to see Darren accompanied by Agent Bridges and the men who had tried to convince her to keep quiet.

"Tell me one thing," Darren said.

"What?" She shook her arm free from his grip.

"Why?"

"Why what?"

"Why would he do this?"

"Who?" Her playing innocent was beginning to annoy him.

"Tim. Why is he doing this to me?"

She smiled slyly. "Tim who?"

"You're pale and blotchy, I'm assuming from the morning sickness, Tim said you were pregnant. Your attempts to conceal your accent only partially succeeded, I'd work on it. Your husband is good at what he does. There's no doubt about that. But I'm better, and I can assure you that he's made a mistake here."

"It doesn't matter anyway; it can't be undone now. There'll be someone up to take you in later. Good luck, Clark, Tim sends his love."

She turned to leave and was surprised to find no one tried to stop her. She glanced over her shoulder to see Darren standing, not all tense and angry as she'd hoped, but with his arms hanging loosely by his side and a look of abandonment and betrayal on his face, just like Tim had predicted. She watched as the female Agent took Darren's hand and pulled it across her stomach so she could hold it in both of hers. The other two Agent's placed their hands comfortingly on his shoulder before reluctantly turning to leave him with the female Agent as they returned to their work.

Darren released Chris's hand and pushed his way through the crowd. He held the tape up for her to go under before following her. She turned to face him to comfort him somehow but found that he'd walked over to where the body had been less than ten minutes before. He knelt on the floor and took an evidence bag from his pocket into which he scooped a small portion of the blood-stained gravel. He paused as he lifted-up a leaf to reveal a lipstick without a cap. He turned to face her and shouted her over frantically before asking her what coloured lipstick the victim was wearing. Chris replied that her lips were red with lipstick and not with her blood. Darren raised what appeared to be a dark purple lipstick, found underneath the victim, which he stated would hopefully belong to the killer.

On the way back from to the office, Darren took an unusual route through a wooded area. He, however, did not take advantage of the open roads to express anger as Chris thought he would. Instead, he drove a little under what he was permitted and took in the views. Silently grateful for the break, Chris sat back in her chair and put her window down enough to let in fresh air without cooling the car too much. She turned and saw Darren was deep in thought.

She placed her hand on his arm and smiled affectionately as he looked at her. He took her hand and set it on his leg where he put his on top. She turned her head back towards the window to continue watching the trees go past. She felt his hand lift from hers but soon heard the reason why. The radio, which he turned high enough to drown out the sound of the wind rushing through the open window, began playing, his hand soon rested on hers once again.

The journey was completed in silence, the music being the only exception until they got back into the city. His hand was needed on the wheel, leaving her to pull her's across the car. The window was rolled up, the music turned down, and the silence remained. Chris dared not ask if he was okay for fear of his response. He was to be arrested for a crime - crimes - which he hadn't committed. It was true that his alibi for the victim in Tennessee was next to none existent, but since then the killings had continued while he was in not only her presence but the presence of other members of the team and Frank himself. One of the victims had been killed while he and Chris were at thirty-thousand feet, they couldn't pin this on him like they would like to.

They reached the office at around 12:30 and were soon at their desks completing the paper-work for the morning's case. Frank came rushing out of his office and immediately requested that Darren and Chris join him in his office. They obliged and closed the door behind them after being firmly told to do so. Darren asked what was wrong. Frank explained that he'd received a call from the Head Detective in Tennessee and had been told that two of his Agents have already left for New York and would be bringing Darren back with them, no objections, that was the way it was going to happen. They were to drive just over nine-hundred miles. The team had only fourteen hours to find the killer or Darren was to be arrested and charged with the murder of Sarah. Frank conceded that there was no way that they could blame Darren for the other killings under the circumstances and could not understand why they were charging him solely for the murder of his wife, primarily when it was clear that it was the same killer for them all and not a copycat.

There was a knock on his office door. Crowley waved Nick in. As soon as he had, he rushed over to Frank and whispered something in his ear, something which made Frank's face drop and turn pale as he glanced out of his window into the bullpen. Darren looked over his shoulder to see Isabelle standing in the middle of the bullpen, her arms crossed and a stern look on her face.

Darren met her in the middle of the room. He could feel the eyes of the other Detectives on him as he had no choice but to ask Isabelle if she would like to sit down and if she'd like a drink. She took his seat instantly but was reluctant at first to accept a drink but soon changed her mind. Despite taking the glass from Frank willingly, expressing her gratitude with a smile which made Darren sick, an unsure look remained on her face as Darren watched as she wiped the moisture from the lip off the glass that was left behind after almost every sip she had, how unusual.

Isabelle revealed that she'd had received a call from Tim, saying that early the following morning, Darren was to be arrested in connection with the case of her daughter's murder. She repeated once more what she'd said over and over for the last year. That it was his fault. "I just never knew how much of a part you played in her death." She had the nerve to wipe a forced tear from the side of her nose, an act no-one but the occasional Detective who had overheard the conversation seemed to buy.

She left abruptly after giving her glass one more wipe.

They watched as she left, all breathing a sigh of relief when the elevator doors closed, banishing her face from their view.

Once Isabelle had left, Darren found it hard to concentrate on any task he was given to do. Still, he completed his work, albeit a little slower than usual, but was still able to somehow join in on the jokes shared by the team. When he laughed, he found he was genuinely laughing at what they were saying. It wasn't until after the pain in his stomach induced by excessive laughter had died that he was cruelly reminded that he only had about twelve hours until he was to be charged with murder.

There were moments where silence hung over the bullpen as each team member thought about how bad the upcoming future was, how ridiculous the accusations were.

Darren glanced over at the glass on his desk. There was a faint mark where Isabelle's lips had pressed against the glass as she had drunk the water. Something bothered Darren about the glass.

For some unknown reason, as unusual as Isabelle's reluctance to accept it, he asked that it remain there, refusing the cleaner permission to take it.

Chris sat in front of him on his desk, obscuring his view, he could no longer see the glass and was strangely glad, he looked up to Chris and smiled. She asked him if he would like to join her for lunch. He grabbed his wallet from his top drawer and his jacket from the back of his chair before they made their way to the elevator. Nick and Jason emerged from the elevator, they'd just been to lunch and stated that the bagels from the truck down the street were delicious and left them with a recommendation of which fillings looked fresh.

Neither of them could have begun to imagine what was to happen in less than ten minutes.

Chris glanced behind them once they'd entered the alley before she pulled Darren back and placed her hands either side of his face. She playfully commented on their lack of time to 'have fun' the previous evening. She pulled his face into her as she felt him press himself against her.

He placed his hands on her hips as he walked her back towards the wall. Their hands wandered as their tongues fought against each other. Darren would have liked nothing more than to make love to her at that moment, he knew she felt the same too, but they were in the wrong place, it would just have to wait until later that night, as long as the detectives from Tennessee didn't get there before then. They smiled at each other before they continued to walk on hand in hand. Chris felt Darren run his thumb over her knuckles affectionately. She squeezed his hand gently in response.

The air around them cooled as they passed through the alley towards the food truck. They were halfway through the alley in its darkest point when Darren heard a crashing noise and suddenly felt Chris' hand leave his as she fell to the floor.

He turned to see Isabelle standing above her with a broken vase clutched firmly in both hands. His blood ran cold with rage as his mind formulated an uncountable amount of ways in which he could make her pay for everything. None of it mattered to him anymore, not now she'd hurt Chris. He'd get her somehow, just for this, this was worse than all of the years he'd spent stuck with her, combined. She was smiling broadly as she turned her head towards Darren.

Everything around him seemed to slow. He knelt by Chris' head as he felt on her neck for a pulse. Darren took his phone from his pocket and called Nick before placing his phone on the other side of Chris' head out of the view of Isabelle. He stood after checking Chris was alive, she was just unconscious.

He stood back as Isabelle suddenly lunged at him with the broken vase, the razor-like edges just inches from his face. She jumped forward once more, this time catching his cheek with the largest of the edges. He immediately felt his cheek warm with the blood coming from the surprisingly deep laceration just under his left eye. He took his gun from its holster and extended it towards her, pointing it between her eyes. She fell silent, and Darren was able to hear the faint voice coming from his phone. He revealed their location out-loud, much to the confusion of Isabelle.

What seemed like minutes passed, before Isabelle stood up straight and smiled at him, knowing that he wouldn't be able to pull the trigger. Nick and Jason soon appeared at the entrance to the alley behind Isabelle. They slowly approached and stopped a few feet behind Isabelle. Isabelle was somehow aware of their presence and their exact positions as she turned briskly and threw the vase to the floor between them, causing them both to instinctively jump out of the way of the fragments which had begun to fly through the air. They both shouted aloud as fragments stuck in their legs. Isabelle pushed an injured Nick to the floor as she ran past him and towards the street.

"Isabelle, stop!" Darren shouted.

Somehow, things seemed to slow further. She did not slow and showed no signs of stopping at all. He shouted to her once more and found that he could not stop her, he was unable to wound her. Darren heard a rumble from behind him and jumped at the sound of a gun-shot. It hadn't come from his gun. He watched as Isabelle fell to the floor, her hands wrapped around her left calf. Reality caught up with him as he suddenly heard the screams of pedestrians who had heard the shot. He felt a hand on his shoulder and turned to face Frank. Nick and Jason got to their feet and embraced briefly once establishing they sustained nothing but flesh wounds.

Everyone gathered around Chris who was still sprawled out on the cold floor unconscious. Darren heard Frank call for an ambulance. He then informed him that there should be one arriving in just under five minutes. Darren sat by Chris, removed his coat and lay it over her; he was careful not to touch the open wound on the back of her head. He longed to hold her, to place her head in his lap and wait for her to wake, but he couldn't move her, the impact may have caused more damage than the eye could see, the vase hadn't been a small one. He placed his hand on hers. It was cold.

Frank told Nick and Jason to go back inside and have the medic see to them but his relief, found that both men didn't want to leave until Chris was taken to the hospital, he wasn't surprised.

They sat against the building to the left of the alley and kept their eyes on Chris. Frank remained standing but ensured he stood close to Darren. Within minutes, the musical ringing of the ambulance began to sound. Frank rushed to the end of the alley, past an angry Isabelle who was cursing him with every step he took. He met the lead paramedic and quickly explained what was needed. He watched as two men and a stretcher ran towards the darkened part of the alley and another began to tend to Isabelle.

Frank ran the two blocks back to the precinct where he instructed the medic to follow him back to the alley along with two officers. Nick and Jason were seen to almost instantly, their wounds were cleaned and bandaged in time for them to watch as the paramedics loaded Isabelle and Chris into the ambulance. They watched silently as Darren, and one of the Officers climbed into the back before it drove away.

Darren kept his eyes on Chris, determined not to give the smiling Isabelle the satisfaction she'd get from catching his eye and grabbing his attention.

In the hospital, much to his delight, Isabelle was taken one way and he and Chris another. His facial wound had been tended to quickly and had thankfully only needed three stitches. Chris woke not long after she was placed in a bed. Darren had rested his head on her leg and suddenly felt a familiar touch on the back of his neck as Chris began to fiddle with the curls that resided there. His heart began to pound at the sight of her awake. He took her by the hand as he filled her in on what had happened.

A Nurse had already cleaned the wound and explained that there would be no need to shave any of the surrounding hair off to stitch the wound up. The Doctor came in not long afterwards and stitched up the wound. Once a scan had been undertaken to ensure that there was no damage sustained to the brain, the Doctor explained that Chris would be able to go home if everything else was right. She returned from her scan with a smile as the Doctor explained that there was no fracture and no internal damage. They kept her for another two hours to ensure that nothing changed before they released her with the strict instruction to go home and rest.

As they left the hospital, Darren took Chris in his arms as he gently kissed her. She extended her arms around his neck. After a few seconds, she mumbled something as she pulled away and nodded in the direction of the Officer approaching them.

The Officer's name was Granger. He was the one who was under strict instructions to bring Isabelle to the precinct once the Doctor authorised it. He gave Chris his best as he made his way back inside, saying that he'd see them later when he brought Isabelle in.

Darren and Chris got in the car. Darren was convinced to take Chris, not home, but to work where she could rest on the sofa in the bullpen. He was at first understandably reluctant but was eventually convinced. Chris used the 'Invalid Card' as Darren put it, to get her way with the music choice. She took an album out from the glove compartment and put it in. She smiled as she did so. It was revealed why when she played the disk, it was one of Darren's and her's favourite songs. Josh Groban's 'Hidden Away' began to play, to which they both sang along while smiling at the words.

Chris did as she said she would and lay on the sofa in the bullpen as soon as she had reassured everyone that she was okay.

Darren sat at his desk, grateful for the fact that he could see the sofa and therefore Chris, from where he was.

He suddenly remembered his promise to speak to the victim's mother. He asked Frank where she was. He told him that she was currently in the relative's room. He thanked him and began making his way towards the relative's room. Upon entering the room, she confronted Darren with the accusation that he was precisely what the reporter had said.

He sighed as he sat a few seats away from the woman. He waited patiently until she'd said her piece before he explained that the woman who had told everyone those things wasn't entirely honest either, she was a reporter from Tennessee, not from New York and that most of what she had said, was wrong. The woman smiled softly as she apologised and said that it was unfair that she accused him of something so serious without even knowing the details. Darren moved to the seat opposite her and rested his elbows on his knees. She closed her eyes as she apologised once more, it had been a long day, and she shouldn't be taking it out on him.

275

She looked at him sceptically before asking what I was all about, what the so-called reporter had claimed. She withdrew her question before Darren had time to answer, once again apologising, saying it was none of her business and that she should never have asked.

Darren assured her that it was okay and that he'd tell her everything, well, he knew and so did she that he would not tell her everything, just enough to clear his name. He explained that he was married to the first victim, as the reporter had said, but other than that, everything she'd said was wrong. He also let it slip that he was to be arrested for the murders despite it being physically impossible for him to have committed them all, explaining that he was in another country at the time of one of them.

Nicole expressed her disapproval at the accusations and asked if they had any idea who was killing the poor girls. Darren sadly revealed that they had no idea, he did not disclose that were theorising that it was a woman, he didn't want to upset her or get her hopes up for it to be a false alarm, a mere coincidence that female DNA, they had found the same DNA on the lipstick itself, was found at two scenes. They talked for almost an hour until Frank popped his head in and asked how Mrs Greene was doing. She thanked him for allowing her to remain there throughout the day. He answered comfortingly that it was nothing and that if she wanted anything, she should ask. Darren was briefly disappointed to find out that Nicole's son had arrived to pick her up, they were going to go and tell the victim's grandmother and grandfather about her death. She thanked Darren for his honesty and hugged him before she left, saying she would be back to thank him personally when they find the killer. She emphasised the when, stating that there was no if, about it, she believed in them all.

They had been told to go home at 17:30 but had all refused because Isabelle still hadn't been brought in. It wasn't until 18:23 that Frank received a call from Officer Granger that said he was bringing a rather angry Isabelle, in cuffs, to the office.

Isabelle.

Darren diverted his eyes back to the glass sitting on his desk. He yearned for it all to go away, for the Detectives from Tennessee to turn around and stop their crazy journey. He prayed the mark on Chris' head which Isabelle left behind would vanish soon along with the pain.

His mouth dropped open as he thought of something unthinkable, but could it be? He stared at the glass a little while longer until he could bear not knowing much longer. He picked up the glass and stood swiftly. Everyone asked him what was wrong, but he did not tell them. "Work with me. I need to know something. I need to do this." He was desperate not to go to jail now, so they followed him down to the lab where they were met by Alice who had the results on the shade of lipstick fond at the scene. "Alice, I need to know if the DNA on this glass match that of the skin found under the victim's nails and the lipstick, soon, please."

Everyone stood and stared, something within them all told them what they had considered long ago but had dismissed with little thought. Was it possible? Of course, it had always been possible, and not entirely unbelievable.

Darren wandered over to the window in the corner of the room. It covered the corner of two walls and overlooked the streets to the west and the north. They were three floors up, so he was able to see for quite a while. He watched a mother and child. The child had spilt ice-cream down their shirt, and their mother was trying her hardest to clean it off without losing her temper. The child, who, as Darren could now see more clearly, was a young girl, was running her fingers through her mother's fringe before she began fiddling with the hair that fell in front of her mother's ears. Her mother said something to her which caused her to look down and her feet, probably out of shame. The mother got up off her knees, picking up the baby wipes she'd used before she told the child to stay where she was while she walked the five paces to her left where she then put the wipes in the bin. Her child obeyed and waited patiently for her mother to return. When she did, the young girl picked up her mother's bags, one strap in each hand and held them up for her mother to grab. The mother appeared to smile as she took the bags, threw them over her shoulders and then took her daughter by the hand affectionately. Darren turned from the window, happy with the result of the incident. All was forgiven.

Chris joined him by the window and smiled comfortingly. A beep came from the machine, the one which Alice had put the DNA samples in a minute before. She said that she had done the test and that she just needed to print the results.

Everyone remained where they were by the computer and the window until Alice came back into the room with a single sheet of paper in her hand. She walked over to Darren and handed him the paper. He noticed that she did not meet his gaze. He held the results to his chest as he turned to face the window once more.

Was he stupid? What possessed him to think that it could be Isabelle? Would she even do such a thing?

He held the sheet away from his stomach so that when he cast his eyes down, he would be able to see immediately whether or not it was her. Would she do such a thing? Yes, she would and-

She did.

His heart began to race, and tears sprung to his eyes as he read and re-read the results.

It was Isabelle, the DNA matched, Isabelle had killed them all.

He turned to the others and told them. They stood and stared at him, unable to comprehend what they had been told. Nick was the first to speak. He said that despite having cases where a mother had killed her child, there was something sick about this one, it wasn't just her daughter that she'd killed. There were others, other innocent women.

Chris was the next to speak. She reminded everyone that Isabelle would soon be there. Nick and Jason smiled sympathetically at Darren before leaving Chris with Darren.

Alice went too as she returned to her office to update the case file. Chris threw her arms around Darren and held him close. To her surprise and relief, he broke down. She was grateful that he was no longer holding in the grief which had controlled him for almost nine months before, he finally knew the truth. He fell to his knees. She followed him down and held his head to her chest comfortingly as she whispered over and over again that it was going to be okay, and that they were going to get her, it wasn't long until they'd have her.

By the time they re-joined the team in the bullpen, Frank had informed Nick and Jason that Isabelle had arrived and was on her way up in the elevator. Darren proposed that they shouldn't tell Isabelle that they had got her DNA and had connected it to the victims. He suggested that they try her for assaulting an Agent and then see where it goes from there.

Frank asked Darren if he would like to interrogate as he was the lead investigator on the case. Darren said that he would.

The elevator doors opened to reveal Isabelle with Officer Granger. He walked her out into the bullpen which she'd stood in earlier that day.

Frank could hardly believe the cheek of the woman, to come in smiling the way she was as if she was proud of what she had done. Her face hardened when she saw Chris, apparently disappointed that she was there. She commented on how unsuccessful her attempt to get rid of Christine was before smiling at the rage it sparked in Darren. Would

Darren be able to handle interrogating her? She stood before him and observed him, waiting for him to speak.

She waited patiently before appearing to flinch as Darren raised his hand in a gesture towards the hallway.

"This way."

As Officer Granger lead Isabelle down towards the interrogation room, Darren began to follow behind. Frank called him back and suggested that he go home for the night, they could keep Isabelle there for him to speak to in the morning. It had been a long day, and Frank had quietly confided in Darren not long before, that if Isabelle refused to talk about the killings and the detectives from Tennessee showed up before they charged her, then he probably wouldn't have another time to stay in his own home, at least for a while. The suggestion that he and Chris should go home was quickly accepted, and they left with Nick and Jason. They arranged to be in the office by 06:00 the following morning. Frank waited until he'd convinced Isabelle to wait overnight without causing a fuss before he went home himself. He knew Darren could handle the pressure of the case, but could he handle interrogating Isabelle? Frank knew she wouldn't be playing fairly, and not friendly.

Darren and Chris had decided that it would be best if she went home, to begin with so that she could collect some things. The real reason was however unspoken, they both knew that she would stay at hers for a couple of hours to allow Darren some time alone, in-case things didn't go according to plan the following day.

She drove to his after a couple of hours, getting there just before 21:00 where she found him in happy spirits as if he'd completely forgotten about what had been happening. He was hot and sweaty when she arrived. He explained that he'd been on the treadmill for the last hour.

They embraced fondly upon her arrival before they made their way upstairs. They decided that they'd watch a couple of episodes of some program or other when they returned downstairs, but first, Darren needed to shower.

Chris sat crossed legged on the toilet seat as Darren turned on the shower and climbed in. "Why do you think she did it?" Chris asked after a couple of minutes.

"You mean Isabelle?" Darren asked, but continued before getting a reply, "I don't know, I hope we'll find out."

"We will find out," Chris stressed as she tried to convince both him and herself that Isabelle would talk.

He turned to face her. "But suppose we don't, Chris, what happens then, the evidence isn't enough to convict her, and I doubt she'll take any more lives if she knows we're onto her."

"Darren," Chris stood and sat on the edge of the tub, "she'll talk, we'll make sure of it. We need to be positive and not think about what could happen and think more about what should happen."

He slumped against the wall, flinching at the cold of the tiled surface before tipping his head back and closing his eyes tight. He laughed aloud before opening his eyes and turning his head towards Chris. "I suppose. I guess I just haven't had that much luck when it comes to Isabelle. I'm just too used to losing out against her."

Chris held her hand out for Darren to take and when he did, she assured him once more, "She'll talk." She smiled.

Silence fell between them. Darren playfully bit his bottom lip before gently tugging at Chris's hand. Her mouth dropped open in amused shock before she stood and slowly stepped into the shower to join him. She wrapped her arms around his wet neck. He pulled her under the water, soaking her clothes through until they were stuck against her equally wet body. She felt Darren's hands begin to unfasten the buttons on her blouse as she pressed her lips to his with an eagerness he reciprocated willingly.

Her arms left the warm, wet comfort of his neck as her blouse was peeled from her body. The procedure was tiresome for her clothes did not come away quickly, but laughs and looks of amusement were exchanged during the unusually romantic occasion.

They made love passionately against the cold of the bathroom wall, both clinging to the other as the harsh reality set in, this may be their last night together, and they were to make the most of it, every minute of it.

Afterwards, they dressed and made their way back downstairs where they watched a single of episode of some program neither of them had previously watched and of which they still didn't know the name. They lay on the sofa, their legs entwined as they secretly reminisced over their time together. Neither of them paid any attention to the TV as they silently relished each stroke of a hand, each gentle squeeze and every mumble of gratitude and love exchanged in the brief time they lay there.

They went to bed just before 22:30 where they both lie, neither knowing the other one was awake. Darren held Chris in his arms as she held his hand under her chin. He lay behind her and pulled her closer to him, so they were pressed firmly together. She pushed herself into him in a reassuring and comforting gesture as she finally closed her eyes, kissed his hand and inhaled his sweet scent once more before dropping off. Darren soon followed and was happy to find his sleep went uninterrupted. There were none of the usual thoughts of Isabelle or the equally unwanted dreams about his past. They slept peacefully until their alarms sounded at 05:00 the following morning.

CHAPTER 18

"MRS JAMES, WE'RE HERE because of your actions on the 31st January 2017, yesterday." Agent Thompson explained.

"Okay." Isabelle did not seem to mind.

"What drove you to commit the crime, that is, what made you attack Agent Bridges yesterday afternoon?"

"Clark, skip the formalities, you know why I did it."

"Please, Mrs James, it's Agent Thompson in here."

"So formal." She moaned.

"I'll repeat the question, what led you-"

"Alright, alright, I'll put it into words for you since your simple mind cannot figure it out for itself." She smiled. She stuck out her bottom lip as she mocked him when answering, "I was upset about the death of my daughter and felt betrayed that you should have moved on so fast, so, I decided to, I don't know, 'betray you'." She shrugged.

"You do realise Mrs James that your actions will have consequences, you will serve time, and you will be requested to write a formal apology to Agent Bridges."

"That cannot be protocol."

"Oh no," He finally raised his gaze from his pen and paper. His eyes met with Isabelle's as he continued, "it is a request I made that the Chief of Police has approved. You cannot leave this room until Agent Bridges receives either a written or spoken apology which she deems acceptable."

"Well, that ain't going to happen, never."

"Then I'm sorry, but you won't be leaving this room. Goodbye Mrs James." Darren began packing up his things.

"Wait, fine, I'll apologise." Isabelle half stood.

"I'm happy to hear it. I'll send somebody in to take it down."

"Aren't you going to take it down?"

"I don't think that will be appropriate now, do you?"

"Listen Clark, I don't give a shit about the formalities, now I know you think you're 'it' in this room, but I know that deep down, you're still the weak-minded little boy that I took in and I know that despite your objections, you will still do as I say. You are to take down my apology and give it to that slag you've been banging, and then you're going to come back in here and sort this mess out." She sat back in her chair with a huff before objecting loudly when Darren stood and left the room.

Darren entered the observation room to find Frank and Chris recovering from their fir of laughter.

"Some slag you've been banging? Oh, even for Isabelle, that was a little harsh." Chris laughed.

Frank wiped his eyes. "The look in her eyes and the twang of the 'g' in 'banging' somehow made that hilarious."

He exhaled, and his smile vanished slowly. "But even I have to admit that that was below the belt, and uncalled for." He straightened his suit out before he entered the interrogation room to warm Isabelle on the use of language such as that which she had just demonstrated. Frank popped his head around the corner of the observation room to inform Darren that Officer Granger would soon be arriving to take down the apology. Darren thanked him before he returned to the interrogation room.

"What are you trying to achieve from this Clark?" Isabelle asked in a raised whisper from across the table.

"Justice, that's what we all aim to achieve every time we sit in this room."

"How does that normally work out for you?"

"Pretty well, and this time will be no exception."

Isabelle was about to comment when the door opened to reveal the officer who had arrested her the afternoon before. She sat back in her chair in unwilling defeat as the officer pulled up a chair on Darren's side of the table.

The apology took just over twenty minutes to write, but three versions later, the wording was no longer offensive and was presented to Agent Bridges and was accepted for formality sake it. There was no reason for Chris to accept the apology and everyone knew it.

Agent Bridges voiced her forgiveness through the speakers in the interrogation room shortly before Darren left and asked Isabelle what she would like for breakfast. There was a choice of a cheese and ham sandwich or nothing.

"I'd rather starve." She decided.

"Very well Mrs James, but we're not done with you yet, we've still got much to talk about, so if I were you, I'd accept the sandwich."

A moment of panic spread across her face before she hung her head momentarily. She raised it once more as she answered, "Fine, but you know I don't like cheese."

"A ham sandwich then?"

"Yes." There was no chance of a "please" or a "thank you".

"It'll be here in about ten minutes." With that, he left, leaving Isabelle in the silent room under the watchful eye of Frank as Chris joined Darren for breakfast in the kitchen.

"Now that yesterday is sorted out, I hope she'll be less resentful if we ask her about the killings," Chris said as they sat at the table.

"And if we can't get anything from her and the detectives from Tennessee arrive early, at least she'll still be going down for something." Darren sat and stared at his sandwich, unable to eat it for fear of what could happen.

"We'll get her. I know we will." But she still wasn't convinced, and she too had lost her appetite.

Darren raised his head and suddenly realised where they were. "This is the place we first met," he chuckled, "we're even sitting in the same seats as we were then." Chris placed her hand on his and ran her thumb over the back of his hand.

"And we're going to be able to sit here again. We have to believe that."

"I know." He agreed as he kissed her gently on the hand.

But did he? Chris knew that despite his determination to not allow the possibility of jail scare him, Darren was scared. They knew that Isabelle was going to be difficult, especially as she knew that Darren would go down if she didn't talk.

He stood slowly before standing behind Chris, his hands on her shoulders. She placed her hand on his and once again reassured him that they were going to get her. Darren took hold of the chair and turned it so that she was facing him. He took her face in one hand and placed the other gently on her arm. She closed her eyes as their skin touched. He kissed her gently on the lips. There he lingered until he knew that it was time to talk to Isabelle. He tipped his head towards hers so that their heads were together.

"I love you." He whispered.

She took his face in both her hands as she drew his lips up to hers once more. "I love you too." She said before letting go. He smiled affectionately before leaving the kitchen towards the interrogation room.

"He does love you, you know." Nick came from behind and sat beside her. He smiled comfortingly before placing an arm on her shoulder and drawing her towards him. She let her head fall onto his shoulder as she closed her eyes and slowly exhaled.

"I know," she whispered, "more than I could ever love him."

Her answer had confused him. "I thought you loved him."

"I do!" She voiced as she realised how it had sounded. "With all my heart."

"Then how-"

She stood and faced him, "He just has a bigger heart." She patted his hand thankfully before leaving the kitchen to find Frank.

"Mrs James, there are a few questions I need to ask you before you go," Darren said not long after he'd sat back down.

"I've got nothing more to say to you." She gave him a long hard look before returning her gaze to her hands.

"I'm sorry to hear that, but you've got to remain here and listen to what I have to say whether you wish to make a reply or not."

"What right do you have?" She demanded.

Darren couldn't believe the cheek of the woman. "What right do I have? What right do you have?" He cleared his throat before apologising for his comment.

"I have nothing to say to you." She repeated.

"Fine, I'll talk, you listen."

"Do as you please Clark."

"I want to talk to you about the night Sarah McAvoy died."

"You-" She was lost for words as if she was unable to comprehend why he would want to talk about such a thing. "Why do you want to talk about that?"

"I feel as if there are some unresolved feelings regarding that night, don't you?"

She appeared shocked, that much was obvious, but still, she remained quiet.

"Where were you on the night of Sarah McAvoy's death?" He did not attempt to meet her eyes, from knowing what was to come, he figured it would be easier to defend himself against her remarks if he did not look at her.

"Where was I? Where were you? It's your fault that she's dead. If only you would have remembered that you were meeting her, then she would never have been killed!"

"I'm sorry you feel like that, Mrs James. I'll ask you again, where were you on the night of Sarah McAvoy's death?"

"I was at home."

"Alone?"

"Yes, alone." She snorted. "Your presence in our family meant that my husband couldn't be with me at home, I was alone."

He sighed. "Your husband was arrested for a crime he was caught committing, and there can be no denying that he was guilty."

"Still, I don't see why you're asking me where I was, and you still haven't said where you were."

He finally raised his head from his paperwork, "I was at work, many people can account for my presence."

"Are they the same people who have sent the detectives from Tennessee to come and arrest you?"

"That is of no concern to you."

"That answers that question then." She smiled slyly.

Darren sat back in his chair and rolled his eyes. He sighed deeply as he turned partially towards the mirror behind him, behind which he knew Christine and Frank were watching.

"Mrs James, were you aware that your daughter was pregnant at the time of death?" Darren knew precisely where he was going and hoped that she did not.

"I was, yes."

"May I ask if you are aware of whom the father of the child was?" She hesitated before answering that the father was Darren. "I am afraid I must tell you that the father was, in fact, a fellow officer and friend of mine."

"Why- I-" Her mind went blank as she attempted to answer. "I did know yes." She conceded.

"You knew?" He could not hide the shock from his voice, maybe that's why she did it, it was time to ask.

"Of course I knew. She had many other lovers excluding you, not that you could be called a lover."

It was time. "How did her infidelity make you feel, Mrs James?"

"I was ashamed of her, infidelity is a sin, and she knew it!"

"Such un-pure behaviour, how did you manage, knowing that such a person was not only living but was associated with you as she was your child?"

"Barely, she was living in sin, sin I tell you! Disgraceful child!" It was evident that Isabelle was on edge, his next question had the power to either push her over or make her realise just how close she was.

"Sinning, unworthy of heaven." He said simply.

"As the Bible says." Her eyes were red and tears had begun forming in the corners, but she appeared angrier than she did upset.

"The association with Heaven, is that where the 'ironic' angelic theme comes from?"

"Yes." She replied. She inhaled quickly upon realising what she had done. Frank and Christine exchanged a shocked smile behind the glass. Her eyes widened as she stared into Darren's, unable to comprehend how on earth he had come to know, she had always been so careful.

Darren clenched his fists under the table in an attempt to control his temper, she had confessed, and despite not needing further explanation, she owed it to the parents and the friends of the other victims to explain why she did what she did.

He heard the door open behind him and was joined by Frank and Chris. They both stood next to him silently as they waited for him to ask his next question.

"So, let me get this right, she killed her daughter because she sinned?" Nick was astonished to discover the motive behind it all.

"Yes, and the rest of the victims were either prostitutes, women who are selling their bodies, or women who reminded her too much of Sarah," Darren explained soon after he re-joined the team in the bullpen.

"That's messed up," Alice commented.

"Yes, thank you for that analysis, Alice," Frank said sternly. "Mrs James has been charged with assault and nine counts of murder. She'll be transferred over to the Metropolitan Correctional Centre later this afternoon."

"And until then?" Chris asked.

"And until then, she'll be held downstairs," Frank answered. "Well, isn't this brilliant timing, those young gentlemen over there look like they're here for you Darren." Darren stood quickly. "I'll go and talk to them."

"Thank you, Frank." Darren put his hand briefly on Frank's arm.

Frank placed his on Darren's back and smiled. "I'll not be a minute."

Darren and Chris sat back at their desks to continue filling out the case files. Within two minutes, Frank walked past him with the two Detectives from Tennessee. They were heading towards the holding cells, Darren noticed that one of the Detectives, was Tim. Frank would show the men the video recording of the interrogation before letting them watch Alice as she checked the evidence. They would then go with Frank to the holding room itself where they would have a short conversation with Frank while Isabelle was present before asking her a few questions to see if her story matches that on the interrogation video, even if she changed her story, so she sounded innocent, it wouldn't matter anyway.

Darren hung his head and took a long, deep breath. It was almost over, he was, however, careful not to become too thankful, they hadn't gone away yet. He glanced over at Chris. It was so unfair, the things that had been happening to him wouldn't have bothered him as much if he didn't have her. It wasn't fair on her. She hadn't deserved any of it, not Isabelle's comments or the drama of the case itself and especially not the attempt on her life. He made a mental note to apologise to her when - if they look Isabelle away.

It was just after 12:00, and he was beginning to get very hungry. He tried to forget about his stomach while he finished filling out all that was required of him. By 12:45, Frank and the Detectives had finished and were making their way back towards the bullpen. Frank introduced them to Darren, not as the previous suspect of course, but as the lead investigator. "Darren Thompson," Darren said as he shook the other Detectives hand willingly, but he was careful not to make eye contact with the man who he had once called a friend.

"We're sorry for the misunderstanding." The other Detective, Detective Jones, said.

"It's fine, I completely understand."

"I just wish there was something we could do to make up for the upset your arrest may have caused."

Darren finally looked at Tim. "As I said, it's fine Detective Jones, honestly. There's nothing you can do. But Tim, call me petty, but I think it's only fair that you apologise," he lowered his voice, "not just for the lies you probably told the Chief, but for everything, for Sarah, for doing that to me."

He stood in silence, Darren sighed, he knew that Tim wouldn't apologise.

"Apologise for what?" Jones asked.

Darren was initially reluctant to reveal his reasons for asking, but he was tired of being made to feel insignificant, his past would not determine his future, he would not allow his real friends to see him beaten by those who had done him wrong. He turned to Jones and explained why he was asking Tim to apologise.

"Well Tim, apologise to the man, it's the least you can do."

Tim reluctantly apologised, Darren didn't believe a word of it. Tim began to leave but was called back by Detective Jones. "You've got a lot of making up to do, if the Chief finds out what you did, he'll have your badge, and from what I've heard, it will be well deserved. I'll be more than happy to take it from you myself. I'll see you in the car."

Darren thanked Jones for everything as he walked him out. As Darren re-joined everyone, Frank let them go for lunch. Frank led, followed by Nick and Jason side by side, Chris and Darren walked behind. They walked in silence until they were out of the building where Darren slipped his hand into Chris' as they continued walking. She slowed after a while, and when he turned to ask her what was wrong, she pulled him closer and wrapped her arms around his neck before kissing him passionately. The stood in their silent celebration until they heard Nick clear his throat. He was standing before them, Jason a little behind, looking at them, eyes wide, in amusement.

"This can wait until you two get home, come on, lunch is on me."

They laughed as they caught up with Frank who hadn't seemed to notice their brief absence. He had seen but had walked on, everyone following him closely as he felt a warm paternal feeling grow inside him as he thought of how happy everyone must be at that moment. He smiled to himself as he listened to them all behind him, laughing and joking about nothing in particular. He heard them talk about that Saturday. He felt a hand on his shoulder and turned to see Darren. They continued walking, Darren next to Frank with the others still behind.

"I'm sorry, but I've completely forgotten what time dinner is on Saturday," Darren confessed.

"I thought dinner could start at about 18:00 if that's okay with you," Frank answered.

"That's fine. I'll be there." Frank put his arm over Darren's shoulder as Darren put his on Frank's back. The paternal feeling was there once more, this time it was stronger than it had ever been, but he didn't mind, next to the love he felt for his wife, it was the most wonderful feeling in the world, and he hoped it would never leave.

"Frank?"

"Yes, Darren?"

"Thank you." They stopped briefly as Darren thanked him with a smile that told him everything to which he was referring. Frank tapped Darren on the back twice before they continued to walk on, their arms now by their sides.

Darren glanced over his shoulder at Chris who was still laughing with Nick and Jason. It warmed his heart to see her smiling. He hoped she would do nothing but from then on.

CHAPTER 19

I N THE MONTHS BETWEEN March and December, things around the office seemed to quicken. Cases seemed to come and go, they were all simple and were solved almost as soon as they were reported. They were grateful however that their success rate had improved in the last few months. Isabelle was formally convicted and sentenced to four life sentences in prison, but, understandably, everyone found it hard to forgive and forget. Apologies were delivered personally to the friends and the family members of each victim, along with a complete explanation of what had happened, they were to know everything, there was no reason they shouldn't know why they lost their loved one, and no-one had any intention of keeping anything from anyone.

Darren had been guaranteed that there was no chance Isabelle would be able to apply for bail, ever, she would be in for life, as she should.

One September lunchtime, Darren introduced Leon and his Aunt Sam to Chris' parents. The six of them spent the afternoon together walking through central park. Chris' mother, Flo, and Darren's aunt soon left the group to look at some flowers on sale on a near-by market stall, leaving Leon to walk with Albert. Darren and Chris had already created quite a distance between them and the others. The day wasn't significant at all, but each party member thoroughly enjoyed every minute of it. That was the day that Darren realised what he wanted in life, it was the day he asked Chris to move in.

"Have you ever seen two people more in love?" Sam asked Leon once she and Flo had rejoined the men.

"Never." They smiled as the followed behind Chris and Darren on that September day, overjoyed at the fact that Darren was finally happy.

Nick and Jason went on their holiday to Mexico before finally deciding to adopt a baby girl soon after returning home. Things seemed to be falling into place for everyone, even with Alice, she was soon over her crush on Darren and willingly moved in with Steven when asked in early November. Soon after Isabelle's conviction, Darren began playing a more prominent part in his company. He took a week off every two months to travel to London and check everything was in order.

Everything ran smoothly for a few months until a letter arrived through Darren's door in the first week of August. It was from Isabelle herself, requesting that Darren visit her in Prison. He obliged so that he could see her once more before he shut her out from his life properly. He'd gotten her now. There was no way that she could change that, it would be the first time he could talk to her as him and not as who he used to be. She no longer scared him, she no longer had any power over him, and she now knew it.

It was strangely warm on the morning of his visit although the forecast had promised rain all day. He had to wait a few minutes after his arrival before Isabelle was seated before him. She looked much older, she had not styled her hair, her face was not done up, and her signature purple lipstick was nowhere to be seen. He should have wished to be happy to see her in such a state, but instead, he found he felt a little sorry for her but could not explain why. He set his thoughts straight, she had committed a crime, and for which she was being punished, therefore, there was no reason why he should feel sorry for her.

Darren found their conversation to be annoying and quite pathetic, they talked about normal things for once, she asked how things were at work, he answered honestly but knew that she didn't care. When asked why she had asked for him to visit, Isabelle finally apologised for what she had done. She uttered one line over and over, "Thou shalt not kill", a sin she now realised was higher than that of infidelity. Darren felt the need to comfort her despite every ounce of his being urged him not to. He did something he had never done before to Isabelle, he placed his hand on hers and met her gaze before smiling sympathetically. She put her hand on his and to his surprise, her eyes filled with tears as she began apologising for how she had treated him when he was younger.

Despite the hatred for her remaining, Darren found she was sincere with her apology to him. He told her that everything was okay, in his mind, it was all forgotten, everything but the crimes she had committed, he could forgive her for abusing him, but not for killing innocent women, no matter how much he tried, he couldn't. He didn't want to.

He let go of her hand and stood to leave. He said goodbye, but she had one more request to make of him. She asked if he would come again, to which he replied that he would come every time she requested it. As he was leaving, he realised something. He loved Isabelle. He loved her like someone would love an Aunt or a cousin. She wasn't his mother, his love for his mother could never be compared to that which he had for Isabelle. Isabelle was not his mother, but still, she had been his guardian for ten years and some sick and twisted reason, he loved her.

She requested his presence twice more in the space of four months, he went both times, as promised. Nothing significant happened on his visits, they just talked for half an hour at a time about nothing-in-particular until the warden was instructed to send everyone away. Leaving her didn't make him sad, but something inside him always wanted another minute or two, a brief extension so he could study her expressions more, figure out whether or not she held the slightest regard for him, figure out whether she honestly did feel sorry for what she had done.

He had three visits in total, no more, she didn't ask him again. On their last visit, he'd seen something in her eyes, he saw regret, she did feel something for him, and she sincerely did regret what she had done to him. As soon as he saw this, he and Isabelle had exchanged one final look, he'd seen what he needed to, and she knew he had too. She could leave him alone now; now she knew he'd forgiven her for her behaviour towards him. There was never a reason behind what she did to him, but she always managed to make one up. She did feel sorry for how she had treated him, but something inside her was proud of what she had managed to do to Sarah and the others. Her sentence, her sins, they were small prices to pay to remove such people from the world. She knew that everyone had some evil inside them, everyone, even Darren. The girls may not have already done something wrong in their lives, but they would have. Isabelle felt that she had done God a favour by preventing such events from occurring. It never occurred to her that what she had done was so much worse. She knew it was terrible, but she never even thought that what she had done was as bad as it was, and she never would.

⇜ CHAPTER 20 ⇝

S NOW HAD BEEN FALLING since the early hours of the morning. Everywhere was now covered with a thick white blanket of snow that extended as far as the eye could see and stretched across the horizon were black strips where the roads had been cleared. That Christmas Eve, they spent the evening at Darren's as they had the year before. Once again, they occupied the floor and not the chairs as they fussed over Nick and Jason's baby girl Georgie. It was almost a month since they began taking care of Georgie and they were excited to spend Christmas with her as a family.

Nick leaned in towards Darren. "When?" He asked. Darren jokingly wafted him away telling him to be quiet. A few minutes later Jason came into the kitchen and asked him the same question.

"Shh," Darren urged, "could you be any more obvious?" He laughed as he handed Jason a bowl of chips.

"I'm just excited." Jason smile.

Darren put the bowls on the coffee table before he slumped beside Alice and smiled at her childishly. "So, tell me everything, I feel like we haven't talked in a long time."

"That's because we haven't." She sat up straight against the chair and turned to face him. "What do you want to know?"

"How are things going with you and Steven? Are you fully settled after the move?"

"I am, yes thank you. Things are going great. We're so comfortable with each other, and I never knew I could feel like this and I never even began to think that I would ever find somebody as wonderful as Steven, he truly is the best man I've ever met. You know the other day, well, he made the most beautiful chicken stew. There it was, freshly served with a side of fresh bread when I walked in from work. The table looked amazing. It was romantic, I almost cried."

"That does sound nice. You're lucky. He genuinely sounds like a lovely man."

"He is."

"But he's lucky too; you're just as amazing as he is."

A look of gratitude spread across her face as she placed her head on his shoulder briefly. "Something tells me you've found the one." He assured her. She could not hide the joy. A smile remained on her face even as the conversation shifted towards work.

They began talking about her new intern, a man who could only be described as clumsy. He mixed up evidence and always managed to spill her coffee in the morning. Still, he was kind enough and in the last couple of weeks had improved substantially to the point where he was only an occasional inconvenience. Geoffrey had started working for Alice just over two months ago and in that time, he had managed to make a good impression on everybody, including Frank, he was very good at solving cryptic messages when Darren wasn't around and excelled in human biology despite having a degree in chemistry. They had invited him to dinner, but unfortunately, he had to return home to Indiana, he was only 22, and his parents still expected his presence at their dinner table come Christmas Day.

"How are you and Chris?" Alice asked. "I hear you're going to-"

"Shh!" Darren interrupted quickly.

"Speak of the devil," Alice whispered to him as Chris smiled at her from across the room and stood to join her. She sat on the other side of Alice as Darren stood to leave. Alice turned to Chris and asked about her father.

Steven watched as Alice sat with Chris, he felt his lips curl into a smile each time he saw her smile or heard her laugh. He truly was a lucky guy. His parents were to join them for dinner the following afternoon. He just hoped they were going to like Alice. Darren sat beside him and asked him how his job was going. He replied and told him that he had been promoted recently to head waiter, a position which had a 30% increase on his previous wage, he was thinking about moving. He had some money, quite a bit, saved up and he knew that their apartment was barely big enough for the two of them, should they someday decide to start a family, they would need a bigger apartment or even a house.

Once Alice joined Darren and Steven, and Chris decided to talk to Helena, Darren decided to go over to Nick and Jason, leaving Steven with Alice. He asked them about their plans for tomorrow. They told him that since it was Georgie's first Christmas, they were going to make it extra special. They'd done the house up entirely with decorations, and they had bought her more presents than they dared admit. They said that despite initially wanting it to be the three of them for Christmas, they would like it if Darren and Chris would pop by at some point during the day, to which Darren replied that they would.

When Nick asked Darren what he and Chris were doing for Christmas this year, he told them that Chris's parents who had recently become friendly with each other once more were coming over as well as his Aunt Sam and Leon from London. All round, Christmas sounded like it was going to be perfect for everyone.

By 20:30, Nick and Jason had put Georgie to bed in the spare room and were back downstairs with everyone else. They all decided that it would be a great idea to watch a Christmas film. They agreed on 'It's a Wonderful Life' before they finally took their place on the sofas and chairs and settled down to watch it.

Throughout the film, Frank's eyes wandered from person to person as he watched them embrace the person they love. He watched their facial expressions as the scenes changed from a happy one to a sad one and he viewed them as they wept as the film ended. But by the time it had finished, he found he, as was everyone else, was beginning to fall asleep.

As Darren looked around, he saw that Frank was the only one of them not to be crying. Still, he looked moved. Darren attempted to move but found that his legs had gone to sleep. He lifted himself from the chair with his arms, disturbing a now dozing Chris as he did so.

Jason watched as Nick yawned. He smiled to himself as he silently reflected on the last eleven years of his life, the time he had spent with Nick, and now they had a daughter, everything was, and he prayed that it remain so.

Frank had gotten up first and had turned the film off, put it back in his box and put it back on the shelf, carefully ensuring the alphabetically organised DVD rack remained undisturbed.

He then made his apologies before announcing that it was the time that they went home, Helena, like Chris, was beginning to drop off and he was getting tired too. They said their goodbyes, wished everyone a Merry Christmas and handed out presents which they had forgotten to give at the beginning of the evening.

Darren walked them to the door where he was asked again by them both when he was going to do it. "Guys, seriously, I'll let you know. I'm going to wait until everyone's gone home and we've finished tidying up."

"Good luck." Frank wished as he took him in his arms fondly. Darren kissed Helena on the cheek before running to the kitchen. He brought back a plate of the roast potatoes he'd promised her. Once Frank and Helena had left, Steven and Alice decided that they'd better be getting home. Soon after they'd gone, Nick and Jason emerged from the spare room after waking Georgie.

They made arrangements with Chris and Darren for lunch the day after Boxing Day before they left them alone.

Chris began tidying the living room. Darren watched for a few seconds before he passed her and made his way to the DVD shelf. He took out a CD and put it in the DVD player. Within seconds, Glenn Miller's 'Moonlight Serenade' began playing.

He watched as he saw Chris stop momentarily before continuing with a smile on her face. He walked over to her slowly before holding out his hand for her to take. She smiled shyly before slipping her hand inside his. He pulled her gently over to the area behind the sofa where they would have plenty of space.

He placed his hand on her waist as she put her's on his shoulder. Their feet began moving in time with each other as they started waltzing around the room. She tucked her head under his chin as she smiled broadly to herself, she had never been as happy. Darren thought the same as he went over his speech in his head, perfecting every detail to prevent any mistakes that may occur hopefully.

They danced in silence, holding each other close until the song ended. She raised her head, so their eyes met. He kissed her gently on the forehead before wrapping both his arms around her tightly.

Soon after returning home, Nick and Jason had put Georgie to bed in her cot before climbing into bed themselves. They lay awake for the next hour, talking over their life together and where it was to go from there. They knew that nothing was set, they were going to take every day as it came. They'd live spontaneously, not making plans for anything that exceeded six months in advance. One thing was sure, they knew they'd be together for the rest of their lives and that they would live carefully and save enough money to ensure Georgie would be able to go to College wherever she pleases if she pleases.

They finally settled just before midnight when Nick turned to Jason. "Do you think she'll say yes?"

"She's got no reason to. She loves him, more than she knows. They're going to be fine, just like us." Jason kissed Nick affectionately on the lips as he assured him once more that everything was going to work out, for everyone.

As he lay awake with Helena asleep next to him, Frank thought about his family and what they had been through and what they had overcome in the last year. He loved them all as his children, and he was proud of them when they achieved something and ashamed of them when they disappointed him. He loved them more than they would ever know.

Darren and Christine continued tidying the apartment with the music playing in the background, Darren started in the kitchen while Chris stayed in the living room.

By midnight, everything was tidy, and they had readied themselves for bed.

Darren waited eagerly for Chris to return from the bathroom. He placed it under his pillow as she re-entered the bedroom. She climbed into bed next to him and snuggled up to him.

Nerves overcame him as he sat up boldly in bed. She sat up too and asked him what was wrong. Suddenly, his nerves disappeared as he realised that there was no need to be nervous, it was the right time to do it. He turned to face her and took her hand in one of his as he slipped his hand under his pillow and took the box in his hand. He kept his hand hidden as he cleared his throat.

"Chris, I cannot begin to explain how much you mean to me. You've been there for me and have had to suffer for it. I've known for a while that you're the one for me, and I know that you know that too. When I was younger, I always found myself trying to make everyone else happy, and as you've probably already figured out, that didn't always work out very well for me. After my parents died, I never thought I'd be happy again, but not long after I met you, I realised that maybe I could be. I almost feel guilty for being so happy without them. After seeing the way my father was with my mother, the way that he loved her, I knew there was such a thing as love. But then they died, and I married Sarah. I convinced myself that the mere idea of love was all in my imagination. It was my simple view that made me think that love was real, make me think that my father loved my mother. Until I met you, I was convinced that I'd never find someone, and when you burst into the kitchen that morning, I realised that there were kind people in this world, not just those who pretend to be your friend, who pretend to love you and put up with you because they want your money, but truly kind people."

He took a deep breath. "Anyway, I love you Chris, and that's why," he watched as her eyes widened as he took the box out from underneath the pillow, "I want to spend the rest of my life with you, as your husband and you as my wife." Her eyes filled with tears as she smiled broadly. "Christine, will you marry me?" Darren asked quietly.

Chris's breathing became uncontrollable as her heart began beating faster than she'd ever known it to do before.

She placed a hand on his cheek as she swallowed hard.

She found her voice and replied, "Darren, this last year has been the best of my life. I don't know what I'd do without you, and when I think about what my life would have been like without you, it hurt's here," she took her hand off his and placed it over her heart, "and I find it hard to breathe. I can't bear to think about my life without you, and I too would love to spend the rest of my life with you, as your wife. Yes, I'll marry you!"

Her hands began to shake as Darren slipped onto her ring finger, it was the most beautiful ring she'd ever seen, it was everything she'd always wanted, and as she looked back at Darren whose face had also become streamed with tears of overwhelming happiness, she knew she was getting more than she'd ever wanted.

Darren was much more than she could have ever hoped for. He was nicer than he should be, he was sweet, and he was more thoughtful than any other guy she had met. As she looked into his beautiful eyes, she knew how lucky she was to have found such a man so amazing. They knelt on the bed as they embraced eagerly.

Their lips found each other for what seemed like the millionth time in a desperate kiss as Darren lay Chris on the bed and held himself above her.

Unknown to them, their encounter that night would blossom into much more. They were to be a family much earlier than they expected, but neither of them minded, secretly, they both wanted nothing more despite the lack of planning.

It seemed as if from that moment on, the past was the past. It had seemed that the last year had been a war between a future and a past, but now it was over, the future had won, it looked bright and promising for all, and there was no reason the past should return and fight again.

Lightning Source UK Ltd.
Milton Keynes UK
UKHW01f2317170918
329072UK00001B/11/P